PIECES OF EIGHT

ALSO BY STEVE GOBLE

The Bloody Black Flag

The Devil's Wind

A Bottle of Rum

PIECES
OF EIGHT

A Spider John Mystery

STEVE GOBLE

SEVENTH
STREET
BOOKS®

Published 2021 by Seventh Street Books®

Cover design by Jennifer Do
Cover illustrations © Shutterstock
Cover design © Start Science Fiction

This is a work of fiction. Characters, organizations, products, locales, and events portrayed in this novel either are products of the author's imagination or are used fictitiously.

Inquiries should be addressed to
Start Science Fiction
221 River Street
9th Floor
Hoboken, New Jersey 07030
PHONE: 212-431-5455
WWW.SEVENTHSTREETBOOKS.COM

10 9 8 7 6 5 4 3 2 1

978-1-64506-036-9 (paperback) | 978-1-64506-037-6 (ebook)

Printed in the United States of America

For Mom and Dad.
I love you, and I miss you.
And Mom? Sorry about all the cuss words.

I

SEPTEMBER 1723

Spider John Rush mopped his brow with his sleeve, hummed a dance tune, and lifted his face to greet the freshening dawn wind. That's when Calvin Garrick toppled silently from *Minuet*'s main topsail yard.

"Jesus," Spider muttered, dropping his saw into the tool chest and rushing forward—but it was pointless. There was no lucky grab of a stay, no divine gust of wind to push Garrick beyond the gunwale and into the sea where he might—might, perhaps, if he could knife into the water rather than smack it flat—survive a plunge from that height.

No.

The man had fallen silently, unmoving.

Calvin Garrick plummeted headfirst to the hard deck, and Spider stopped short just before the impact. The ship's carpenter averted his eyes and winced at the horrid crack of skull and neck and the thud of the man's body and legs that immediately followed, like the second note of a drummer's flam.

He'd managed not to see the horrible end of Garrick's fall, but he could not keep himself from imagining it, and that was bad enough. Spider prayed the spray he felt on the back of his head was wind-borne moisture from the Atlantic, but he knew it was not; the breeze was only now beginning to rise on a sea so gentle the weather deck was nearly level with the horizon. The drops that fell on him were certainly Garrick's blood.

The carpenter braced himself, then slowly turned and looked at the body. He'd seen plenty of death in his day; his former life as a reluctant pirate had revolved around violence, and he'd learned to do the bloody work quite well in order to survive. Still, a death like this in the midst of a calm sea kissed by morning sun staggered him.

It staggered others, too. *Minuet*'s sailors all stopped working. The straining sways, slackening sails, and the lapping of sea against hull were the only sounds.

The light September wind chilled the sweat he'd earned by sawing spars, and Spider wished he'd brought his coat from the forecastle, but he'd not needed the extra warmth while laboring. He certainly needed it now, looking at the dead man, whose blood ran slowly to starboard.

He had not known Garrick well. Indeed, he was not familiar with anyone among *Minuet*'s fifty-odd crew save for the companions who had come aboard with him—brash young Hob, one-eyed ancient Odin and, the newest addition to his merry band, lovely Ruth Copper.

Those fellow travelers, like Spider John, all had piratical pasts. *Well,* he thought, *Hob and Odin certainly did.* Spider had sailed with them and knew it to be true. They'd dodged sharp blades and hot lead together many times since meeting about a year ago aboard the pirate vessel *Plymouth Dream,* and he had come to depend upon them. Shared risks forged strong friendships.

Ruth Copper, on the other hand, was a bit of a mystery.

Ruth's piracy claims were only that, claims, and she never included much detail. Indeed, she was as secretive as Odin, who never shared his real name and who might claim to be Scottish or Irish or English or Welsh, depending on the direction of the wind. The woman's secretive nature, and the cool head she kept when things got rough, were the only real evidence Spider had that she had ever sailed in pirate waters. Those, and the fact she'd survived the skirmish when vengeful pirates had come sweeping across the grass in the night at Pryor Pond, where he'd met her. Spider's part in that battle had been elsewhere, but he'd seen Ruth's cuts and scrapes afterward and had no reason to doubt she had fought. And she must have fought well, for she had lived. There had been no good place to hide that night.

So, we're pirates all, he mused. Or former pirates, as he frequently reminded Hob and Odin. Spider assumed the others felt somewhat adrift, as he did, here aboard a merchant vessel bound for the Colonies to engage in honest trade, her holds full of letters and metal wares and expensive English clothes rather than plunder gained from pillaging such vessels on the high seas. Spider wanted to belong here, on an honest ship, but could not quite convince himself that he did.

Strike that, he thought. *Maybe this is home, after all. A man's life leaking out all across the deck is a very familiar sight. Maybe I'll never escape such things. Maybe they'll always haunt me.*

Spider yanked the sweat-dampened red kerchief from his head. He grimaced at the drops of Garrick's blood on it before tossing it aside in disgust. He knew the back of his shirt was splattered, too, but he could not afford to discard that. He had only two.

The wind rose, just a little. He wished for rain, something to help wash the deck, but he knew the sky wasn't going to provide that today.

The hands would have to do that, with buckets of salt water and stones to scrape away the stains.

Sad duty, that, and one Spider hoped he would be able to avoid.

Spider knew very little about Garrick, but he'd seen the man go about his daily work without complaint, and heard the man pray each morning, and watched him whittle a whalebone into a nice serving spoon for the woman at home. Spider had a woman waiting, too, or so he hoped, and that was enough for him to feel some kind of bond with Garrick. Spider touched his chest and felt the heart-shaped pendant beneath his shirt. He'd carved that for Emma.

Spider prayed silently that he'd get to hand it to her, rather than die at sea the way so many men did. The way Calvin Garrick had.

The stunned silence among the crewmen gathered about the dead man slowly gave way to calls for the captain, and to whispers.

"Did anyone see what happened?"

"Damn tragic, this is."

"Maybe he went up there drunk," answered another. "Fool, if he did."

"You stow that, damn you. He was not a hard drinker. A sensible man, and a good one."

"Could happen to any of us," said another, wiping his brow. "It is risky work, aye? A bit of daydreaming, a slip of the foot. Any of us. Bless his soul."

That ended any talk of Garrick being at fault.

And it wasn't his fault, by thunder, Spider knew. *Calvin Garrick was not at fault at all.*

"Damn, Spider John," Hob said, rushing to Spider's side before he got to "amen." Spider threw a heated glance at the lad, who lowered his eyes quickly and muttered "sorry."

Spider sighed. *And well you should be, young idiot.*

The name "Spider John" belonged to a wanted pirate, one of the men who had survived the capture of *Red Viper*—*Plymouth Dream* had been rechristened by a new captain after a brief and bloody insurrection—almost a year ago, and the man who, in making his escape and avenging his best friend, had slain the Naval officer and spy responsible for his friend's death. No one aboard *Minuet*, save for Spider's friends, knew the carpenter's true identity. Here, he was known under the borrowed surname of Coombs. Hob should have known better than to speak the words "Spider John" aloud.

But it was a moment of stress, in the wake of a violent death, and no one was paying any attention to Hob anyway. Spider punched Hob gently on the shoulder. "No one heard you, boy," he whispered. "All attention is on the dead man."

"How do you suppose he fell?" Hob brushed long blond hair from his light blue eyes. "A good sailor, he was, by all accounts, anyway. At home up there, he was."

Spider nodded. "Aye. None spoke ill of him, not in my presence. And if he couldn't handle the work up there, you can bet Odin would've cursed him more than once. Odin has no patience aloft."

Spider cast a glance upward. Odin and a couple of others were descending, the one-eyed rigger more slowly than in the past. He seemed to be breathing hard, too. The years finally were showing in the old man. Odin stared back at him with his lone eye, framed by lank gray hair dangling like seaweed draped across his ancient head. The scarred right side of Odin's face, torn and burned long ago by the blast of a cannon if the old man's stories were true, gleamed with sweat that made the red crust brighter than normal. Odin shook his head slowly, as if to say he had no idea how Garrick had plunged to his death.

"Odin would not put up with a lubber up there, no doubt," Hob conceded. "He shared a biscuit with me once, Garrick did. He had some honey, too, from home. It was lovely. Not a single maggot in it. The honey, I mean. The biscuit had a few."

"Aye," Spider said. "Put my saw away proper, will you, lad, and gather the spars? I sort of dashed the saw into the box when I saw the man . . . when it happened."

"Aye," Hob said, disappointed at being given a mundane task. Tall, strong, and broad-shouldered, Hob figured he was built for finer things than hammering nails and sawing planks. Hob would never make a good carpenter's mate, no matter how hard Spider tried to instruct him. Spider followed the boy—young man, rather, he had to remind himself—to the toolbox.

Hob deftly placed the saw into its proper place, but ignored the stack of sawn spars. His mind was elsewhere. "How did he fall?"

"I do not know, Hob." Spider gazed upward into the rigging as the crewmen on deck surrounded their dead shipmate. *But I have an idea about that.*

"Tragic."

"Damned gentle sea, to be tossing an experienced hand off his perch like that," Spider said.

"Aye," Hob replied. "Was he drunk?"

"Don't know," Spider said. "But I can find out. Gather that wood, stow it proper." He nudged his way forward. Spider was not as tall as his shipmates, but working wood and wielding swords these last several years had made him strong, and a carpenter commanded a certain amount of respect at sea, thanks to his sorely needed skills. Spider had no trouble forcing his way through the gawking hands to reach the dead man's side.

He had considerable trouble kneeling by the dead man's crushed, misshapen head and lowering his nose toward the man's mouth. But he did it, and he detected no scent of rum or whisky or any other strong drink. All he could smell was blood.

Spider felt the need for a jolt of alcohol in that very moment, but he had promised Hob and Odin that he would drink less. His drinking had caused them problems in the past.

Spider was sober now, though, so he immediately recognized the stern voice of Edwin Bellows and got away from the body before the crowd parted for the captain.

The old man stood over the corpse and muttered a prayer. The captain's gray-bearded chin quivered, and his hard sapphire eyes examined the faces of his crewmen. "What transpired here? Did anyone see him fall?"

"I saw it, cap'n," said Burke, a dark-haired salt with a pocked face and eyes the color of a glass of porter. "He was at work on the topsail yard, and he just dropped. Maybe his foot slipped."

The men in the trees looked down at their dead shipmate, after no doubt making sure of their own footholds.

"More than thirty yards onto unforgiving English oak," the captain muttered. "Dear Lord."

The captain looked up from the dead man. "Mister Gordon!"

The first mate, thin as a twig and tall, pushed through the crowd. "Aye, cap'n. Sorry, sir, I was in the hold. Barrel leaking."

"Prepare this man for a burial," the captain said. "Clean him up, see to his belongings, prepare a shroud. I shall read a verse and we shall commend him to the sea in one hour's time."

"Aye, sir."

"In the meantime, let us catch this rising wind. Send the men who were on the topsail with him to my quarters, one by one, as soon as we have enough canvas on. I want to hear from them first. Then have the men who knew Garrick best come speak with me, as well. I must write a letter to his family. Do we know where his family resides?"

"Plymouth," the mate said. "A wife he has, and two little ones. Aye, sir, we'll do right by him."

"This deck will need scraped clean," Captain Bellows said, glancing at the blood. "Ask for volunteers. It will be an unpleasant duty. But if there are none, choose men to do it."

"Aye, sir." Gordon got to work.

The captain turned to go but stopped in front of Spider. "Your britches, man, they are crimson."

Spider looked down at his own knees, soaked in the dead man's gore. "Aye, cap'n. I tried to see if there might be life left in him."

The captain stared at Spider for three heartbeats. "Kind of you, man, but . . ."

"I know, sir. There was no saving him."

"Go put on fresh clothes, John, if you have them."

"Aye, sir." Spider turned and headed toward the forecastle. Passing Hob, he paused. "Did you stow the timber?"

"I . . . I saw to it that the job got done."

Spider glanced amidships where he'd left the spars. Two men had gathered them up and were now strolling across the tilted deck toward the lumber hold.

"Did you trade them some of my tobacco again, Hob?"

The young man glanced down toward his feet. "Whisky, sir."

"You have whisky?"

"No, sir," Hob answered. "I know where to acquire some." He could not quite avoid grinning.

Spider sighed. "Well, you did not trade away my stuff, so I reckon I'll count that as progress, of a sort. Fetch me a brand from the cook, boy. I need a pipe. And you can just ask for the brand, you don't have to cat-sneak in there and steal it."

"Aye." Hob looked disappointed.

"You are carpenter's mate, and I am ship's carpenter, so I do not care that you find your duties boring," Spider said. "Do as I say, or I'll flog you, but if you do it and I finally get a good pipe going, and perhaps a tot to drink, if you can spare some . . ."

"I am certain I can," Hob said.

"Once I have some Virginia tobacco burning and some whisky, I'll tell you about Calvin Garrick's murder."

"Murder?" Hob's eyes widened.

"Aye," Spider said. "I have no doubt of it. Go, fetch that brand, and then meet me in the forecastle."

2

By the time Spider had donned a clean shirt and britches and wrapped himself in his sea coat, Hob showed up in the forecastle with a hot brand in his hand and Odin in tow. They had the cramped space to themselves, as everyone was either seeing to his duties or talking about what had happened to Garrick.

"Aren't you supposed to be aloft, Odin?"

"No one tells me what to do, Spider. I'll go up when we're done here," the old man said. "This pup Hob tells me you are talking about murderous nonsense. Why in all the bloody hells do you want to do that?"

"I can tell you later," Spider whispered. "We are not on a bloody pirate vessel anymore, you understand that, aye? If the cap'n tells you to do something and you want to do something else, you can't just slit the man's throat and then elect a new cap'n. You have to obey orders, damn it."

"If someone wants to chase me up to my post, let them grab a sword and try. Now what the hell are you thinking, Spider?"

Spider shut his eyes and swallowed the curses he wanted to hurl at the old fool. *I'll just tell him quick and then he'll go up before he's missed. That'll be faster than trying to cram sense into his hard skull.*

"I think Garrick was murdered," Spider said.

Hob poked Odin's shoulder. "How many bloody hells are there?"

Odin blinked. "What?"

"You said all the bloody hells. How many are there?"

"How should I know?" Odin laughed. "Blackbeard only sailed me into three of them! Ha!"

Spider sighed, took the brand from Hob and fired up his clay pipe. The stem had broken recently, so it was shorter than he liked. He tucked it into his mouth as far to the left as he could in hopes the smoke would not roll up into his eyes. "I don't know why I don't toss you both to the sea and let the whales bugger you."

Odin's eye widened. "Spider, do you not know the plan? It was your plan, after all, I'd think you might know it. We're leaving the pirate life, staying away from trouble and you're going home. That's the plan."

Spider inhaled deeply, exhaled, and smiled. "Rum, Hob?"

"Whisky," the boy said.

"Aye, yes, whisky. I forgot. I've been thinking on other matters."

"Aye," Odin said, "thinking. We could all do with less of that nonsense, Spider John."

"We're all getting a bit careless with old names that might get us hung if anyone overhears them," Spider said quietly. Then he sucked hard on the pipe, exhaled a fog of smoke and took a deep swallow of Hob's stolen whisky. *God, that's good*, he thought.

"I'll be more cautious," Odin said, looking around to see if anyone else might have overheard. "We're alone here, though, so all should be well. And all will stay well if you don't drive us off course, Spider. John, I should say. Fuck. I hate pretending we are not pirates, goddamn it!"

"What do you blather about, Mister Hughes?" Spider winked upon uttering Odin's fake name, then popped the pipe back into his mouth.

"We are bound for Boston, aye? Not bloody far from Nantucket, aye? The island where your woman waits for you, or, at least you think she does, although it has been a damned long time and you are not worth waiting for. And she's got your little boy, right?"

"All true," Spider said. He wondered if his son, maybe nine years old by now, would grow to be taller than him.

Odin nodded. "So, here we are, honest as we can be and forgetting all our pirating, sailing aboard a sweet little ship to the life you've been pining after ever since I met you, and most bothersome that is, I might add, and now you start talking about murder. Bloody hell, man, must we shake you? Slap you? Douse you in the cold sea?"

Scottish, Spider decided. *Today, he sounds very Scottish.*

Spider removed his pipe and sipped from the flask. "A man was murdered. A good man, near as I can see. Do you not care about that?"

Odin spat. "Ha! I have not known the bastard Garrick even two weeks, Spider, and I've seen a lot of murders in my day. I sailed with Blackbeard, I did! I saw him murder a dozen men in a day. It is no matter to me if Calvin Garrick got murdered, he isn't any more dead that way than if he just fucking fell!"

"Listen, mate . . ."

"No! You listen!" Odin spat on the deck. "It is no matter to me whether *Minuet* reaches Boston or goes off to the bloody Mediterranean to rob the sultans. But it matters to you, you lobcock, and if you go about talking about murders and such, you will rile things up and men will sharpen their steel and slice your goddamned neck while you sleep. Or we'll have the goddamned Navy crawling all over this ship so they can write reports or whatever to the Admiralty. Is that what you want? A bunch of men in uniforms who might figure out you sliced the neck of the man who killed your friend?"

The two men stared at each other as pipe smoke swirled about the cramped forecastle. Hob sat on a bunk and watched them.

"Is that what you aim for, by God?" Odin whispered it, and put a hand on Spider's shoulder.

"We'll fight them off," Hob said, beaming as though he looked forward to the opportunity. *The young fool probably did*, Spider supposed.

"I'm not planning to ask a lot of questions or stir the pot," Spider said. "I am just telling you, Garrick was murdered."

Odin blinked. "How do you know that?"

"I've seen two men plunge from the trees in my day," Spider said, sucking on the pipe. "One was on *Lamia*, when I sailed with Bent

Thomas, and the ship took a bad dip after a broadside poked a hole in our hull. The other was before that, on *Lily*, when George Looman went up top drunker than I will ever be. Anyway, both those men screamed like a goddamned gale all the way down and flapped their fucking arms like they could fly and snatched at every line they could see, no matter how far out of reach."

"So?" That was Hob, his forehead scrunching beneath his blond locks.

"So," Spider said, "Calvin Garrick fell like a sack of grain dropped into a hold. No sound, no movement, no reaching out to grab a ratline or anything. Just . . . dead silence."

Hob and Odin peered at each other. "It is true," Odin said. "Aye, that is right. He was dead on the way down." He turned toward Spider. "I still do not care. I still do not think we need to go about saying that he was murdered."

"Aye," Hob replied. "Odin is right, I think. We can keep silent until we reach Boston, and tell the captain then. Or let him discover what happened on his own. He's a smart man, Captain Bellows is. Maybe he will discover what happened without any help from us at all."

Spider, lost in his own thoughts, seemed not to hear.

"It should be simple to reckon this out," Spider cut in. "The killer had to be on the same beam with him, right? Probably stabbed him or clubbed him. A hard shove would not serve, because that would not have killed him, aye? He'd have made all that noise we talked about if he was living. So a stab or a thunk, then."

"Aye," Hob said. "That seems likely."

"So, how many men were working that beam with him?"

"Three others," Odin said. "Woodley, Simon, and Gray, it was."

"Did you see any of them with a cudgel or dirk?" Hob's eyebrows arched and his eyes widened.

Odin ran a callused hand roughly through Hob's thick hair. "They all have knives, fool. They're sailors."

"Aye," Hob said, pushing Odin's hand away. "Don't do that. I'm not the ship's cat."

Spider nodded. "Every hand has a knife, aye, and I suspect that is how the deed was done. If he was clubbed, hell, that would have been noticed, surely? You can stab a man smooth and quiet, if you know how, but you have to hit him damned hard if you kill him with a chunk of wood or something. Need to take a big swing. Hard to hide that, I would think. Someone likely would have noticed."

Odin nodded. "I think someone might have seen a clubbing, likely, aye."

"So probably a knife." Spider stabbed the air with the stem of his pipe. "That would make a mess, though. A man would have to be stupid to wipe it on his shirt or breeches, and stupider still to carry it around with a man's blood on it, aye? If it had been me, I'd have flung the thing into the sea while all eyes were on Garrick's fall."

He clamped his teeth on the pipe stem. "We shall not find a weapon, I reckon. But," he pointed at Hob, "let's keep watch for anyone who says he lost a knife, or hasn't got one, or asks Mister Gordon about getting one."

Hob nodded. "That is good. Aye."

"In the meantime," Spider continued, "we'll have to figure out which one of those gents had a reason to kill him."

Odin scowled. "Why do we have to do that? Everyone thinks he just fell. I say we just pretend we think that, too. That will keep us out of trouble, by God."

Spider ignored the one-eyed man. "It is a calm day, still morning and the wind just starting to come up, so he had not been up there long, and he did not smell of booze."

"I trust you for smelling liquor," Hob said.

"Silence, boy."

"And I know he slept," Hob continued. "He snores, he does. Snored all the night, so he wasn't up drinking nor nothing."

"Good," Spider said. "Excellent. You do pay attention to things at times, Hob."

Odin blinked. "I still do not care, and I don't know why you would care, either. I say, keep your head down, don't get involved in the affairs of other men, and get back to the Colonies and hope your woman even remembers your name. Hell, if you are not in a hurry to see her, I'll go find her myself."

Spider clutched at his shirt and felt the heart pendant, ignoring Odin's last comment. "She'll remember me," he said. "We married, and she bore my son."

"Ha!" Odin snatched the flask from Spider and took a swig. "You could not have been much older than this whelp"—he pointed at Hob—"when you tupped her, and you have been away eight or nine years, aye? Married her right before you left for the sea and then never come back. That's a long time."

Aye. A long, long time.

"You want any chance of a life with her, you'd best not start poking your nose into a murder. You do that, and someone will take offense. If you don't get killed or arrested before we raise Boston, you'll have the cap'n bringing on the authorities after. We don't like being around lawmen and Navy officers, you might remember. You, me, Hob, we've all done some pirating, aye?"

Aye, Spider thought. *I remember. I remember the bright sun gleaming on* Lily's *sails the day* Lamia *chased her down. I remember the nine-pound balls that cracked* Lily's *mast. I remember Bent Thomas and his savage crew leaping over our rails, howling like wolves, waving sharp steel and thundering guns. I remember the screams of* Lily's *crewmen as they went overboard, and the laughter of Bent Thomas and his men. And I remember Thomas telling me I didn't have to die if I'd serve him as carpenter. I remember making that deal with the devil, and vowing I would escape that life and get back to Em and my baby boy.*

But Bent Thomas would not let me keep my hands clean. Everyone fights. Everyone kills. Everyone shares the guilt.

And everyone can hang when we get caught.

"Aye," Spider said. "I remember."

"Then hammer things, and cut planks, and mind your duties," Odin said. "Let Calvin Garrick sink into the sea and to hell with finding out how he died."

Spider inhaled until the pipe fired bright and then slowly died. "I suppose we can't really change anything, can we?"

Odin smiled. "He's just as dead, whether we catch his killer or not."

The three friends sat in silence for a while. Spider took another swig, then handed the flask to Hob. The lad took a long swallow.

"You drink like a man," Spider said.

"I am a man," Hob answered.

"Ha!" Odin grabbed the flask and tilted it up, pouring the last of the amber fluid into his throat.

Spider slapped his knee.

"Hob, they'll be stitching the man into the shroud by now. Go help them."

Hob nodded. "I will. But why?"

"I did not see a stab wound or anything. See if you can do better than me."

"God damn it," Odin muttered.

"Aye." Hob started to rush off.

"Wait, boy. Look right here," Spider said, placing a hand at the base of his skull, toward the back. "Or here," he added, touching a spot low on his back. "Someplace Garrick would not see a blade coming. That's how a sneaky fellow would do it, right?"

"Aye." Hob was excited now; this task was much more interesting than fetching hammers or measuring lumber. "That's how I'd do it."

"You are a goddamned fool, Spider John."

"I probably am, Odin. I probably am."

3

*T*he men stood in ranks amidships as Calvin Garrick's shrouded remains were carried on a plank toward his deep ocean grave. The chill Spider felt was not from the September air.

Captain Bellows read solemnly, in a voice that rose and fell in volume with the gentle waves. Spider thought he'd heard the text before. Ecclesiastes, he believed.

"I said in mine heart," the captain said, seemingly more from memory than from reading the battered book in his hands, "God shall judge the righteous and the wicked. For there is a time there for every purpose and for every work."

"No purpose for my work. It was wasted effort," Hob whispered, after pushing his way through the assembled men and taking up a place next to Spider. "Everything was mushed up, his neck shoved down into his shoulders and his back sort of snapped. There was no way to find a knife wound."

"Shhhhhhh." Spider glanced about, but no one seemed to have noticed Hob's words. He caught the eye of Ruth Copper, though. She'd traded her breeches and flintlocks for dresses and flowered hats after they'd all managed to steal enough coin to pay her passage aboard *Minuet.* Odin's plot, that had been. He'd spent just enough time in Plymouth to know where lads did a bit of gambling, and he, Spider, and Hob had remained sober long enough to aim some guns and make off with a fat pot with little trouble. It had been a sweet little crime, and Spider still felt shame at how good it had felt to pull it off. *Forgive us, Lord. It was for a good cause, Lord, truly. Ruth don't want to be a criminal any more than I do. If one last crime leads to a life without crime, that's a gain, right?*

She looked quite fetching this morning, he decided. It was a pleasant diversion from the death rites, and Spider immediately felt guilty once he caught himself being distracted.

Ruth looked away from him. *Was she having similar thoughts?* He wondered.

Ruth had said she had unfinished business in the Colonies, and family in Virginia, but she would not say more than that. Spider and Ruth had unfinished business between them, too, or so it felt to him. She always seemed on the verge of saying something, and he always felt as though he was betraying Em whenever he was with Ruth—even though things had never gotten so far. *Well*, he thought, *except the time she doffed her blouse and tried to catch me off guard. But that had ended in drawn weapons, not lovemaking.* The lovemaking had happened only in some dreams, and in distracted thoughts.

Damn it, Spider John! A man has died here today. Heed that, not the girl.

The captain had closed the Bible. "God, I think, will judge Calvin Garrick a good man. That, certainly, is how we shall remember him. And so now we commend our brother to the deep, and to his Heavenly Father. Amen."

A chorus of amens followed the captain's words. The board tipped, and the dead man slid into the waiting sea, with scrap metal and holystones tucked into his shroud to make sure he went all the way down.

A moment of silence followed. Spider tried hard not to think about the decaying corpse, and the hungry fishes, and the crabs and sea worms.

"Back to duty," Captain Bellows said. "Mister Gordon, choose a man to fill Mister Garrick's role aloft, if you please, and let us get sail up quickly. We miss a good breeze, but we are ahead of schedule and I intend to keep us so. Mister Garrick would not have wanted us to miss a good breeze, I should think, nor to give up bonuses."

"Aye, sir."

The captain's jaw worked back and forth for a moment. "I think an extra ration of grog, this evening, that we might drink to the man's memory."

"Aye, sir," Gordon answered. "It is a hard day. Seitz?"

The sea cook's mouth barely moved within his great wealth of dark beard. "Sir?"

"See to it the men have an extra tot, and don't water it too much."

"Aye, sir," the cook said, marching off to see that it was done.

The captain turned aft, toward his quarters.

"If you please, sir, I think Jim Trawley would be a good choice on the topsail yard."

Spider turned to see who had spoken. It was Isaac Gray, one of the crewmen who had been on the beam when Garrick had toppled from it. Gray had a grin that was too wide for his face, and squinty eyes. Spider thought the man looked rather like an imp.

"Sailed with him before, I have, and he's not skittish to be up so high." Gray nodded for emphasis. "He can handle the work, I'll vouch for it."

"Mister Trawley, come forth," Gordon ordered.

A tall man, wide of shoulder and sporting a deep white scar on his bronzed cheek, stepped forward. "Aye, sir?"

"Are you ready to work above? We can get by with one less deck hand."

"I like it up there, sir. A man can see far."

"Indeed." Gordon nodded. "It shall be so, then. Mister Gill?"

Hob's gaze fell to the deck. "Aye, sir."

"You shall take Mister Trawley's spot on deck. Mister Coombs, you can fare well enough without a carpenter's mate, I trust? For a while, at least? The ship is in excellent shape."

"Aye," Spider said. "I can handle my chores without him." *Hell, I often do.* "If I have a need, I'll ask for him. It won't hurt him to work a bit harder." Then he whispered to Hob. "You are better at hauling on a rope than cutting wood, I dare say."

"Aye," Hob said. He looked at Spider and spoke so softly the carpenter had to lean in to hear the words. "Sorry I could not find a knife wound."

"No matter," Spider muttered. "It's murder, nonetheless."

"Do we tell the captain?"

"Let me think on that," Spider said. "As our one-eyed friend says, that might cause us trouble. A great deal of trouble, the kind that could get us hung along with the murderer. Aye? So, go see to your boring duties."

4

Spider spent the rest of the day sawing spars to proper length, and making his inspections of hull and bulkheads, and watching Gray and his mates, Homer Woodley and Ronald Simon. They reefed the sail at Gordon's order, and Spider noted that the three of them spoke to one another a great deal as they worked. Trawley, the new addition, seemed to be conversing freely as well. They all were too far aloft for Spider to hear what they were saying, though.

Spider wiped sweat from his brow. Soon, the bell would clang and the watch would change. He looked forward to a meal, a drink, and a pipe.

Spider looked upward again. There was little room up there; men stood upon lines suspended below the spars, working almost elbow-to-elbow. It was close labor, requiring a good deal of teamwork.

That realization led him to a conclusion. He glanced toward Hob, who was placing holystones in a chest after an afternoon of scrubbing Calvin Garrick's blood from the weather deck. Spider had spent a good deal of time this day studying Hob, and he noticed that the boy had paid close attention to the men above. Had Hob stumbled upon the same point he himself had noticed? He would know soon enough.

The members of the evening watch, preparing for duty, were finishing up their meal of salt pork, crusty bread, and rum mixed with water when the bell rang.

"To duty lads!" Mister Gordon bellowed, and men moved to

comply. The men aloft started downward. Odin, working the foremast topsail, clambered down slowly. *Careful, old man*, Spider thought.

Spider sighed. Odin claimed to have sailed with Blackbeard, and Spider had seen him tie knots with great dexterity and race much younger men into the trees. The idea that Odin might finally be showing signs of having lived through all those years, all those battles and tall tales—the notion made Spider John wince. Such things could not be. Odin was a legend who had strode across the bloody deck of *Queen Anne's Revenge* with bloody Blackbeard himself. Odin was supposed to endure forever.

Spider also watched Trawley, Gray, Simon, and Woodley descend. They took their time, talking among themselves. Hob was at his side before the first of that group—Simon—set foot upon the weather deck.

"I'm hungry," Hob groaned.

"You are always hungry," Spider replied. Let us get in the line." Sailors from the day watch were gathering to collect their meal and grog.

"Aye," Hob answered. "I had a thought, Spider."

"Did you, now?" He leaned closer and whispered. "And if you don't want your balls made into a toy for the ship's cat, you will damn well start calling me John."

"Sorry." Hob lowered his voice. "You realized there is no goddamned way one of those gents killed Garrick without the others noticing?"

Spider grinned. "Aye. I had the same thought. Too close up there for something like that to go unnoticed. You are smarter than I thought, Hobgoblin."

"Stop calling me that. It makes me feel like a child."

Spider sighed. Hob was right, of course. Spider looked on the lad as a son, filling a void left by the real son he'd never really known. That probably wasn't fair to Hob or Johnny, he knew. "Well enough. You've grown into a man, with the right to be called what you will. I will try to remember."

"Good," Hob said.

"And you try to forgive me if I forget once in a while," Spider said.

Hob merely groaned. They stopped talking once they fell into line for their meals.

"Have you decided what to do?" That was Odin, cutting in line behind Spider. A couple of men groused at that, but Odin merely stared at them with his one good eye, waved a knife, and shouted "Ha!" The complainers decided not to press the issue.

"I have decided," Spider said. "I am going to eat. I am going to drink my grog. I am going to fire my pipe. And then I am going to have a discussion with the cap'n."

"Don't get us hung," Odin whispered.

"Aye," Spider said.

The three of them remained quiet until they reached Seitz. They took up wooden bowls and cups from a barrel, then the German poked a fork into hunks of pork and bread to serve them. Spider's pork slid off the fork and onto the deck after giving his bowl a glancing blow.

Seitz went on with his business, rather indifferently, as Spider stood in place.

"Well? Move along, John," Seitz said.

"I want my pork."

"I gave you pork."

"You missed my bowl, and I think Hughes is standing on my pork."

"So?"

"So give me a goddamned hunk of pork that ain't got goddamned boots all over it."

Seitz pointed toward the gray mass at Odin's feet. "Your pork there. Eat it."

Spider seethed. "Listen, man. I know all this meat is tougher than a cedar shake. I know the one on the deck probably ain't no more dirty than the ones in your kettle, even after he's squashed it. But putting a damn chunk of meat in a bowl is a fairly easy job and you managed to foul it up anyway, and I don't feel like plucking my food from the deck. So, if you please, give me a hunk from the kettle. The cat can have what you dropped."

Men in line behind Spider grumbled as the two men stared at each other.

"Aye," Seitz finally said. "Hate to waste meat. But I give you new pork."

"There has never been new pork in your bloody galley," Spider grumbled. "Methuselah threw this crap to his dogs."

Seitz plopped a new chunk into the bowl, and Spider sniffed it and scowled. "Thank you, though."

The cook's mate ladled grog into their cups, full to the brim this time so they could drink their respects to Calvin Garrick. They found a spot on a trunk by the larboard gunwale and sat to eat. "Goddamned sin against rum, this is," Spider said after his first sip. "Watering good rum, goddamned crime." He took a deeper swallow. "At least they gave us a good pour."

"Those three, the ones who were up top with Garrick when he fell, they keep to themselves," Hob said. Those men were getting their food now, and exchanging a few words with Seitz.

Spider nodded. "Aye. They like Trawley well enough, though. Odin, can you hear what they talk about up there?"

"No," the old man said. "They talk, but they don't do it loud. It is much like the way we keep to ourselves, us three," Odin said, looking around.

"Aye," Spider said. "I had that thought, too."

"I think they may be pirates! Like us!" Hob's eyebrows lifted at the thought.

"Like us?" Odin's words were clear, despite being uttered around a hunk of tough pork that might have served to plug a small hull leak below. Spider gave up on trying to bite through his and lobbed the meat over his shoulder to splash into the Atlantic.

Spider wagged a finger. "We are former pirates, Hob."

Hob nodded. "So you say, John. So you say. Former pirates."

The old man grinned. "Once a pirate, always a pirate," he muttered.

"If they be pirates, or former pirates, do you think Garrick somehow realized that?" Hob took a bite of bread, then continued with his mouth full. "Maybethaswythaykillim."

Spider stared at the lad. "Talk after you swallow that, you lobcock."

Hob swallowed. "Maybe that's why they killed him. He figured out they were pirates."

"Maybe," Spider said. "The trick will be this. How do I tell the cap'n about this killing without him finding out that we are former pirates, too?"

"Do we have to tell him anything? Ha!"

Hob punched Odin's arm. "Garrick shared some damned good honey with me!"

"Pardon my damned soul if I don't want to hang over a god-damned chunk of bread and a few drams of bee shit!" Odin had whispered it, but it still sounded like a shout to Spider. "And he didn't share no honey with me, now did he?"

"Silence, you buffle-headed loons! I need to think!"

Spider set his wooden bowl on the deck beside him and licked the salt from the pork off his fingers. Then he reached up to the band of his wide-brimmed hat, donned because the air had become quite chill, and found his clay pipe. "Go fetch me a brand, Hob."

"I am not your slave," the lad said.

"Go fetch me a brand, I said. And then I have a secret mission for you. Hurry!"

Hob scurried off.

"What the hell are you on about, John?" Odin scratched his ruined face.

"What do you mean?" Spider filled his pipe from a pouch on his belt.

"Secret mission? Jesus!" Odin sounded decidedly Scottish at the moment.

"Where are you really from, Odin? You never say."

"Maybe I'll tell you one day," he answered. Then he winked, and when the lone eye vanished for a moment he looked even more frightening than usual. "And maybe I won't tell you. Depends on if it ever needs to be told. Ha!"

Hob returned with a short stick, flaming at one end. Spider took it and soon had his small pipe glowing red. He chucked the brand over his shoulder and into the sea.

"Well, then, you've got your smoke. What is my mission, Spider?"

"Everyone is eating, or working," Spider said. "Get to the forecastle, and if it is empty, peek into their chests. Gray, Woodley, and Simon. And Trawley. Garrick's, too, though that may be picked over by now. See what's there. While you do that, I will go have a word with our cap'n. Odin, you stand watch for Hob and give him a fair warning if anyone approaches."

"Aye." Hob ran off.

"Are you really doing this?" Odin snapped his fingers in the carpenter's face as he said it. Spider sighed.

"Aye," Spider said. "Hob is going to inspect the trunks of the men who were up there with Garrick when he fell, and those of their new friend and the victim, too, and maybe find some indication they are pirates, or killers. Something to tell us why the man is dead."

"Meddle and you'll get us dangling, Spider John. Mark my words."

"No noose for you, Odin. Or Hob. Do not fret. When I talk to Cap'n Bellows, I will not mention you and Hob."

Odin spat a fat wad of pork gristle onto the deck. "Don't know why you need to talk with the cap'n at all," he said, "and he knows you and Hob and me came aboard together. If you hit a lee shore and he reckons you for a pirate . . ."

"Former pirate," Spider whispered.

"They hang you either way!" Odin smacked his own forehead with the palm of his hand. "If they figure you were a pirate, they will figure the same for me! I don't want to hang for a man we met two weeks ago."

Spider closed his eyes. "Calvin Garrick deserves justice."

"Let God do it," Odin said. "Not us."

Spider rose. "I will not pull you into this," he said.

"See to that!"

"Keep watch for Hob, if you please." Spider strode aft toward the quarterdeck, where the captain paced in deep thought. "We don't want him getting stabbed nor hung, do we?"

"I might stab you," the old man growled, but he moved toward the forecastle.

Before Spider reached the ladder, Ruth Copper called him.

"Will you finish my grog, John?"

5

Ruth's perfume mingled with the scent of the booze, and Spider could make out the blue in her eyes even in the dim light. Her eyes were the kind of blue you could not help but notice.

"Well, if you do not wish to drink it." He took the cup and drained it.

"I knew that would tempt you," she said, leaning her head a bit sideways so the dark hair dangled and shimmered in the lantern's glow.

That's not all that tempts me, he thought. *Was she being so alluring on purpose?*

"Thank you," he said, waving the empty cup.

"I have seen you conferring with your shipmates," she said softly. "A bit secretive, I should say. One suspects a conspiracy of sorts."

"Well, we have things to reckon over," he replied.

"About Calvin Garrick's death." She leaned forward slightly and looked him directly in the eyes, as if to find the truth there no matter what he might say. She said it with such certainty that Spider wondered if she had been listening to them somehow.

"Aye."

"You believe he was murdered."

"Aye."

"Do you not worry?" She asked it softly, before turning to stroll away.

Spider followed. "Worry?"

Ruth took a deep breath. "You are headed back to your woman, aye? Em? And the rest of your family?"

Spider could not decide if her words had a tinge of bitterness, or if he was imagining that.

"Well, yes. I am going to see Em, and my son, but I have no other family on Nantucket, other than her father and her brother. I grew up near Salem and in Boston. Went to Nantucket to help build whaleboats. Em grew up there, though."

"I see," Ruth said. "You've always made it sound like home."

"It is where Em is," he said.

"Well." She paused, then looked at him.

"Murders mean investigations, courts. I know something of courts. My father was a judge. Witnesses will be needed. Accusers will have to be on hand, to testify. Such folk might not be allowed to go running off to Nantucket. Not soon, anyway."

"Surely, a man will be allowed to see his wife and child."

She turned suddenly, and they stood close together. "An accuser might be delayed. And a killer might make use of that time." Her eyes widened, and seemed to be saying more than her lips did.

"If you are thinking the killer might decide to cut my tongue out, or worse, to keep me from telling my tale, well, I can take care of myself," Spider whispered. "You know this to be true."

"Your actions risk more than your life, John." She shuddered. "Your friends would share that risk, too."

Spider nodded. "They are not ones to shirk from risk."

"No. They certainly are not." Ruth paused and bit her lip. "John, I am thinking about your woman, I am not . . ."

"You are what?"

"I am not so certain she waits for you, John. All those years? And you both so young when you left? But if she did wait, well."

"Well?"

"Then you do her wrong," she said, nodding as though she'd just come to the conclusion. "You do her wrong, I say, if you get tangled up in trials and testimonies and, and fighting and such. You should fly to her, if she truly has waited for you! Damn you, it is what I should want if I were . . ."

Her forehead wrinkled sternly.

"If you were what?"

"If I were waiting for my man to come home from the bloody sea."

She turned and marched off, heavy skirt swirling, before Spider could say another word.

6

*S*pider asked permission to mount to the quarterdeck.

"Come," the captain said, gruffly. Spider wished he'd noted the captain's stern countenance before he'd sought the man's attention, but it was too late to change his mind. There was nothing else to do now but climb up and find out what irritated the man.

Whatever it was, it seemed directed at him. The captain's eyes stayed on Spider, and the man's scowl cut deeper lines in his face and brow.

Spider's mind ran through a list of possible crimes. Had he left a hammer on the deck somewhere? Had he neglected a repair? Had he ordered Hob to do something and then forgotten to check up on the young fool?

He couldn't think of a damned thing.

Spider reached the captain's side, and noticed the man glanced quickly about, presumably to gauge whether they might be overheard.

Good Lord, this must be bad. Has someone aboard pegged me as a pirate?

"John," Bellows said more quietly than might be expected, given his demeanor. The man's habit of working his lower jaw back and forth as though he was passing a quid of tobacco from one cheek to the other made him look as though he was working up a powerful lecture at all times, and Spider suspected he was in for a storm.

"Cap'n," Spider said, removing his hat and adopting a respectful attitude.

The captain looked him in the eye and then—actually smiled.

"She is pretty, that girl, so I do not blame you for your attentions," he said, almost whispering. Bellows glanced back at the wheel to assure himself the man there was not eavesdropping. "But I wish you to consider my position."

Spider nodded. "Of course, sir." *Was the captain thinking of bedding Ruth himself?*

"A pretty girl on a voyage of any kind can be trouble," the captain said, "particularly if she travels alone. That is never a good idea, a woman alone on a ship. That's perplexing, mind you, and I was quite concerned and I tried to dissuade her of it, for it can be damned bad luck, they say."

"I've heard that, sir, aye."

"I am not superstitious, John," the captain continued. "I do not go about fretting over ghosts and curses and broken mirrors or black cats. But there is the kind of bad luck that comes when you do unwise things. Perhaps, I've done an unwise thing in accepting her as a passenger."

"I am not sure I follow, sir."

"Do you not?" The captain actually grinned, then grew stern again. "I had misgivings, but she paid good money and insisted she would be quite safe, and she seemed confident. I ignored my misgivings and welcomed her aboard. Well ..."

Bellows stared at Spider and raised his eyebrows. "I can see, John, that she is not safe after all, at least as far as your intentions."

Spider realized his feet were shuffling a bit, and willed himself to stop. "Intentions, sir? Cap'n, I have no intentions."

The captain's head tilted sharply, and the stern expression returned. "Do not lie to me, John."

Spider swallowed hard, and said nothing.

Captain Bellows glanced up at the sails, turned his face to the wind for a moment, and nodded in satisfaction. "Her sails and courses all are as they should be," he said. "John, a pretty girl on a ship can be managed, so long as the hands all realize she is beyond reach to each and every one of them. Do you understand?" The jaw worked hard as the captain stared at his carpenter.

"I believe I do, sir." Spider nodded.

"So long as none of them can touch her, the men will behave. Oh, they will complain among themselves, and they will spit overboard in frustration, and they will certainly watch her comings and goings with great—indeed, lewd—interest, but they will behave, if they know what is best for them. But when one man seems to be fulfilling that desire and the rest are not, well, let us say, jealousy is a fire that makes a kettle boil over."

"Aye, sir."

"A ship is a kettle, John. I do not intend to allow my kettle to boil over."

"Aye, sir."

The captain nodded solemnly. "I'd not want to see you defending yourself from a jealous shipmate, John. I can't afford to lose the services of you or any other soul aboard to injury. Not after we lost Calvin Garrick, may God grant his soul peace. And even if it never comes to a fight, I don't want bad feelings roiling about, John. It makes for an unlucky ship. Men grouse, when they should be working. They lie awake, dreaming of revenge or worse, instead of resting. I will not have that."

"Aye, sir. I take your meaning, sir."

"Be sure that you do." The captain sighed. "So keep your distance, and keep the peace on my ship, and once we reach Boston, well," he smiled again, "I wish you joy."

"I will heed your advice, cap'n."

"Good. You are a fine carpenter, Mister Coombs. I should hate to have to replace you."

"I should hate that, too, sir." It was true; Bellows had shown himself to be a fair man, and Spider had sailed with many who weren't.

Bellows nodded. "So, you've heard me out, and now, I suppose, it is time for me to hear you out. You came seeking me. What presses on your mind, John?"

"Aye, sir," Spider said. "Well, it concerns Mister Garrick, sir, and the manner of his death."

The captain had been eyeing the rigging again, and listening to the backstays humming in the wind and the creak of the mast, but now he turned his full attention to Spider John. He leaned close and growled in a low tone. "What do you mean, by the manner of his death?"

Spider forced himself to look the captain in the eyes, though he feared he was on the verge of irritating him again.

"I believe it was murder, sir." He'd whispered it, but it still seemed thunderous on the quiet sea. Spider cast a quick look at the helmsman, whose attention seemed focused on the rolling waves.

"Murder?" The captain stepped backward as though Spider had swung a cutlass at him. Then he mastered himself and stood still, once more the man in complete control.

"I shall go to my cabin, Mister Coombs." The captain whispered it, without looking at him. "Wait until the bell strikes the next hour, then come to me, and we shall discuss this beyond the reach of prying eyes and ears."

"Thank you, sir." Spider nodded, and turned to go.

"Mister Gordon!"

"Aye, captain, sir."

"I shall be in my quarters. *Minuet* is in your hands."

Gordon, amidships, smiled and nodded. "Aye, sir."

Spider John descended to the weather deck. Hob was waiting for him.

"Well, boy?"

"Don't call me boy," Hob growled. "And we had it right. Those men are most definitely pirates, or I ain't never ducked a cutlass."

7

Spider took his carpenter's mate by the arm and guided him toward the mizzenmast. "And what makes you declare that? And speak quietly, damn you, or I'll whip your ass red with your own cock."

Hob gave Spider a look that plainly said he did not believe Spider could best him in a fight, but otherwise ignored Spider's jab. "I declare they are pirates because I know a damned treasure map when I see one! And I saw one, I did, in Gray's chest!"

Spider looked about, held up a hand to silence Hob as a seaman strolled within earshot, then leaned toward the lad when the interloper had vanished. "Treasure map, do you say?"

"Aye," Hob said, his excitement evident despite his conspiratorial whisper. "I am not much of a reader, but I have seen charts before and I recognized the drawing of Hispaniola, I did. And there is an island drawn far and away south by southwest of Hispaniola, marked by an X, and a tiny place it is, nowhere near as big as Hispaniola. And then, there's a box with another map and an arrow that points to the X. There's a sketch of that island, I think that is what it is. It's got hills and a spring, it looks like, and there is an X marked on the island near the spring, to the east. I am certain it means there is a treasure there!"

Spider sighed. "I have told you this before, Hob. Men make maps for a lot of reasons. It does not have to be a pirate hoard of gold. And drawing up a map only gives other people a chance to find your gold, aye? I'd trust my memory, and never draw a fucking map, if I was hiding my treasure."

"You don't have any treasure worth burying," Hob said pointedly.

"That is gospel, I suppose."

"Anyway, I know this is a treasure map." Hob nodded defiantly. "I know you hate guessing. Well, I am not guessing. I know I am right."

Spider nodded. "And how do you know you are right?"

"There was a goddamned chest drawn right next to the god-damned island!"

"A chest?"

"Aye. It was drawn on the map. I am guessing it be full of gold! Why else would anyone draw a chest on the map?"

"Hush!"

"Sorry," Hob said. They fell silent as a pair of seamen lugged a small keg toward the galley, and moved aside as the ship's cat chased a chicken past their feet.

"I hope the cat doesn't mean to eat that chicken," Spider said, "despite what happens to any eggs Seitz touches. I don't like birds, but I like eggs."

He was happy to see the cat, a black-and-gray creature that no one aboard seemed to like much, scurry away as Gordon stepped between it and the bird.

Hob, however, ignored the drama. "But gold, Spider! Gold!"

"Aye, so you reckoned. Was anything written on the map?"

"There was a row of shapes, like boxes and circles and such. In a row, though, like letters. Near the island. It was poorly drawn, it was, but it looked to me that the island was far and away from Hispaniola, like I said."

"Shapes?"

"Aye, but arranged like letters in words and sentences. I think it is a code, I do."

"Maybe a name, maybe latitude and longitude, but in code," Spider mused. "Well, my young swashbuckling friend, this is, indeed, sounding like a treasure map. But these are not exactly strange waters, aye? An island would be known to many sailors, would it not?"

"I said it is a small one, Spider. Some boring place no one would heed."

"Aye." Spider nodded. "I suspect a fellow on the account with a fair amount of gains might hide it on some damned scrap of an island that no one visits."

"I knew it!" Hob kept his voice down, but he jumped as he said it.

"Suspecting and knowing are not the same thing, but you may be right." Spider ran a finger through his long beard. "And you said there was a spring, so it might be a place men visit to take on fresh water. But I could see some bastard burying stuff there, even so. He could add to his hoard and take on water in the same trip. Maybe some cap'n knew the place for its spring, and thought it a good hiding place, too."

Hob rubbed his hands together. "I truly wish I could read that code."

"Aye. The code is what interests me. If Garrick somehow stumbled upon such a map, well, greedy men might kill him because of that."

"Aye," Hob said. "Men have been killed for less."

"Have you got the map?"

Hob punched Spider square in the chest. "Am I a fool? No, I do not have the map. If I took it, they'd know someone had been spying, aye? We don't want that, do we? So I left it be."

Spider punched him back. "Good boy."

"Good man, you mean."

"Good man. I wonder if Garrick saw something, or heard something? Where is Odin?"

"Those lobcocks are on the foredeck," Hob said. "Odin is hanging near them, spying."

The ship's bell sounded.

"It is time I went to speak more with Cap'n Bellows," Spider said.

Hob looked dubious. "Are you going to tell him about the treasure map?"

Spider sighed. "I have no bloody goddamned idea at all what I am going to tell him. But I certainly won't tell him you've been poking about in other men's belongings."

8

The swinging lantern's uncertain light and the captain's never still lower jaw gave the man an almost demonic aspect.

"Murder, you said." The captain sat behind his desk, hands clasped upon it. "Murder."

"Aye, sir. I believe it to be so."

"That is a terrible accusation to make against any man," Bellows said. "I suppose you have some proofs of it, before you go about breathing such a word? You have not uttered this to anyone else, have you?"

"No, sir."

The captain nodded. "That is good. And you have proofs?"

"Well, somewhat, sir," Spider said. "At least, I have noticed a few things that make it seem like a murder when you knot them all up together."

The captain closed his eyes and lowered his head. Spider supposed he was praying. Finally, the man raised his head. "What things, carpenter? Knot them up together for me."

No longer addressing me as John, Spider thought, *but as carpenter. Reminding me of my place, he is.*

"Aye, sir. Well, first there was the plunge. Very quiet and still he was, not even trying to save himself. I never saw no one fall so, not without a struggle to grab something. Anything. Made me think he was dead already, before he fell."

"Good Lord, man," the captain muttered tersely. "I hope you have more than that. You said murder."

"Sir, I should add . . ."

The captain scoffed. "Belay that! Mister Coombs, I once served aboard one of His Majesty's frigates. I was a mere midshipman, and might have advanced further in the king's service had I not been fortunate enough to be hired by Mister Morrell and . . ."

The captain paused. "My history is not relevant, and I shall not bore you with it. But I learned a great deal in the Royal Navy, where there are honest-by-God surgeons to attend the men, and I saw one fellow—with my own eyes, I saw him!—fall dead right to the deck in the middle of telling a tale about his damned dog! Alive with one breath, he was, and undeniably, undoubtedly dead with the next. The surgeon, a princely gentleman named Upjohn, he was, I hope he still is among us and not gone to the next world himself . . . well, he examined the poor dead soul and told us it was his heart. It just stopped working, he said, as hearts sometimes do."

"Very sad, sir."

"That is not my point, John," the captain said softly. "My point is merely this: Men die. Sometimes suddenly. Hale and healthy in the morning, a corpse by midday. It is shocking, but it is true. Mister Garrick might have suffered such a fate. His heart might have decided his time was up, and if that happened, well, he'd fall silent the way you described, would he not?"

"I reckon you are right, sir."

The captain nodded his head. "You are young yet. Not quite thirty years, are you?"

"As near as I can count it, aye, sir."

"Well, work upon the broad sea long enough, and you'll see strange things. Things like men dying without apparent cause. There is no need to invent reasons for it. Certainly, there is no need to look for a murder."

I've seen more men die than I've seen years, Spider thought. *And I've seen conspirators huddle together, just like the men who were up there when Calvin Garrick fell.*

Spider John cleared his throat. "Aye, sir."

"So what would you have me do, Mister Coombs? Accuse someone of murder on the basis of what you've presented to me here?"

Spider dared not mention the map Hob had found.

"I reckon not, sir."

The captain stared at him a long while. "I feel you are not telling me all."

Spider swallowed. "Cap'n, sir, I might have been hasty. I just get a general feeling from those gents. And that silent fall bothered me."

"Those gents. It would have to have been one of those men on the spar with him that killed him," the captain said, his jaw working again and his hands tightening their grip upon one another. "Woodley. Gray. Simon. Those gents came to me with recommendations, John. They were well spoken of. I do not dare accuse them, nor do I think you have the right of it, mind you, but . . . well, you are diligent in your duties, never need to be reminded of them, and I do not think you say such things without turning them over in your mind. But, well, you knelt by the man, didn't you? I recall your britches . . ."

"Aye, sir."

"Rushed in to help, and saw up close what befell, you did. Perhaps, John, the sight has unsettled you. Perhaps it has you imagining things."

"Aye, sir," Spider said. "I've not seen a great deal of death."

I hope that sounded convincing.

The captain nodded. "Well, you are a good man, John. You did well to bring your thoughts to my attention, and you did so with discretion. Therefore, I would deem it unwise to ignore your observations entirely."

"Aye, sir." Spider nodded. "I mean, thank you, sir."

"You understand me, I think? If we accuse on the basis of what you've said, we risk impugning innocent men. I will not do that. False witness, that would be, and I endeavor to live by the Commandments. And should we accuse them, we would need to lock them away, and guard them, and we are already short of hands. A deck hand is now working aloft, and your mate is hauling lines, Mister Gordon tells me."

"Aye, sir."

"So, we will not make a show of investigating these suspicions. That would cause more trouble than having the girl aboard. But if you give me your word to remain silent," the captain paused until Spider nodded in ascent, "and I mean silent as you'll be one day in your grave, carpenter, then you and I can quietly keep our eyes on these gents, and we can listen for loose talk or animosities. If I see or hear something amiss, I shall act. I promise you that. If you see or hear something amiss, you shall inform me. Quietly, of course."

"Aye, sir." Spider nodded again. "That seems a wise course."

"Very well. Are you certain you have told no one of your suspicions?"

"I have not, sir." *The lie seems a minor sin compared to your past ones*, Spider told himself.

"That is good, John. See that you don't. If flirting would cause dissension aboard *Minuet*, I think a murder accusation would provoke outright violence, so not a word, man. Not a word."

"Aye, sir."

"Very well. Pay attention, as will I. If they be killers, justice shall be done upon them. In the meantime, we shall not lose hard workers to the brig, nor shall we sow discontent among the crew. Am I understood?"

Spider nodded. "Aye, sir."

"Very well. Dismissed. I've told Mister Gordon to make sure we've some rousing music tonight. I hate sailing under a gloom. It has been a hard loss. It always is when a crewman is lost to us, but . . . well, we must sail on. Listen to a fine fiddle tonight, John, and forget conspiracies for the moment."

"Aye, cap'n."

Spider emerged onto the weather deck, and sighed. He'd done his duty.

He stepped forward and caught sight of Isaac Gray, staring at him from the larboard rail with cold, coal-hard eyes. The ever-present imp grin was still there, but there was nothing friendly in it.

9

Spider headed toward the opposite rail, and noticed Odin was already there. The one-eyed man fell in beside Spider and the two strolled forward. Samuel Bush, a fine fiddler when he wasn't hauling on ropes or scrubbing decks, was tuning his instrument somewhere on the foredeck. The ship's cat wailed a discordant answer that confirmed Spider's low opinion of cats.

"I'd rather we had a dog," he grumbled.

"Dogs make noise, too, Spider," said Odin, who'd been known to let a cat curl up on his lap when he thought no one would notice. "Gray saw you on the quarterdeck with the cap'n, earlier, and he paid close attention when you went to see him just now. He did not get close enough to the cap'n's door to eavesdrop, because I got there first. Ha!"

"Well done," Spider replied. "Did you hear what was said?"

"Most of it. Thanks for not mentioning me."

"Most welcome. Looks like rain there, south."

"We'll tack soon, no doubt, and ride before it." Odin glanced over his shoulder. "Gray is not following us, but I think his mates are up there listening to Sam."

"I think I'll fire some tobacco and listen a spell, too," Spider said. "That man can play." As if to prove Spider's assertion, the fiddler launched into something brisk. The hand claps and foot stomps were almost spontaneous, and the cat launched itself into the nearest hold.

Spider did not recognize the song, and he was convinced the musician was improvising a great deal, but the tune sounded vaguely Irish.

The carpenter went into a bit of a dance, partly because he was enjoying the music, but mostly as an excuse to spin around and see what Gray was up to.

Gray had not moved from his spot, but his eyes were locked on Spider.

"Bastard seems suspicious, he does."

"Aye," Odin answered. "You didn't go asking people questions about murder, did you?"

"No," Spider said. "But Gray might have noticed us whispering together. Or maybe he just has a guilty mind."

"He has a treasure map, too," Odin muttered.

"Hob told me." He stepped toward a gent who was lighting a smoke, and snatched his own clay pipe from the band of his hat. "Share the fire, Roberts?" Spider plucked some tobacco from his pouch and stuffed it into the bowl. "Thanks." Soon, he had a cloud wafting over his head.

"That'll help me think," he said. "A bit of rum or whisky would help, too."

"I am all out," Odin said. "And I suspect you know why."

Spider just winked in reply.

Bush had moved on to a jig, and was dancing and playing near the forecastle as crewmen clapped. "He played that one before," Spider said. "Calls it 'Soggy Biscuits,' says he composed it. Look, there's our friend."

Hob was on the foretop with Ruth Copper, who swayed prettily to the music. Woodley, Simon, and Trawley all huddled together near the foremast, and spoke in tones low enough to force them to lean heads together in order to hear.

"Do they look like conspirators to you?" Spider began climbing to the foretop.

"Do we look like conspirators to them? Ha!"

"Cap'n had me half thinking I was wrong, that maybe Garrick just had his heart go. Doctor Boddings, that old son of a bitch, said once it could go that way sometimes, a man alive and then he's not, just so."

"Was Boddings drunk at the time?"

"Probably," Spider admitted. "He seemed to know his trade, though." Spider wished he had a flask, to toast the memory of the retired Royal Navy surgeon and former shipmate aboard *Plymouth Dream*. "Anyway, cap'n did not seem to think there was much to my suspicions, but Gray watching us and these gents all whispering and such makes me think I was right after all."

"They look like killers to me," Odin said. "They remind me of us. Ha!"

"Belay that, you old warlock."

Spider kept watching Woodley and the others, and noticed they quickly hushed as Seitz approached them. The cook had a chunk of cheese, and shared bits of it with the conspirators as they listened to the fiddler.

"He doesn't drop their food," Spider grumbled.

Once they reached Hob and Ruth, Spider sucked on his pipe and pondered. After blowing out his third voluminous cloud, he signaled his friends to lean close.

"Well, I think this pipe has cleared the fog in my head and I have reckoned on something. It is a rather troublesome something, too, I dare say."

Hob whispered: "What is it?"

"What," he said, "do men with a map pointing them to an island of treasure also need, I ask you?"

They all stared at him.

"They need a ship," Spider said. "They need a goddamned ship."

10

The shipmates spent the next few minutes in silent thought before Hob whistled a low tone.

"You think they mean to take *Minuet*?" Odin scratched his chin.

Spider nodded, and thanked God for the music and clapping hands that covered their conversation. "If you had a treasure map pointing to the Spanish Main, but you were on a vessel bound for Boston, what would you do?"

"I'd take the ship," Hob said. "I'd take the bloody ship."

"Aye," Spider said, looking over his shoulder to assure himself no one was listening. Fortunately, most attention was still on the fiddler, who was playing wildly. More than a few eyes were locked on Ruth, too, he noticed.

"I can't navigate," Spider whispered to his friends, all leaning close together now, "so if it was me, I would wait until we hit the Colonial coast before I pounced. I can't navigate, but I can follow a coastline."

"That is trickier than you think," Odin said. "Shoals and currents, mind you. You can't just point south and keep the land to starboard."

"Well, aye," Spider said. "I reckon you are right. So, can any of these gents navigate?"

Hob shook his head. "I have no idea."

"Nor do I," Odin said. "They know their work in the trees, I know that. But I have no idea what else they know."

Spider pondered all that. "So, then, if taking *Minuet* is their plan, they could strike at any time if they know how to sail her. If they can't navigate, then probably they'll ty to arrange passage to the Main when we hit Boston. We might not be facing any danger at all if that is the way of it."

"Aye," Hob said, clearly enjoying this talk more than carpentry. "But we don't know, do we? Maybe Woodley or Gray or one of them can chart a course."

"Maybe. Did you spy any charts, Hob, other than the one? A compass, or anything of that sort?"

"No."

"Any weapons in their trunks?"

"No, John, not a one."

"So maybe those are hidden elsewhere," Ruth said. "If they plan a mutiny, they'll need guns."

The crew yelled as Bush finished his tune with a flurry of notes that ended way up the fiddle's neck. Once the applause was done and the musician had started a more somber tune, Spider continued whispering.

"Guns hidden elsewhere, or else they are not yet in hand. Might be they plan to steal from the ship's stores."

"Maybe I should steal the ship's guns first," Hob said.

"Maybe," Spider replied. "We just might find a need for them." His hand brushed the hilt of his knife, a Spanish dagger he'd purchased in Plymouth before their departure. It was made for throwing, and Spider was quite expert at that, but he'd had damned little time to practice with this one. "Guns might come in handy, indeed."

Ruth ran her hands through her hair, which was somewhat unruly in the breeze. "Should we inform Captain Bellows?"

"What, tell him Hob was sneaking about in men's chests? No." Spider sucked on his pipe, and was disappointed to find it was spent.

"Maybe the cap'n is part of their conspiracy," Odin suggested.

Spider looked at the old man. "You think so?"

"He's already got a ship, hasn't he? Ha! And these bastards have no guns hidden in their chests, aye? Maybe they aren't armed to take the ship because they already know they don't need to take it."

Spider blinked. "And the cap'n steered me away from the idea of murder right quick, he did. You might have smoked out the truth here, by thunder."

He'd heard similar tales many times during his years plying the sweet trade. A merchant vessel got under way, and her captain waited until an opportune moment to suggest a new course and a new mission, plunder on the high seas. If he had a few men already in favor of such a plan, and a few ready to join in once the dreams of riches took hold in their minds, a captain could turn his crew from honest sailors to sea brigands with little trouble. All it took was persuasion, and maybe a few primed flintlocks.

If such a captain had a treasure map—or was working with crewmen who had one—he might not even need the threat of guns. Many a man would willingly chase gold on the seas, where witnesses were few and the law's reach was often uncertain.

Spider closed his eyes and tried to recall his private discussion with Captain Bellows. After a minute or so, he looked at his friends.

"Well, fate pisses on us again, lads, and this may all be more of a goddamned maze than I thought."

"Maybe the captain is in on their plan," Odin repeated.

"Aye," Spider said, shaking his head at Hob before the young man could berate Odin for repeating himself. "The cap'n may well be involved. It is not something we can dismiss, anyway, and it means we dare not say anything to him. If we tell him our suspicions, and he is, indeed, working with those murderous bastards, well, we might wake up dead."

Hob winced. "And you already told him we think Garrick was killed."

"Aye," Spider said. "I did that."

Ruth exhaled, after apparently holding her breath for a while. "Well, what shall we do?"

Spider shrugged. "I say we arm ourselves and keep an eye. If they try anything, we stop them."

"We could stop them now, and take their map," Hob suggested.

"Hell, we could take the ship south and find the gold ourselves."

"No," Spider said. "This ship is going to Boston, even if I have to take command of her myself. If you have any dreams of sailing her to Hispaniola in search of gold, you'll belay that until I see my wife and child."

"Aye," Hob said. "Fair enough. I wasn't thinking."

Ruth stared at Spider for three heartbeats, then strode away purposefully.

Spider watched her go. "Did I say something wrong?"

"I can sometimes reckon the wind, John, and I can always reckon your next move on a chessboard," Odin muttered. "By the way, you still owe me a bottle of rum for that game in Lymington. But ask me why a woman does anything? Hell, I do not know. Neither does God. Ha!"

II

Spider was still yawning from a fitful sleep—interrupted at some point as Hob woke him to report he'd had no luck finding where *Minuet* stored her pistols, information he conveyed with a ridiculous pantomime, so as to avoid waking anyone else. Spider was keeping a watchful eye while painting a hatch cover that had not held up well when Calvin Garrick's blood had been scraped off it, when he noticed Gray on the deck, flashing a signal to Ronald Simon above. It was just a quick gesture, but Spider had used such silent communication before, and he recognized the casual acknowledgment in Simon's deep-set eyes. Spider had no idea what the two fingers meant, but doubted it meant anything good.

Simon was high on the ratlines, nearing the main topsail yard, but he stopped ascending when the signal came. Homer Woodley and Jim Trawley were supposed to be going aloft, too, but they were still on the weather deck, and Gordon had not yet noticed. That was because Gray was distracting Gordon.

Captain Bellows paced the quarterdeck. If he knew something was about to happen, he betrayed no sign of it.

This is it, Spider thought, and flashed a sign of his own to Hob. The young man gave him an almost imperceptible nod in return and moved toward a tool chest.

Spider dropped his paintbrush and moved closer so he could hear what Gray was saying. He went to the rail and pretended to knock spent tobacco from his pipe into the sea. He had picked a spot behind Gray.

"It hurts, it does," Gray said, rubbing his left shoulder. "I don't know how I hurt it, but it hurts."

"Well," Gordon said, "I suppose we can have you rest, if we must. The sea is in an easy mood this morning. But we are short of hands, so mend quickly, if you please. And you'll have to work hurt if we have a sudden need."

"Aye, sir, I know that."

Spider spared a quick glance toward Woodley and Trawley. Those two were ascending to the quarterdeck, where Captain Bellows talked with the helmsman. The attackers had pistols, and climbed quickly.

They strike now! And we've not acquired any weapons!

Spider noted another signal from Simon, who had come lower on the ratlines and apparently was acting as lookout. Spider, in turn, flashed a thumb at Hob and pointed to the captain, not bothering with secrecy any longer. The lad understood quickly, pulled something from the tool chest and headed up the ladder to the quarterdeck. He would be approaching the captain from the larboard side, opposite of Trawley and Woodley.

Hob carried a small grappling hook, attached to a short coil of thin rope.

Spider looked for Odin, but the old man was high on the foremast and concentrating on his work. *Minuet* would be putting on more canvas at any moment to catch a rising wind, and Odin had charge of the men on the topsail yard. The complex assembly of beams and sails and lines between them made communication almost impossible, and Spider realized Odin would not be involved in this action.

Damn, he thought. The old son of a whore might repeat himself a lot, but he was damned handy to have around when the blades flashed and the pistols thundered. Spider would bet all the pieces of eight he had on the old bastard when it came to a fight. Odin dearly loved action, and years fell away from him when instinct and experience took over.

But for this fight, Odin was too far away.

Spider spun quickly to see if other crewmen were sending signals or exchanging quick glances or reaching for guns or knives. He had no idea how many men might be in on the conspiracy, but *Minuet's* sailors were going about their normal business, waiting for the word from the captain to put on more sail.

He turned his attention to Gray, and saw him grip the handle of a pistol tucked beneath his shirt, behind his back.

To hell with secrecy!

"To arms!" Spider snatched up a belaying pin.

At Spider's alert, Woodley and Trawley rushed the captain on the quarterdeck.

Hob charged from the opposite direction, wielding his hook and line. He carried the hook by its shaft, as though he gripped a cutlass hilt.

Captain Bellows, who had been gazing aloft, snapped to attention at Spider's call. He looked at Spider, though, and did not notice his attackers.

Trawley, however, noticed Hob.

Gray turned toward Spider and raised his gun.

Spider stepped forward, wielding the belaying pin. This would not be the first time he had used one as an improvised club.

Spider struck, hard, and Gray's knees buckled before he could fire his pistol. The gun was in Spider's hand and Gray was on the ground even before Gordon realized what was happening.

A gun thundered on the quarterdeck.

"Hob!"

Spider watched as Hob ducked low beneath the rising gun smoke and the captain leapt away from his attackers.

Spider had no idea whether the gunshot had been aimed at the captain or Hob, but it apparently had hit no one.

The foes clashed in the space Captain Bellows had occupied just a moment before. Hob planted his shoulder hard into Trawley's hip. At almost the same moment, he sank the grappling hook deep into Woodley's thigh. Trawley fell hard against the rail as Hob rolled across the deck, pulling on the line and yanking Woodley toward him like a hooked fish. Woodley fell and flopped.

In an eyeblink, Trawley was leaning on the rail and clutching his hip as Woodley rolled and clasped his left leg, blood spurting around the grappling hook lodged in his thigh. Hob held Woodley's dropped flintlock—which had not been fired—on the both of them.

"Cap'n, sir!' Hob offered a short bow, but kept his attention on the duo he had felled.

The captain, astonished, said nothing.

Spider, who had seen Hob fight before, still shook his head in amazement.

Gray, prone on the deck, stared past the flintlock Spider aimed at his face.

"I reckon you all lost this fight," Spider said.

Gray winced and snarled.

Bellows, his eyes darting back and forth between Spider and Hob, worked his jaw as though his eternal salvation depended upon it. He seemed genuinely shocked, but Spider wondered if it was all a ruse. Bellows could have planned to have his mates stage a mutiny and put a gun to his head, forcing him to capitulate in the eyes of his crew. Some threatening words, a bargain made under duress, some well-crafted words from the captain, and suddenly *Minuet* could be a pirate ship.

Spider grinned. If that was, indeed, the plan, he and Hob had sunk it.

Spider hollered up at the captain. "These men plotted to take your ship, sir." He pointed at Simon, up on the ratlines. "That one, too."

Bellows seemed confused, but he mastered himself. "Mister Gordon! Place these men in irons! And that one, as well!" He pointed at Simon, who seemed to be trying to decide whether to climb down or simply launch himself into the sea.

"Aye, sir." Gordon gave his orders. Gray rubbed his head, and Trawley howled as Hob shoved him to the deck beside the bleeding Woodley. Simon had no choice but to climb down to the men waiting to bind him.

Captain Bellows saw that everything was under control. "Mister

Coombs! Mister Gill! I would very much like to know what has transpired upon my vessel!"

"Aye, sir," Spider said.

"Cheers for John and Hob, lads!" Spider did not see who had yelled it. He glanced around quickly at the crewmen taking up the cheer, to see if any did so reluctantly, or even refused to join in. He saw nothing suspicious.

"My cabin, now. The both of you," the captain said to Spider and Hob. "Mister Gordon, take the pistol from Mister Coombs, if you please. And you, boy, give me that."

Hob handed over the weapon, beaming so broadly that being called a boy did not seem to bother him at all.

Spider watched the men go back to their duty. One man, Seitz the cook, walked toward the galley, but he kept his eyes locked on Hob. Spider watched him, until Seitz stopped and turned his black-bearded face back toward Spider. To the carpenter, it seemed the cook's gaze paused a bit before moving on. Then the broad-shouldered fellow went back to his galley.

"Hob," Spider said when the young man joined him, "have you ever noticed Seitz with any of our mutineers?"

"The cook? Seitz doesn't like anyone."

"Aye, but he nibbled cheese with those lads while the fiddler played," Spider said. "I didn't get any cheese, did you?"

"No."

"Seitz was just paying a great deal of attention to you, just now, before he went back to his pantry full of rocks he calls biscuits."

Hob took a bow. "Naturally," he said. "I was amazing."

Spider nodded. "Aye. How the devil did you manage that?"

"I had the grapple ready, since I couldn't find us guns. I have a handspike tucked away elsewhere, too, and a screwdriver that's a bit sharper than it used to be. That's in one of the jolly boats."

Spider shook his head. "You had something hid away anywhere you thought you might need it?"

"Aye," Hob said. "Did you not do the same?"

"No, goddamn it." The carpenter spat, then laughed. "Well, Seitz took notice of your work. If he should happen to bake you up a little reward, like a nice puddin' or something..."

"Do you think he might?" Hob's eyes gleamed.

"Aye," Spider said. "I think he might. If he does, don't eat it."

12

For once, the captain's jaw was still. His face was granite, and his eyes never strayed from Hob's face. He sat at his small desk, while they stood before him and the ship gently rocked. Spider could feel *Minuet* turning to take advantage of the freshening wind.

Finally, just as Spider began to suspect the man really was working with the mutineers, a wide grin cracked Captain Bellows' stony countenance.

"I do not believe I have ever seen anything to match what I just witnessed, son," the captain said. "Hobart Gill, that was courage. And speed of mind! You probably saved my life, son, and you did it with a damned rope and a hook! I do believe you have missed your true calling. You should join the Royal Navy and fight the king's enemies, by God, not saw planks and fetch tools. France, Spain, would cower in the face of such daring!"

Hob gulped. "Thank you, sir."

"How did you surmise their intention?"

"Well, cap'n," Hob said, smiling. "That's not the first . . ."

Spider coughed, hard. "Forgive me," he said after interrupting Hob. "I had a bit of tobacco or something choke me. Now, how did you know their plan? You spotted their guns, didn't you, Hob? That's what set me going against the other fellow, Gray. I noticed his gun, I did." He raised his eyebrows, and hoped the young fool caught on. *The cap'n doesn't need to know how you learned to fight like a demon on the bloody deck of a goddamned pirate ship, boy, no matter how much you'd love to tell him.*

Hob glared at Spider. "Aye." He turned to the captain. "Aye, sir. I saw they were wielding guns and headed toward you, and I could not reckon any good reason for that, aside from mutiny. So I thought they were up to something evil, for certain, and rushed forward."

"Well," the captain said.

"And you were between me and them, sir, until you realized the danger and moved, sir, and so they were unaware, of me coming toward them, I mean," Hob said. "So that was an advantage. It was all easier than you might expect."

"Such modesty." The captain sighed. "There were two of them!"

"Aye, sir. But, I had luck."

The captain did not seem inclined to wonder why Hob had been carrying a hook, and Spider jumped in before that question arose. "It was bold, Hob. It certainly was."

"Bold!" Captain Bellows nodded. "Bold, indeed. It took real bravery, son, and a cool head. I might be dead, and the ship theirs, had you been even a little slower or a tad less courageous. I believe you would go far in the king's service. You would not remain a midshipman for very long, I dare say."

The captain stared at the squirming Hob. "I know an officer, a man with whom I sailed. I could pass along a good word for you. It would give me joy to do so."

Hob hesitated. "Thank you, sir."

The captain seemed to suddenly remember something. "Your actions were commendable, as well, Mister Coombs. That was well done."

Spider nodded. "Thank you, sir."

Gordon appeared at the cabin entrance. "Captain, sir."

"Yes, Mister Gordon?"

"We've got them in irons, under guard. We improvised a bit of a brig, sir, in the main hold. The fellow with the speared leg has lost a lot of blood, especially after we took the hook out of him. He looks bad, and, well, I've a fear he will not make it to port."

"Understood," Bellows said. "Waste no sympathy on him, Mister Gordon. He might have avoided his fate if he had not tried to take our ship."

"True, sir," Gordon answered.

"How about the other man Hob bested?"

"Trawley's leg is odd twisted and swollen. Broke his hip on the rail, sir, when this lad battered him. He'll live, I think, but he seems to be in a great deal of pain."

Hob grinned just enough for Spider to notice it.

"Gray has a lump on the skull, but otherwise seems fit," Gordon continued.

"It would save us a great deal of trouble if they'd all..." The captain stopped himself, and glanced heavenward for a moment. "Not a very charitable thought on my part. Well, we'll have to spare hands to guard them, won't we, and find ways to do the work with fewer hands. Our early arrival in Boston is in peril, Mister Gordon."

"Aye, sir, I'm afraid so."

The captain looked disappointed. "Well. What of the fourth fellow, Simon?"

"He swears he was not involved, sir, and says these two"—he pointed at Hob and Spider—"are liars."

Spider raised his eyebrows. "I saw the man signal the others just before the attack, cap'n. He was their lookout. That's why I was watching Gray when he reached for his gun. They signaled each other, they did."

"You may have spared me a lead ball in the head," Gordon said, almost whispering. "And you damned near took one yourself. I believe I'll take your word over Simon's, John."

"As will I. I owe you, John," Bellows added, turning to look at Spider. "I've a mind to pay you out a bonus upon arrival. A bonus to both of you. Mister Gordon, how goes the ship?"

"Northwest by west, sir, under topsails."

"Fine. Carry on. Let's get all we can out of this fair weather. It may not last."

"Aye, sir." Gordon returned to his duties on deck.

"I am serious about a bonus, John. It won't be enough to express my full appreciation, but I will see the owner in Boston and I believe he will agree you two have earned more than a carpenter's wage, and a carpenter's mate's."

"Thank you, sir," Spider answered with a nod. "I did my duty, sir, no more than that."

Captain Bellows turned his gaze upward toward the grating that allowed air and light into his cabin and sighed heavily. Then he lowered his head and looked at them each in turn. "Do either of you have a supposition regarding their reason for mutiny?"

Hob blinked. "Sir?"

"Why did they try to take my ship?"

Spider tried to maintain a stony expression. *Do not mention the map, Hob. Do not mention the map.*

"I do not know, sir," Hob said. "Who can tell what a criminal thinks? Perhaps they planned to go pirating."

Spider nodded. "It seems likely, sir."

"And regarding your earlier suspicions of murder—Hob, I am trusting you on this and commanding you to speak not a word—well, perhaps Mister Garrick overheard these fellows plotting, or something of that sort. He worked aloft with them. He might have noticed or heard something they'd have preferred to keep to themselves."

"Aye, sir," Spider said. "I believe you have it reckoned correctly, sir."

The cramped cabin grew quiet. Then Spider blew out a gush of air. "Sir?"

"Yes, John?"

"If you are in a mood to reward me, I would ask something other than money. I would ask that *Minuet* put in at Nantucket, sir, before she continues on to Boston."

The captain nodded, and smiled. "You have a woman there. Or so I have heard."

"Aye, sir."

"And another aboard," the captain muttered, shaking his head and winking at Hob.

"Cap'n, Miss Copper and I are not..."

The captain waved a hand and Spider stopped talking. "We'll be hanging those bastards in Boston, John. Testimony and all that. Boston is not far from Nantucket. You can see your family after we have settled all the details."

Spider tried to hide his disappointment. *Sailors are away from home all the time. It is the way of things. My situation is extreme, but how can I tell him that? How can I tell him I've been away eight or nine years, thanks to the bloody pirate life, without him asking what I was doing all that time?*

"Sir," Hob said, "John's got a baby he hasn't seen. The timing of it, well, it is likely his new boy or girl is born by now. He's quite eager, sir."

Damn, Spider thought, *Hob's more clever than I thought. And he lies as naturally as a dolphin swims.*

"You did not say so, John." The captain smiled. "I wish you joy, sir, and a healthy child."

"Thank you, sir."

Captain Bellows pondered matters for a few seconds. "Well, John, I do not believe a brief stop at Nantucket would set us back too badly. Provided, of course, there are no delays, nor foul weather, and provided Mister Gordon and I can get enough labor out of this crew to make up for what we've lost. I must see to business first, John."

"Of course, sir."

"But we've had an easy passage and fair winds, and we departed earlier than expected as well. We're ahead of our schedule. I will accommodate your request if we can maintain our pace, John."

Spider smiled. "You are most kind, sir!"

"Hob, I will ask the owner to pay you a bonus, and I will write my friend on your behalf to tell him of your deeds here today. The Royal Navy needs you. Now, back to duty, gentlemen. That goes for me, too."

"Aye, sir," they said in unison before turning to go. Then Spider put a hand on Hob's shoulder and turned back to face the captain. "Sir."

"Yes?"

"These men may have accomplices on board." *And Ronald Simon had not been injured at all. He could still pose trouble.* "I suggest we be wary as to who guards them. Perhaps Hob and I should be assigned that duty. And Mister Hughes, sir." Hughes was Odin's false name. "We've both sailed with him before, and we trust him."

"Those bastards won't escape on my watch, sir," said Hob, with a bow.

The captain's jaw began working. "No, I dare say they will not escape on your watch." He chuckled. "I want them guarded at all times, of course. Hob, you go spell the fellows standing watch now. John, inform Mister Gordon that you shall stand guard when Hob is relieved. As for Hughes, he is quite old. I hired him with misgivings, I must say, but you spoke well of him and I admit he's a fine one with the rigging, and knows his business better than most. But is he fit for such duty as standing guard?"

"Aye, sir," Spider replied. "And those men are in chains, aye? And bad hurt, two of them anyway? Hughes can be relied upon." *Heaven help them if they try anything during Odin's watch*, Spider thought. *And if they do, Odin will likely enjoy it.* "If you depend upon the three of us to guard the prisoners, well, that leaves more hands to do the sailing work, sir."

"Very well," the captain said. "Inform Mister Gordon that Mister Hughes should be part of the rotation. I want one of you fellows on guard at all times."

"Aye, sir."

"It will be more fun than hammers and nails, sir," Hob added.

The captain nodded. "We'll arm you properly, so you won't have to fight with a damned hook. Now go to work, men. And thank you."

Hob was the first to exit onto the weather deck, and he took a bow as another chorus of cheers lifted. Spider nodded thanks at his fellow crewmen, then tugged Hob forward.

"I'll be damned if I'll be a Navy man," Hob said, whispering. "Been running from those fellows my whole life!"

"Aye," Spider said. "And you still haven't learned to saw a straight line, so I doubt you'll ever learn to sail a ship from one shore to another."

"I can learn to navigate, by God."

Spider laughed. "Yes, if you were interested enough, you could. I am certain of it. I will bet we can find an old salt or two to teach that in Nantucket. You'll probably not want to repair boats with me. That would bore you."

Hob stopped walking and stared at his feet.

"What is it, lad?"

Hob looked up, his face a picture of determination. "I do not plan to abide in Nantucket, Spider."

"You do not?"

Hob grinned. "Hell, no. Spider . . . I am going to grab that bloody treasure map!"

13

"**Y**ou and Hob are the only thing being talked about on this ship," Ruth said.

Spider had found himself a perch on the bowsprit, away from all the shoulder slapping and questions. Those things annoyed him, and he wanted to think.

Ruth was a distraction, too, but he found himself not annoyed by that.

Ruth had clambered out to stand beside him, her dark hair and gray skirt flapping in the wind. She had a sea coat, but that wouldn't warm her legs. Spider shuddered, imagining how cold her legs must be. But if she minded, she did not show it.

"Aye," Spider said.

Somewhere amidships, Bush fiddled a tune too lively for Spider's mood.

"So why aren't you down there, drinking up the admiration and the grog? Why do you sulk here?"

The carpenter spat into the evening sea. He cast a glance toward the foretop, where men danced to the fiddle.

"It came to me today that this journey means some partings," Spider said, in answer to Ruth's question. "I don't know why I did not reckon it earlier, but it does. Hob, he ain't a carpenter and he won't find adventure on an island full of sheep. He's going to sail on."

"It is in his blood," she said.

"Aye." He popped his pipe back into his mouth and drew from it deeply. "Fool, I was, thinking I might drag him away from his dreams. Gold and glory, that's his lot, he'll tell you. Ran off to sea against his own family's wishes, and couldn't wait to go pirate if you ask me. He sees the riches, not the bloodshed."

"One day, he'll grow to see things your way," Ruth said. "He looks up to you, I hope you know. Almost like a father."

Spider laughed bitterly. "Looks up to Odin, too. That old man's talk about Blackbeard and treasure chests carries more weight with Hob than my hammers and nails."

"For now, perhaps. But Hob will learn."

"If he lives long enough," Spider said softly. "He's down in the hold standing guard now, armed like a pirate and full of piss. I am to relieve him soon. Odin was to stand guard, too," he whispered, "because we don't know how many others can be trusted. We had it arranged with the cap'n, but Mister Gordon counted heads and changed the cap'n's mind. All those mutineers worked aloft, so we're short of hands in the trees and Odin can't be spared for guard duty."

"Could I help?"

Spider glanced at her. He had not known her long, and she spoke little of her past, but she had proven her ability to fight back in England, and she handled herself on a listing deck or a bowsprit like a seasoned sailor. "I do not think the cap'n would approve," Spider said. "Remember, you are a passenger, and no one needs to know you can fight."

He winked. "And as long as nobody does know that little secret, well, it could make for a nice little surprise later, if we find ourselves needing such. We don't know that we got all the mutineers. I no longer think the cap'n is part of the scheme—he'd have set his own guards on the prisoners, not me and Hob, if that was the case—but, well, we still might see surprises before we reach Nantucket."

Ruth nodded. "Aye, there is some sound maneuvering. I shall keep my talents for bloodshed a secret, but I shall remain alert. I already have a knife strapped to my leg, should I need it." She lifted her skirt just enough to show a small punch dagger—a nasty little weapon with a blade that could protrude between the fingers of a clenched fist—in a leather holster on her goose-pimpled shin, then dropped the garment quickly. "It is a tiny thing, but you well know I can get close enough to a man to use it."

She winked. Back at Pryor Pond, where Spider and Odin had rescued Hob from a madman, Ruth had gotten close enough to surprise Spider with a knife thrust more than once.

"Glad you did not stab me when you had the chance," he said.

"I still might," she said, chuckling.

"So with Odin needed up there, it is just me and Hob on guard duty, standing long watches. Hob actually enjoys it."

"He would be bored in a wood shop. You've said so yourself."

"I know," Spider said. "I just thought . . . I do not know what I thought. I guess I did not think."

"Odin is not one to settle in one spot, either, I suspect." She tucked her skirt under her and sat beside him, clutching a stay. "Give me that." She reached for his pipe.

Ruth inhaled, and the bowl's fire lit up her face. She blew out a stream of smoke and returned the pipe to him. "Thank you."

"Welcome. No, I don't suppose Odin will want to sit around watching me do real work and make babies with Em. He probably will stay with Hob, and the two of them will haunt the Spanish Main and cross swords with all manner of brigands and thieves. They will rank with Ed Teach, Calico Jack, Bartholomew Roberts, Stede Bonnet, all the bloodiest bastards."

"I hope they meet better fates than those fellows," she said.

"It will take a lot of prayers," he said.

Spider scanned the waves. "Beautiful, is it not? When she's in a pretty mood, like this, anyway."

"You sound as though you aren't ready to leave the sea behind yourself."

Spider glanced out over the ocean, his gaze trailing the low sun's red ribbon across the water. "I do love the sea," he said. "But she's already taken more from me more than she's gave me. I have missed years with Em and Little Johnny. I do not wish to miss more."

Ruth's silence seemed to be saying something.

"Tell me, girl," Spider said. "What is it you wish to say?"

"Just don't be surprised, Spider, if she isn't what you think her to be. People change, and you have been gone a long time."

Spider considered that, and stared westward. "I've been hoping a long time," he said. "Sometimes, that hope and a cutlass was all I had to keep me alive."

"I suppose." Ruth swallowed. "But think on it. Are you the same man you were when you left?"

He laughed. "Hell. I left as a carpenter's mate who would scarce harm a mouse, and now I am a wanted man—pirate, thief, killer."

"So consider that she has likely changed, too, in all that time. She might not be the same woman she was when you left." Her eyes contained an unspoken thought, but Spider did not ask about that.

"I have to see," he said. "You may be right, by thunder, but I have to see for myself. And I have to see my boy, at any rate, even if Em has forgotten my face. Even if she chases me away."

"I was harsh to you earlier," she said, climbing up to stand once again on the bowsprit. "I did not mean to be so. You are a good man, Spider John."

She left him, alone with his pipe and his thoughts.

14

Hob nodded, reluctantly removing the sword belt that held a serviceable cutlass and a pistol. "It felt good to be armed again. That's primed and ready to fire," he said, handing the belt over to Spider. "But these lads are not going to give you any trouble, I dare say. They've had enough of trouble, haven't you, lads?"

The prisoners said nothing.

"Aye," the carpenter replied. "They do not look very dangerous now."

Spider was grumpy after a restless sleep. "Go enjoy some food. Only two weevils in my bread today." He handed Hob a fresh lantern to replace the nearly dead one hanging on a hook.

"I don't mind weevils," Hob said, laughing. "Probably eaten hundreds. And Seitz did not make me anything as a special reward, neither. He paid me no attention at all."

"Good," Spider said, casting a glance toward the prisoners to see if the mention of Seitz drew a reaction.

It did not.

The lad climbed to the deck above, leaving Spider in the hold to guard the four men. They were chained together, attached at wrists and ankles, and tucked between stacked crates on one side and barrels on the other. With hands bound behind them and ankles lashed tightly with rope, the prisoners posed little danger. Spider could not rule out the possibility of a rescue effort by some unknown conspirator, however, so he would be ready.

He strapped on the weapon belt, outside his coat, and made sure his hands knew exactly where the sword hilt and pistol butt were. Then he blew on his hands to warm them, before inspecting the flintlock. It was a good English gun, and primed as Hob had said.

Next, he checked the sword. It was heavy for his taste, and longer than he liked for such cramped quarters. He decided he would go for the knife first, if he needed a weapon.

"You've handled a sword before," Gray muttered.

Spider did not acknowledge him. Instead, he crouched, then straightened up and stretched his legs, then inspected the prisoners more closely.

Woodley certainly would never fight again. Even in the uncertain light of the swinging lantern, Spider could discern the blood-sopped bandage on the man's leg, and the beads of sweat on his face, and the labored breath. Spider had seen men die slowly of wounds before, and he did not think Woodley would live through the night.

Trawley, the man who had broken his hip and twisted his leg badly when Hob rammed him against the rail, did not seem to be in danger of dying, but he was not ready to fight. His britches had been cut away to reveal a swollen purple knee, and each time the man tried to find some measure of comfort in the cramped space, he winced with pain and reached for the hip. Spider reckoned he might never walk again.

Gray had taken a hard thump on the head, but seemed unhampered.

"I'll remember to hit you harder next time," Spider muttered.

"I'm going to kill you," Gray said through his dolphin grin.

Spider looked at Simon, the uninjured man. "I suppose you want to kill me, as well?"

"I just might do that," he said. "You lied about me, got me down here with these murdering thieves."

The night had remembered this was September, and the relative warmth of the preceding days had vanished with the freshening wind. Simon's eyes added to the chill.

"Well," Spider said, "Try to kill me if you must. I'll warn you, it won't be easy."

"I do not belong with this lot," Simon growled, his face florid. "I did nothing wrong."

Spider shook his head. "I knew you lot were up to something the moment Calvin Garrick plunged to his death, damn you."

The prisoners—even Simon—exchanged quick glances. Spider whistled. "Mistake, Simon. You shouldn't have looked over to your mates when I said that. I sort of wish I had you at a card table. Your face tells a story, man."

Simon moved as though he would rise, but the chains and ropes were not going to let that happen.

Gray shook his head. "Now, let us wait a bit."

Spider paced. "Don't expect a miracle, boys. You'll swing when we reach the Colonies. That's what happens to mutineers and murderers. They hang. I know you killed Garrick."

They stared at him.

"Did you club him, then? Or did you stab him?" He turned his back to them, and took a gamble. *I'll never be able to prove it anyway, and I certainly won't testify. But I want to know.*

"I saw you fling the weapon into the deep, when everyone else was watching him fall, but I couldn't quite tell what it was. Was it a knife, or a sap?"

"I didn't throw a damned thing!"

Spider whirled. Simon had spoken.

Gray spat at his companion. "You foolish bugger, he don't know."

"Well," Spider said. "I do now."

Spider watched as the prisoners exchanged more worried glances. *Here it comes*, he thought. *The bargain.*

"Look," Gray said. "We have something to offer."

Spider had seen it before. Desperate men veering from defiance to haggling as soon as they saw the noose in their future. It was as pathetic as it was predictable, but he'd long feared the gibbet himself so he actually pitied the poor bastards.

"An offer? What might that be?" Spider raised his eyebrows and wondered how much of the truth these prisoners were ready to share.

"We know an island," Simon muttered, giving up any pretense of innocence. "A sweet little island where a pirate captain hid a great deal of treasure."

Spider laughed. "Do you now? And who buried it?"

"Fellow named Moore," Gray said. "I heard from an eyewitness in Tortuga that it was more than a Spanish galleon could carry."

"Did your Cap'n Moore have a Spanish galleon to carry it?"

"He had a small fleet," Gray answered. "Some say five sloops, some say ten. I don't know the truth of that, but I know where they took the goods."

Gray nodded, just once, and licked his upper lip.

"True!" That was Trawley. "It is all true! And you can have a share, if you just free us."

Spider tilted his head. "So, what would be my share?"

"A fifth," Gray said. "Us, plus you, all shared fair."

"Woodley ain't likely to be around to claim his share. His can go to Hob."

"That rat?" Trawley spat. "I am going to peel him like we do to whales."

Spider John laughed. "No, you won't. You couldn't handle him when there were the two of you." He aimed a thumb at the dying man, Woodley. "Now you can't even stand."

"Listen, then, five ways still, aye?" That was Gray. "Me, you, Trawley, Simon and your friend Hob. My point is, there is a hoard of it and you'll be a rich man. We'll all be rich men, if you and your friend are smart enough to keep your mouths clamped tight."

Spider stared at him. *No need to let these men know he had no intention of testifying in front of the forces of the law.*

"I don't much care what happens to any of you. Men that try to kill their cap'n for coin? No. I am not that. I am no saint, to be sure, but I am not that. Truth is, there is not a goddamned thing you can offer me that's better than what I will find at home. Not a thing. And I will love telling the tale in front of a governor or a magistrate. I'll tell it pretty. You'll all swing, lads. The only one who will escape the noose is Woodley, because his justice is swooping in a bit sooner."

Trawley looked at the dying man. "Poor soul."

"Poor damned soul," Spider said. "Now, let's have some quiet, shall we?" Spider tapped the cutlass hilt. "Because I won't mind slitting your throats if you talk again."

No one talked again.

15

Three days and two rains later, Nantucket loomed.

Spider John sat on the foredeck ratlines and stared hard, as though he might see Em and Johnny waiting on shore.

Minuet was north and east of the island, which was just a hump in the distance. "Beautiful, aye?"

"Seems small," Hob called up to him, then pointed north by northwest. "That's the cape away there, right? Is that where Bellamy sank?"

Spider shook his head. "No, lad." Sam Bellamy's short but infamous pirate career had come to a sudden end in 1717, when Satan stirred up a horrifying nor'easter that plunged his *Whydah Galley* beneath the waves near Cape Cod. Spider had heard the story many times. The number of lives lost, and the amount of gold lost, changed with every telling. But most of the men who'd shared the news were consistent regarding the wreck's location. "Sam sank north of the cape, I heard, not south, so you can stop peeping down into the sea. You'll have a long swim from here if you want to go off and find his gold, I reckon."

Hob sighed, and looked again at Nantucket. "It is so small."

"Aye, she's not big," Spider told him. "Not many living there. More natives, that's Wampanoag, than colonists. More sheep than people, too. And everybody walks everywhere, mostly. But she's beautiful to me."

All he could see from this distance was beach and trees, and a few gray shapes he supposed to be homes. He knew he would not see much more even as the ship drew nearer, for the island was sparsely populated. He remembered more white oak and pine, especially north of the inner harbor, than he could discern now. He could not quite make out the new harbor entrance, though he tried. No one used the old harbor at Capaum anymore, the captain had explained, for it had silted up. Spider was eager to see what else had changed in the eight years or so since he had left this crescent-shaped island. It was all he could do to keep himself from jumping into the sea and swimming to Em.

As they drew closer, swaying gently and choosing a course to avoid dangerous shoals, Spider counted ships in the outer harbor. Six, there were, brigs and sloops that probably plied the waters of Boston, Cape Cod, the Vineyard, and Nantucket. The island imported wood, pots, pans, plows, guns, and other such items from the mainland, and sent back copious amounts of wool and whale oil, creating a steady local trade.

Spider turned his head toward the quarterdeck when the captain yelled out. "Lads! Hear me," the man said.

Once he'd adjusted his seat to gain a line of sight through a gap in *Minuet*'s cordage and sails, Spider could see the man's face. Captain Bellows was smiling, and his jaw was shifting to and fro.

"Lads, I have promised our good carpenter a favor, in that he's got a family on yonder island and we owe him much. Where are you, Mister Coombs?"

"He's halfway up the foremast, hoping he can see the breeze lift her skirt. Ha!"

Odin's joke prompted a great deal of laughter. "Three cheers for John Coombs!" A chorus went up, and Spider nodded in appreciation. Then he started his decent.

"There is little on Nantucket for the rest of us, though," Captain Bellows continued, pointing toward the island. "Look for yourselves. Naught but sheep and natives and wool merchants. And here we be, with a chance to deliver our cargo in Boston ahead of schedule and earn a fat bonus, if we do not tarry, despite the misfortunes that befell us. That's a tribute to your hard work, lads, and you are deserving of some rewards. I happen to know we can find strong ale and beef in plentiful measure in Boston."

Someone added: "Women, too!"

This brought another round of cheers, and a more enthusiastic one than the last, Spider thought. The men needed some fun. It had been tough these last few days, short-handed as they were, and the prisoner Woodley had died sweating in his sleep the night before. That had taken all the remaining fight out of the mutineers, and Gordon had assigned fresh guards.

The captain shifted his gaze back and forth, to take them all in. "We draft deep enough to have trouble with the inner harbor even at high tide, gents, so I propose"—when Bellows said "propose," it was understood that he meant "command"— "we anchor among those fine ships yonder and let John take a jolly boat ashore. Then we'll be off as quick as may be. Mate, find some volunteers to row the good man to his woman, if you please."

"Aye, sir," Gordon replied.

More cheers rose. *Minuet's* mood had lifted dramatically.

Spider reached the weather deck and found shipmates ready to clap him on the back. One of those was Odin. "So, you will be repairing whaleboats, then? After the life you've led? Ha!"

"Aye," Spider said. "And rollin' in Em's arms."

"Be romantic and get your britches all the way off that first time," Odin said. "Ha!"

Hob tugged at Spider's sleeve. "I have something for you," the young man said. He peered over his shoulder, then pulled a small roll of canvas from his coat pocket. Spider caught the aroma of Virginia leaf.

"Well, thank you, Hob."

"Tuck it away before anyone sees," Hob answered. "I pilfered this."

"Naturally," Spider said, placing the canvas roll behind him, under his belt and beneath his shirt. He cast a glance around and noticed Seitz's hard eyes aimed at him.

Spider whispered to Hob. "Did you steal this from the cook?"

"No, sir," Hob said. "It's Mister Gordon's."

"Gordon's?"

"He hardly ever takes a pipe, so I reckon he won't miss it."

"Well," Spider said. He glanced toward the forecastle, but the German cook was gone. "Hob, go tell Gordon I'd like you and Odin to row me ashore. No one else."

"Aye," Hob said, running off, leaving Spider and Odin time to talk for a while as the ship worked into the harbor.

"You are just going to fix boats," Odin said.

"Maybe build some. I can do that."

"I see your girl approaching," Odin said. "Not the one ashore."

The old man pointed, and Spider saw Ruth strolling toward him. She looked determined, and quite beautiful.

Odin scurried off. "I'll go get the jolly ready."

Ruth stopped before Spider and performed a slight curtsy. "John."

"Will you help ferry me to shore, Ruth? I know you can handle an oar."

She considered that for a moment. "No," she answered. "No."

Spider looked into her eyes. She seemed to be trying to choose her words carefully. He felt as though he should say something, too, but he had no bloody idea what that would be.

Ruth broke the silence.

"I hope that you find everything to be as you wish," she said. "You have a good soul, John. You deserve happiness."

"Thank you," he said. "I hope you find your family."

"I will." She stared at him for six heartbeats. "Farewell."

Ruth departed, at a much faster pace than before.

Spider went to gather his belongings. Those were scant: a heavily patched second shirt he had not worn since cleaning it of Calvin Garrick's blood, spare britches he'd not worn lately for the same reason, his wide-brimmed hat, a threadbare sea coat that seemed to be held together mostly by crusted salt and old sweat, a spare clay pipe, a few pieces of eight, and a small canvas sack to carry it all in. Those, the clothes and boots he wore, and the knife in his belt summed it up.

He sighed heavily. All those years at sea, and only this to show for it.

Well, he surmised, *I have a great deal more on shore.* He tucked the stolen tobacco into the sack along with his other items.

He donned his coat, strapped the sack over his shoulder, rushed to the quarterdeck, and clambered up the ladder when Captain Bellows nodded permission. Hob and Odin waited by the taffrail, where the jolly boats were suspended on davits. *Minuet* was at anchor now, and her crew was busy calling across the water to sailors on other vessels. There would be many exchanges of news and goods for trade—a spare knife for a good hat, some scrimshaw for baubles from Jamaica, and other such trinkets— but Spider had little interest and little to trade. He just wanted to get ashore.

Captain Bellows strode forward and extended a hand. A small pouch, closed with a leather cord, suspended from his grasp. "Your pay, sir, and a little extra."

"Thank you, sir," Spider said. The sack was heavy, and felt good in his hand.

"The sea is in a quiet mood, John, but still, only two men to row the jolly back seems a couple of hands too few."

"Aye," Spider replied. "But Hob and Mister Hughes are sure hands, and they will handle it well. And they are my best mates, sir. I'd treasure a few private moments with them."

"Very well," Bellows said. "If they wreck my boat, I shall just take it out of their pay."

"Aye, sir."

Spider headed to the taffrail.

"Just going to repair whaleboats, then?" The old man had been repeating himself a lot these past two days.

"Aye, Odin."

"Ready, then, Mister Coombs?" Gordon stepped forward, and Spider nodded.

"Aye, then," Gordon said. "Jump in, Hob."

"Aye, sir." Hob clambered into the jolly boat, and Gordon ordered it lowered.

"You are a fine carpenter, John," Gordon said. "I hope that young man heeded his lessons well."

"He did not," Spider said, laughing. "But he only needs to keep *Minuet* together until you reach Boston, and he can manage that. I doubt you will see him again after this journey ends."

"We'll find a good carpenter in Boston, no doubt. I know some fellows at the shipyards. Enjoy your life on Nantucket." They shook hands, then Spider and Odin clambered down a rope ladder to the jolly boat, where Hob used an oar to keep the small vessel from banging into *Minuet*'s hull.

Soon, the lines were released and the jolly was headed across the waves, toward the mouth of the inner harbor. Spider's beard waved a bit in the breeze, and he doffed his hat so the morning sun could warm his face. He had thought to use the hat to wave at Ruth, but he could not spot her.

"That would be a good spot for a lighthouse," Hob said, looking over his shoulder toward the northwest side of the harbor mouth.

"Aye," Spider replied. "Maybe I'll build one."

Spider noted that Odin matched Hob's steady pace on the oar. He no longer moved as spryly as before, nor thought as quickly, but his body seemed as strong as ever.

"Building boats sounds like boring work," Odin said.

"Aye? You might think so, but I will be happy. I will build boats and send them out against the whales and fix them when they come back. Those that do come back," Spider said. "Whales can beat a boat to death. I will be busy. And Em's pa thinks this place will just grow and grow for whaling. There's plenty of them in these waters, and they were just starting to send ships further out when I left. *Lily* was going to be away for a year or more, that was the plan, before we got hit by pirates." He spat overboard. He'd been gone much, much longer than a year.

"It don't seem much," Hob said, looking over his shoulder. "Nothing much there."

Spider laughed. The early morning sun was high enough now to reveal more than they had seen from *Minuet*'s deck, but there was not much to see. "There look to be more houses than there was when I left." Indeed, he could see plenty of roaming sheep and a few houses that looked almost new. He could not see the house he sought, though. That was over the rise, toward the south shore.

That's where he would go first.

"You gentlemen can still join me," Spider said, quietly, though he knew the answer he would get.

Hob laughed. "I am a terrible carpenter, Spider, and you know it. And what would I do with a sheep?"

"I know what you'd do to a sheep. Ha!"

Hob slapped Odin on the arm, and laughed. "You stay away from the sheep yourself, bastard. Ha!"

They all chuckled. Then Hob nodded at Spider. "You could come with us, you know. We shall arrange for a sloop in Boston, while you spend a few days with the woman. Hell, stay a month, or through winter, even. Then, we'll come fetch you and we shall all go find the gold." He tapped his right boot, where the mutineers' map was hidden. "Your pretty wife won't mind you going away again, not if you come home wealthy. Or bring her, and your boy. Teach Em to fight like Ruth."

Spider tried to imagine Em swinging a cutlass, and could not.

"You plan to steal a ship, do you?" Spider shook his head. "No, my boy. That is not the life for me." He didn't know if living a good family life would balance all the bloodshed of his past, but it was the only course he could think to try. Would it be enough? The decision would be God's, he decided.

"We don't have to steal a ship," Hob answered. "We just have to persuade someone who has a ship to throw in his lot with us, in exchange for a future share of whatever we find."

"That sounds like a good way to get lusty men to sharpen knives and slit throats, Hob."

"We know how to deal with that."

Spider sighed. "I will never convince you, will I?"

"To become a lubber? No."

"Not a lubber, just an honest sailor will do."

"Honest sailors work hard, get hurt, sometimes die poor men. I'd rather work hard, and maybe live as a rich man."

Spider muttered a quick prayer. "I've seen plenty set out on that path. They died poor men."

"They were not me," Hob said, grinning.

"No. They were not you."

He turned toward Odin. "How about you, old friend. You've fought by my side, snuck into unwise places with me and lived longer as a pirate than anyone I ever heard tell of. I think you've earned a rest, don't you?"

"On a little island full of sheep? God damn me, no, ha! I am going to sail until I drop, Spider John, and God help the man I fall on!"

They all laughed again.

"I never made you a chess set," Spider said.

"You never bought me the bottle of rum you owe me, either. Ha!"

The trio remained quiet after that, as they worked the small boat into the harbor, giving wide berth to the tenders working back and forth from ship to shore.

"My," Spider said softly. "Look at all that."

He was peering at a large wharf, jutting out from the west at least a couple hundred feet into the water. Behind it were warehouses, cooperages, and shops that had not been there when Spider had embarked aboard *Lily*. Most of the buildings still sported fresh paint. "Now I know where all the trees went. All that was built while I was away," he said. "A carpenter will have plenty of work here, by thunder! Building whalers, and building houses for all the families. Aim for that wharf. It is new, too."

The boat reached the wharf, built of wood and stone piled between massive pillars of wood, and some boys tossed them a line. Spider grabbed that and tied off while Odin and Hob shipped oars. "I reckon you two can come back and see me some day, tell me about how you outwitted everyone and cheated them of their gold."

"Of course," Hob said. "Tiny place like this, you'll be easy to find."

"Just look for the fairest girl on the island. I'll be by her side."

"We'll just follow the scent of whisky," Hob answered. "That'll be the sure way, I reckon."

Spider clambered out of the boat and climbed onto the wharf's sandy top, then caught the sack Hob hurled at him.

"Farewell, Spider," Hob said.

"Aye," Odin added.

"Farewell, mates. Few men have had better companions, I'd wager. Don't get yourselves killed."

"We're ready for the world, Spider," Hob said. "It's the world that should worry."

Odin grinned. "And we won't have to worry about you ducking out of a fight and covering your face just because you saw a fucking bird, Spider."

Spider laughed. "Aye. I do hate the birds."

"Three men with cutlasses charge you, and you'll shoot one and stab two," Odin said, "but a fucking parrot comes within twenty yards and you piss yourself. Damnedest thing I've seen on the high seas. Ha!"

"Well, you won't need to watch out for me anymore, old man," Spider said. "And I will miss having you two by my side."

"Ten minutes in Em's arms, and you'll forget our faces," Hob said.

"No one forgets Odin's face."

"The half that's left, you mean. Ha!"

"Farewell, friends."

Hob smiled. "Fare thee well, Spider John. Kiss her for us."

Hob let the line slip and the jolly boat drifted away. Then Hob and Odin set to work to return to *Minuet*, and Spider watched them go. He watched until Odin's hideous face was a distant blur, and Hob's bright eyes were just indistinct dots on an indistinct face.

I won't likely see you two again, he thought.

Then, wiping a tear away, he turned to look at the new row of merchant buildings and storage houses beyond the docks and wharves. Ordinarily, treading upon solid ground unsettled him. He did not like being among strangers rather than familiar shipmates, nor the feeling that any moment might bring someone who recognized his face, pointed in accusation, and yelled "pirate."

But he felt none of those discomforts now. Not even the hovering gulls—"winged rats with goddamned stabby beaks and murder in their eyes," as he often referred to them—gave him pause now.

He slung the sack's strap over his shoulder and turned toward the south—and toward Em.

16

*I*t took Spider a moment to decide whether he had found the right house, for there were three others nearby of similar construction and painted much the same way. But he'd put the window frames on this one himself, long ago, and he knew his own work.

The house had stood alone when last he'd been here, eight or nine years ago. The shakes had held up fairly well, although some would soon need to be replaced. The roof and chimney seemed intact, and the front door and the shutters on the two small windows flanking it all had been painted red within the last year or so. Good, he thought, for he'd walked past several homes that showed less care.

Smoke trickled from the chimney, and Spider could smell the burning peat and a trace of cooking meat. That started his stomach rumbling, for it had been some time since he had tasted any meat aside from fish or barrel-stored salted pork or the occasional hen that had stopped laying. He could not determine whether the wind carried the aroma of lamb or beef or goat, but he did not much care. He could pick up the scent of onions, and deduced he was smelling stew.

Loud bleats assaulted his ears. He spun quickly as a trio of sheep zipped by him. Once he regained his bearings, he reminded himself to watch for dung as he walked across the soft soil. A quick glance in all directions told him he was no longer in danger of being overrun by the animals that roamed freely all over Nantucket. The sheep turned toward the watchtowers on the distant south shore, and toward a

Wampanoag who waved at him. "Sorry," the dark-skinned man said. "They do not watch where they go."

"I remember," Spider said, nodding. "I will watch where *I* go."

He turned away from the native and from the towers where men kept watch for the right whales, and then looked back toward the small house. He realized his hands and knees were shaking, and his breaths came in such shallow spurts his pipe was nearly dead.

Em.

He did not know if she was there, in the house, but he knew this was the place to start looking. Ruth's warning came to his mind, but he dismissed it. He had carried Em's memory with him across the seas and the years; whatever she might have become in that time, she would still be some version of the woman he had known. He was certain of that.

He reached into his coat and touched the heart-shaped amulet he'd carved for her. He considered removing the leather cord from his neck, so he could hand it to her the moment he saw her, but decided against that. He would kiss her first.

Still quaking a bit at the knees, he emptied his pipe and tucked it away. Then he went to the bright red door.

He stood there, breathed deeply three times, then knocked.

"Enoch?" It was a gruff voice from within. It was a voice he knew, one he had last heard booming at an open-air sermon the day before he left Nantucket to earn a living on the sea so he could support Em and Little Johnny.

Ephraim Pierce. Emma's father. He was expecting Enoch, Emma's younger brother, about Spider's age.

Spider's knees shook again. He had the right house.

The door opened seconds later. "Enoch!"

The years had been far less kind to Ephraim Pierce than they had been to the house. The face now was carved with deep lines above a beard gone from black to gray, and the blue eyes that had been sharp and clear now were cloudy. Pierce leaned heavily on a silver-headed cane, and put little weight on his right leg. The powerful voice, which once had lifted exuberantly to tell Wampanoags about the life, death, and resurrection of Jesus, now issued only a low growl. "John Rush."

"Aye, sir, I am home at long last," Spider said, removing his wide-brimmed hat. "I am sorry I am not Enoch. Has he gone to sea, too?"

"Aye, gone to sea, the same sea that was supposed to swallow you! Damn you!" Ephraim Pierce slammed the door.

Spider, stunned, stared at red paint.

He had known, of course, that Ephraim Pierce had no great love for him. Spider had gotten Emma with child. Her father had glared at Spider from the moment they'd confessed to him, and throughout the hastily arranged and sparsely attended wedding rituals, and every day after until he'd helped Spider find a berth as carpenter's mate aboard *Lily*. Spider had not expected a warm embrace from the man.

Nor had he expected this.

Spider waited a good ten heartbeats, his mind racing, before he knocked again. "Sir? I want to see my wife, and my son."

The door opened quickly, and the wide mouth of a blunder-buss appeared inches from Spider's face. Pierce glared, teetering now without the cane, and spittle drenched his beard. He put the butt of the gun to his shoulder, struggling to hold it steady. "If you are still here three seconds from now, I will pull the trigger! God help me, I will!"

Spider had stared into guns at close quarters before, and usually had answered with a swift duck past the weapon's mouth and a dirk or flintlock shoved into the attacker's thigh or belly. This time, he stood and blinked as his eyes teared up. He did not for a moment believe Ephraim Pierce would kill him.

"I know I vanished for a long time, sir. It could not be helped. I . . . I will explain in due time. All of it. I will. But I did my best. I sent money, when I could, though opportunities were rare. I trust that it arrived?" That was true; he'd sent coins any time he met someone who was sailing to Boston, with instructions for finding Em on Nantucket. He'd always assumed a certain amount of that never reached her, but it was the best he could do, and he'd prayed that some of it, at least, had found its way home. He had seldom included a letter, because he could neither read nor write, and because he did not want to commit any facts regarding his piratical life to paper, but he'd always trusted she'd know they came from him.

"I've been husband and father as much as I could, goddamn it, sir—pardon that, sir, I beg you—and now I am here to do it better. I will see my wife and child."

"No, you will not." Pierce then roared unintelligibly and squeezed the trigger.

The hammer fell.

There were no sparks.

A misfire.

Spider, shocked that the man had actually tried to kill him, and equally shocked to still be alive, grabbed the weapon away. He threw the gun behind him. "Why?"

"Go to hell," Pierce said, trying to close the door again. Spider kicked hard and the door flew open, as Pierce stumbled backward against a large table. "Go to hell!"

Pierce snatched up a leather-bound volume, and Spider recognized the well-worn tome from which his father-in-law had taught the island natives. It was the same Bible the man had sat reading throughout the night after learning his daughter was going to be a mother.

Spider stepped inside and closed the door behind him. His kick had damaged it, and it would not shut smoothly. A breeze pushed it slightly ajar. Spider ignored that.

"Why do you greet me with a gun?"

Pierce moved away from the table, leaving the Bible there, and stepped toward the large fireplace. The cane leaned against the floor under the now empty gun rack, too far away for Pierce to reach it and use it as a weapon.

Spider was more alert now, and hard-learned fighting habits began working for him again. He did a quick inventory of potential weapons at the hearth, which Pierce might be able to reach with some luck. Pokers. A shovel. A small kettle, where stew boiled, on an iron tripod that could serve as a weapon itself. Tongs and knives on the mantle. And, of course, the fire itself, if he were to be hurled into it.

Spider had stepped between Pierce and the fire before the complete list had run through his head, so his father-in-law had no chance to snatch up any of the deadly implements. Pierce still might try to snatch something from the desk in the corner—a desk Spider had built for him—but all Spider could see there were letters, quills, and ink pots. If a drawer held a pistol or knife or any other weapon, well, Pierce would not get a drawer open before Spider could get to him.

Spider braced himself in case the man tried to rush him. He kept his arms at his side, and ignored the knife on his belt.

Spider was not yet thirty, and Pierce was perhaps thirty years older than that and had led, as far as Spider knew, a bookish life. Now that Spider knew the man's intentions, Pierce posed little danger to a man who'd crossed blades and dodged musket balls across the Caribbean.

Pierce stopped advancing and took the weight off his bad leg, but he breathed hard and his eyes darted about for some sort of weapon. He squinted badly.

"We need to talk, sir," Spider said, fighting to keep his voice calm. "I want to know where Em is, and Little Johnny."

"Em? I want to know where she is, too, damn you!"

Spider gulped. "What do you mean?"

The man's cloudy eyes regained some of the ice-hard look Spider remembered from days past. Em's father spoke. "I mean you turned her into a . . . she's . . . she's a harlot, damn you! God and devil alone know where she's gone or who she . . . who she . . ."

The man dropped to his knees, and prayed through tears and heavy sobs.

Spider gulped. "Where is my boy, then?"

He got no answer.

"Where is my boy?" He said it with menace that time.

Ephraim Pierce would talk only to God.

Spider walked to the table and picked up the Bible. He opened it, and slowly turned the pages. He could not read a damned word of it.

He returned to the praying man's side. "Read this," he said, dropping the book onto the wooden floor. "Read this, and pray. If Em is in some sort of trouble, you need to know this. I will cut through anyone and climb over anything necessary to get her out of it. God's truth. You pray, and you read, and maybe God will tell you that. I am going to go now. I am going to give you time to pray. When I return, you can tell me what you know then. But pray first."

Spider stepped outside, picked up his dropped hat, and glared upward.

I've done bad things, Lord. I know that. But I am trying. You tell Ephraim that. You tell him.

Spider glanced at the tossed gun, but ignored it. He wasn't going to shoot it, and he'd be well beyond range before Ephraim Pierce could load it and try again.

He stumbled toward the southern shore, not sure where else to go.

17

Spider was drunk.

He'd wandered to the south shore, found a man with a flask watching for whales, and traded the remains of his Virginia leaf and his spare pipe for the whisky. East Spider walked, then west, then east again. When he passed his trading partner again, he turned the empty flask upside down. "Any more? Trade a hat for it."

The man, a curly-haired fellow seated on a high perch and wrapped in a heavy wool blanket, had stopped watching for whales and watched Spider instead.

"You drank that fast, friend."

"How long's supposed to take?" Spider tossed the empty flask aside. Unsteady, he leaned against a whaleboat, one of seven upturned on wooden blocks waiting for crews to come running when the next whale alert was raised.

The whale watcher sighed. "Big flask. Ought to last you more than it did, I'd say. Days, not minutes. I'd trade you more, if I had it. My name is Wood," the man said. He stared at Spider a long while. "You seem troubled, if I may say so."

"Troubled. Aye." Spider looked across the sea. *Was Em out there somewhere, with Johnny? Where had they gone?*

Whoops to the west drew his attention. He saw a bonfire, glowing orange and red, and several Wampanoags dancing around it while others used heavy sticks to roll hot stones from the fire onto a pallet. Beyond them, others cried out from a shallow cave in a low hill.

It was a sweat lodge, and these natives were preparing for something important. They would huddle in the cave around the heated stones to purify themselves for whatever was to come. Perhaps they were whale hunters. Perhaps they were raiders, preparing to make war on other natives to the east. Spider had watched rituals like this before, and knew that soon these men would rush into the sea.

He felt a bit like rushing into the sea himself.

"So, what is it that ails you?" The man on the high seat leaned forward. "Maybe I can help. It would pass my time, since whales are swimming somewhere else today."

"You can help if you know Emma Rush," Spider said.

"Emma Rush?" The man grinned.

"Aye," Spider said, slurring. "Emma Rush." He started to describe her—pretty, hair blonde or brown, eyes blue or green, both depending on the light—but the man's quiet laugh made Spider change course. "You do know her?"

"I do not know her," Wood said. "Never did. Never had the money." His shoulders quaked, and his eyes closed tightly as he laughed. "Break your heart, did she?"

Spider stood away from the boat that had been propping him up. He took a deep breath and steadied himself. Wood just laughed.

Spider glared. "What do you mean, about the money?"

Wood looked up. "Just no use finding her if you are out of coin, I mean." He shrugged. "She won't play otherwise." He resumed laughing.

Spider plucked the Spanish knife from his belt and threw it, missing by a wide margin. Wood was laughing too hard to notice.

Cursing, Spider spun about to find a weapon. He knew it was the liquor that had spoiled his aim, so he decided against plucking up a beach rock and hurling that. He needed something more reliable.

Spider looked beneath the boat, knowing he'd find an oar there. He found one. A good, solid oar.

He took it up.

"Come down here," Spider said, vaguely aware that he was slurring. He planted his feet wide apart and prepared his weapon. He knew that he was thinking way too hard about what might come next; the pirate life he was trying to escape had made violence a reflex for him, and he thought it unusual that he was now calculating things such as a balanced stance and the best way to wield his makeshift weapon. *Damned drink. Too much of it.*

He also thought that all this thinking meant he should drop the oar and stumble away.

Instead, he spat and glared at the man on the high seat. "I told you to come down here, and tell me again what you think of Emma Rush."

Wood stopped laughing, though it took an effort. "What, lad?"

"Come down here." Spider held the oar like a quarterstaff.

"Friend," Wood said, holding up his hands in a gesture of peace, "I told you, I did not know her. If you're looking to beat a man who did, there's plenty who . . ."

Spider John growled. *Use the oar to avoid a kick in the face, knock him off his perch, scare the piss out of him and make him talk.*

Spider changed his grip on the oar. Now it was a club, and he lunged forward and swung at Wood's knees.

He knew his plan had gone awry even before the impact, and he landed a much more fierce blow than he'd intended. Spider knew well the sound of cracking bone. He jumped back, almost falling, and watched Wood plunge to the ground, not even trying to break his fall because his hands were trying to clutch his oddly bent knee. The man rolled onto his back and screamed unintelligibly.

Damn! Fuck and bugger!

Spider did a pirouette, looking about to see if anyone had noticed. He had to use the oar as a prop to prevent toppling over, and his sudden movement forced a great horrid belch of whisky out of him. He blinked to clear his eyes, and sighed as it became apparent no one had seen him attack the man. The Wampanoags, shouting and splashing in the distance, were too caught up in their ritual to pay any heed to

Spider and Wood, and their noise provided cover for the injured man's agonized wails.

But Spider knew such luck would not last. He had to silence the man.

The former pirate planted the oar blade at Wood's neck. "Quiet," he commanded. "I don't want to bust your windpipe, but if it takes that to silence you, well, I know how."

Spider then realized he was leaning a bit on the oar, and was damned near turning his threat into action. He lifted the oar away, but waved the blade in the man's face. "Don't make me do it."

Wood gasped, and shook his head violently. He stopped moaning, but tears streaked his face.

"Good. Quiet. I'm drunk."

Spider shook his own head, uncertain why he'd felt the need to announce that. Then he breathed deeply, and tried to focus.

"I want to know a name, damn you, someone who does know her, Emma, and knows where she is," Spider said. "You should not say what you said, damn you. You should not say that. So you best give me the name I want now, because I am damned weary and damned drunk. And you had better give me a name, by God, because you should not say what you said and if you don't give me a name I got nothing, nothing to lose, I say, for killing you."

Wood stared up at Spider and apparently saw no reason to doubt Spider's words.

"Easy. Easy, mate. I'll talk. Jeremy Stoneham," Wood said. His voice was airy, like a bellows squeezed hard. "Jeremy Stoneham took up with her. With Emma. He was with her for a while, before she went away. Jesus! My leg!"

"To hell with your leg. Where did she go?"

"I do not know, I swear it. People say she tired of Stoneham. Ran from him." Wood's words came at an agonizing pace, because he paused frequently to wince and gasp in pain. "I think she, um, she earned money, let's say, but Jeremy always drank it up. Jesus, this hurts!" He clutched his leg. "He didn't mind, you see. The way she earned money. He didn't mind. But he drank it all up. And he can be a mean one, Stoneham, so he probably hit her. That is what people say. He hit her. So she left."

Spider adjusted his grip on the oar. "Where is this filth, this son of a bitch Stoneham?"

"Roger Dawes, he's a cooper, easy to find, and he can tell you about Stoneham. He rents the fellow a room." The man pointed toward the north. "Cooperage is up by the harbor. Stoneham lodges in a spare room above."

Spider looked down on the man, and examined the injured leg. *I hadn't meant to hit him so hard. I was leaving this violence behind. Wasn't I?*

Spider lifted the oar and hefted it over his shoulder. Wood writhed.

"Swear this to me," Spider growled, trying to shake off the anger and liquor. "You will never speak of Emma Rush again. Promise me you understand that."

"Aye," Wood said. "I do."

Spider watched the natives in the water. *Could a man really purify himself that way? Or any way?* He looked to the heavens. "I've prayed a lot," he said, "and things don't get better."

"Pray for me," Wood said, weakly. "You broke my leg, you bastard."

"You will live," Spider said. He turned in the direction he'd thrown his knife, and scanned the beach until he found it. He raised it to show Wood. "God loves you," he said. "I don't usually miss with a knife, so someone is looking out for you."

"Damned drunk bastard."

"Aye," Spider replied, dropping the oar. "Damned for certain. Drunk, too. Might be sober when I find this Stoneham, though. He'll need God looking out for him, by thunder."

Spider flashed the knife. "I wouldn't bet on me missing twice in a day."

He put the knife away, and headed toward town.

18

ction usually burned the drunkenness out of him—or so
Spider often told himself—but he still felt wobbly when
he saw the casks stacked outside a spacious wooden building near
Nantucket's main harbor. Two brigs were anchored there, apparently
new arrivals. Beyond them, fishing boats dotted the water, newly returned from the day's hunt.

A vertical post full of pegs beside the open entrance to the barn-
like building held hoops of hickory and metal, of varying sizes. Heavy
thumps echoed inside. Wood on wood, Spider's carpenter ears told him.

He stepped out of bright sunshine and into the cooperage. Once
his sight adjusted to the change, he saw a ruddy-faced man in the back,
stacking firkins on a shelf. He placed another, well made in Spider's
assessment, onto the stack with a thud like the ones he had heard previously.

"Are you Roger Dawes?"

"I am."

"I am looking for Stoneham," Spider said, aiming for a tone that
would not imply violence but guessing he'd missed.

"Jeremy? What do you want from him? Money? He just paid me
half what he owes, and I doubt he has any more." Sweat dripped from
his brow, and from his tied-back brown hair, and from a small disk
that hung from his left earlobe. He clearly had been working hard. The
man crossed the floor, lifted another firkin, and crossed back, adding
it to the stack.

"I don't want any money," Spider said. "Is he here?"

"No."

"Fuck and bugger," Spider growled, looking around for something to hit or kick but stopping himself before he did so. He still felt the whisky swirling in his mind. *Don't want another failure like back at the beach. Keep a cool head.*

"I take it you have an argument with Jeremy?"

"I need him to tell me some things," Spider said. "Probably will argue as well, no doubt." *A short, bloody argument.*

"Well," the cooper said, taking a cloth from the shelf and mopping his brow. "I am not a friend to Jeremy, exactly, but . . . I knew him in better days, and I hope to see him return to such days. He drinks, too much. He needs to lean on Jesus, if you ask me, not a bottle." The man, a head taller than Spider and considerably wider in the shoulders, had been approaching, but he stopped short. Spider heard the sharp inhalation, and guessed the man had detected liquor on Spider's breath.

He might have noticed the knife in Spider's belt, too.

"A lot of people drink too much," Spider said. "I do not aim to buy him drink. And maybe I know a way he won't drink no more." *Or eat, or dream, or hit my Emma,* he thought. *He won't do anything anymore.*

In the back of his mind, Spider realized he was talking too much. *A cool head, remember? Jesus.*

Dawes looked as though he was thinking. "What did Jeremy do to you?"

"He hit someone I care about."

"Would that be Emma, would it?"

Spider stepped forward. "You know her? Do you know where she is?"

The man shook his head. "Emma Rush? I knew who she was, of course. It is not a large island. Everyone knows everyone, at least, those that live here. It's a busy port, of course, always strangers about."

The man looked at Spider up and down, from the worn boots to the ugly battered hat.

"Aye," Spider said. "Always strangers in a port town. Sometimes, damned impatient strangers."

Dawes gulped. "Emma and Jeremy took up together for a while, and I think it got rough. People said so, anyway, but people talk. But I can't say I knew her, Emma. My wife and I, we're quiet people. We stay out of trouble."

The man's tone implied Emma was not fit company for decent folk, and Spider's reaction must have shown on his face, for the man took a step back. "I judge no one. She was widowed. Her man went to sea and never came back. It happens. And she had a young one, she did, and her mother dead and her father scarce willing to look upon her. Some people tried to help, with food and such, but she was independent, I suppose. Maybe she did what she had to do. God will judge her. I won't."

Spider clenched his teeth, and his fist. *It must have been damned hard for her.* "Do you know where she is?"

Dawes shook his head. "She left the island. She took up with a seaman, Captain Samuel Westcott. He claimed he was bound for England, with rum and tobacco, and she sailed with him on *Margaret*."

Spider's eyes narrowed. "You said 'claimed.' Why that word? Did you not believe him?"

Dawes stammered. "I make no accusation. Do you know him? Is he a friend, or . . . a shipmate?"

"You say shipmate as though it is a foul word."

"Well, Westcott seemed a rough sort. Some say maybe he was headed to the Caribbean."

Spider almost slumped to the floor. "You believe him to be a pirate?"

"I did not say that!" Dawes was staring at Spider's knife.

"You think I'm a pirate, too. I'm not." *Not anymore, I'm not. Unless Em really has run off with a pirate. Then, by thunder, I'm going to be the bloodiest goddamned pirate on the high seas until I find her.*

"I did not say you were a pirate."

"And I don't know this Westcott," Spider said. "But if Emma is with him, I want to find him. You think he's on the account?"

Dawes shrugged. "Maybe. I met him, once, and, well, I believe him to be the sort to turn pirate."

Spider looked at the man's earring. "You sailed, I reckon?"

"Yes," Dawes said. "I did not like it much."

"But you've met pirates."

"Yes," the man answered, after a hesitation Spider couldn't have missed even if he'd been twice as drunk. "And I pray for Missus Rush's sake she hasn't taken up with a bloody pirate."

Spider began pacing. *Was she out there on a pirate ship? Was his boy?* "How long ago was this?"

"A year, I guess, maybe a bit more."

"And her son?"

"Went with her, I hear."

Spider considered all this. He felt the absence of Hob and Odin profoundly. He felt alone in the world.

But mates by my side or no, I'll turn the goddamned Spanish Main red if that's what I need to do to find my family.

"Where can I find this Jeremy Stoneham?"

"Who are you?"

Spider plucked out his knife. "I'm an impatient fellow."

Dawes started at him, and his face reddened even more. "I don't know your grudge with Jeremy, but I don't hold to violence and it looks to me as though you do. I don't want to lead you to him. You look like you mean to kill him."

"I mean to find Emma," Spider answered. "She's not a widow."

"You're her husband?"

Shit.

"No," Spider said, hoping he had not sounded like he was lying. "Not her husband. I'm his friend. I mean to find her, Emma, and the boy. I've got messages for her, and for him. And I'll tell you," he said, feeling the booze swirling in his head, "I may well beat Jeremy Stoneham to death. I hear he hurt my friend's wife. But if he is smart, and talks before I have to force him to, and helps me find her, I might only hurt him bad enough to feel it all the rest of his days."

Did that sound convincing? Or too angry? Hell.

Dawes stared at Spider as though the latter was mad.

Maybe I am.

"No promises, though," Spider said. "Now where the bloody hell is he?"

19

Spider was wandering between two flocks when he saw the man—
not the man he sought, but another, who seemed to be seeking
someone himself.

The thick black beard stood out, even at a distance, and the man
walked with a sailor's gait and wore a sea coat. He walked with determination, too, from the south—where Spider had broken the leg of the
man named Wood—and toward the cooperage.

Spider knelt low, using the sheep for cover, and peered at the
fellow. The man was too distant for Spider to make out his face, but
his blue tricorn was decorated with a deep blue feather and he wore a
dangling earring that reflected sunlight and looked like a tiny sun. The
beard dominated the man's face.

The man was clearly scanning to and fro, looking for something,
or someone.

Is he looking for me? Probably. It would be how my luck usually goes.

That realization prompted a stream of low curses. "Fucking fool
you are, Spider John, fucking fool of a fucking lobcock!" He'd left a
trail of witnesses who had heard him declare violence toward Jeremy
Stoneham. Had he used his real name? He'd almost told Dawes who
he was. He could barely remember what he'd said on the beach, where
he'd clubbed a man.

Odin and Hob were right. I drink too damned much.

And now here was someone following that trail.

"So, fellow," Spider whispered. "It is your good fortune that I have no time to ambush you. I am looking for someone else."

Spider crawled on his hands and knees toward the Widow Coffin's home, and swatted at a sheep that bleated in his ear. "Got no time for you, either, beast."

He got away from the sheep noises and smells as quickly as he could. He would find Jeremy Stoneham, and deal with him first. Then, if he had to, he'd worry about this mystery pursuer.

If it became necessary, Spider would deal with him, too.

20

The first hints of darkness were showing as Spider John peered from his hiding place in a sheep barn, waiting for Jeremy Stoneham to come to his new woman.

"A very tall fellow," Dawes had said upon deciding it would be best to tell Spider what he wanted to know. "Skinny as a mast, his eyes are kind of too big for his face. Keeps his beard short. And he'll be drunk. Maybe drunker than you."

"Tell me more."

"Aphra Coffin's husband went to sea, never came back. Jeremy took up with her after Emma left," Dawes had said. "Well, before she left, to be honest."

"You think Stoneham is with this woman now?"

"I do not know where he is now. Probably scrounging for liquor, no doubt. But he'll be sniffing at her home tonight, I have no doubt of it. East of town, not far from the harbor. Tucked between two barns, one of them half burnt down. Please, sir, tell me. Are you going to kill him? He's not a good man, but he's trying. The Lord forgives. So should we."

Spider hadn't answered that.

Now he waited inside the remnants of the fire-eaten barn, which no longer seemed to get much use but which no one yet had bothered to tear down or try to repair. It still smelled like smoke, though he reckoned the fire had been some time ago.

He shared the space, open to the sky toward the rear where flames had devoured a portion of the roof, with a small dark cat that stood by the door, staring at a pair of brownish hens that wandered aimlessly outside the barn. Spider was no fan of cats, in general, deeming them too difficult to fathom, but he decided to accept this one because the hens would not approach it. Anything that kept birds at bay earned at least some of Spider's favor. His gaze darted back and forth between the widow's door and the damned chickens.

He cursed himself, too, when he realized just how much of his attention he was wasting on the birds. He should be on the lookout for Stoneham—and for the mystery man he'd seen while crossing the pasture.

He'd seen no sign of the stranger since, though, nor had he heard any alarms. So he waited, and wished he'd drunk a little less.

Night arrived, and with it an aroma of meat born on the smoke from the widow's chimney. Spider listened to his stomach churn and tried to remember when he'd last eaten. It had been that morning aboard *Minuet*, the ship that had carried his friends off toward Boston and future adventures. He felt their absence keenly now, as his fingers tapped the hilt of his knife.

He still saw no sign of Stoneham, and no sign of the seaman sporting the blue feather.

Spider watched the house. It was almost a duplicate of Ephraim Pierce's home, although its door badly needed a coat of paint, and its shutters hung crooked. He could just make out lantern light inside, and now and then a shadow moved within. The Widow Coffin, no doubt, awaiting her drunken lover.

The foggy darkness deepened, pierced only by lantern light streaming through the Widow Coffin's now-closed shutters. The moon was out there somewhere, Spider knew, but was yet too low to do him any good. But he'd tried to memorize the landscape as daylight waned, and hoped he could find his way to his quarry, if the drunkard ever bothered to show up.

Spider shook his head and breathed deeply, trying to will himself to sobriety. A meal would help, he knew, but he had nothing to eat. He looked at the chickens again, and fantasized about breaking a neck, plucking the beast, and starting a fire here in his hideaway. That would require actually approaching the hen, though, and he knew he could not bring himself to do that. He wished again that his friends were with him. He could almost hear Odin teasing him about his fear of birds, and Hob bragging about how he'd cleverly build them a fire hidden from the sight of anyone outside. And, of course, one of them would actually throttle the damned bird and cook it on a spit.

A voice from the east ended his reverie.

Spider crouched low. He peered through the barn door, exposing as little of his head as possible, and removed the knife from his belt. He saw nothing but branches swaying in the wind, sometimes blocking and sometimes revealing the lights of homes further east. Those lights were mere spectral orbs in the mist.

The voice, almost as ghostly, was growing louder.

Spider closed his eyes and concentrated on the sound. It was just one voice, he was certain. Someone telling a story to a silent companion, perhaps, or praying aloud.

No, he decided after a few moments. *Singing*, Spider realized. *It's a drunken man, singing.*

The man was having the devil's time holding to the tune. Too fast one moment, too slow the next, and very little of it melodious at all.

Soon, he could make out a lantern, swinging and bouncing in the distance. The light's movement bore no real relationship to the song, but the glow and sound both seemed to approach him together. After a hundred heartbeats, and after the leather of his knife hilt had grown wet in his sweaty grasp, Spider could discern the lyrics.

"*I am Gamble Gold of the gay green woods,*
And I travelled far beyond the sea,
For killing a man in my father's land,
And from my country was forced to flee."

Spider John spat on the barn floor. If this was Jeremy Stoneham, there would be nowhere for the son of a whore to flee.

"*If you are Gamble Gold of the gay green woods,*

And travelled far beyond the sea,
You are my mother's own sister's son,
What nearer cousins can we be?"

The singing man drew closer still, and his dark shape took form in the fog. Tall, he was, and thin. And he was most certainly drunk.

The man paused, raised his lantern, and stared toward the Widow Coffin's door. Then he coughed hard, strode toward the home, and resumed his song.

"They sheathed their swords, with friendly words,
So merrily they did agree,
They went to a tavern and there they dined,
And cracked bottles most merrily."

Spider John rose from his crouch. *I'll crack your skull, Jeremy Stoneham. Most merrily.*

Spider calculated, and once he was certain of his timing he sped toward the singing man. He approached from behind, determined to catch the man before he reached the widow's door. He kept low, and held the knife in his left hand. He would not use it, he'd decided, until the bastard told him where Emma and Little Johnny were. He had no real plan beyond that.

His booze-addled mind became dimly aware that he was a tad off course, and listing slightly to starboard.

Just before Spider reached his prey—it had to be Stoneham, he was certain—the man stopped and turned, nearly falling over. Spider got a glimpse of the man's overly large eyes, and ducked in case the lantern came arcing toward his head.

Instead, the lantern fell as some shadow crossed Stoneham's face. A thud that reminded Spider of Calvin Garrick hitting *Minuet*'s deck was followed by another, and by something that felt like sleet pelting Spider's shoulders and head.

Stoneham fell, the lantern glow reflecting from his eyes and a dot of silver shining on his bloody forehead.

Someone shoved Spider from behind.

Spider turned and started to topple. His right hand reached out toward the darkness and clutched at something hard and cold. He pulled, hard.

"Ow! Damn!"

Spider did not recognize the voice, and he could not make out any details in the dark fog.

Then he felt his knees buckle, and wondered why his head echoed with thunder—and why he was suddenly showered in glimmering silver.

21

Spider never quite blacked out, but he rolled on the ground and heard the soft curses and grasped the back of his head. Something in his right hand got tangled there. He yanked it away, cursing furiously as he ripped hairs from his own head.

He rose, unsteadily, and heard footsteps, which seemed to belong to someone running away. He looked in what he thought was the right direction, but saw no one.

Spider checked his left hand, and was surprised to find he still held his dagger. He checked his right, and found he clutched a gold earring. It was wet with blood, and some of Spider's hair clung to it. It was not his own plain bauble, a simple brass hoop that could be found on many a sailor's ear, but a gold disc stamped with a devil's head. Spider realized he must have yanked it right out of the attacker's earlobe.

Then he noticed the dead man.

The eyes, like boiled eggs popping out of the corpse's face, convinced him that he was looking upon the remains of Jeremy Stoneham. The man's forehead leaked dark blood, which flowed onto shiny stars scattered on the ground.

One of those stars was stuck there, right in his wound.

Spider bent down and picked up a couple of stars.

Coins, he recognized. *Spanish silver. Pieces of eight.*

Dozens of the coins covered the ground, shining brightly.

It was only then that Spider remembered that it was a dark night, and he was standing far from the lights of Nantucket Town, and that the moon was not yet high. Stoneham's lantern had gone dark.

What light do these coins reflect?

He turned toward the Widow Coffin's door, and noticed it was open. A woman stood within, her hand covering her mouth. Her wide eyes quivered in her face. Her left hand held aloft a lantern, which threw forth the light that made the coins shine. Her entire body seemed to be trying to force a word out of her, and failing.

"This is not . . ."

Spider couldn't finish his sentence before the shocked woman finally spoke.

"Murderer," the Widow Coffin whispered.

Then she shouted. "Murderer!"

The shrill scream assaulted his ears, and he wondered if it might be heard as far away as the town.

"Murder!"

Hell, they might hear that on Cape Cod. Jesus!

He ran.

22

He ran in the dark for a couple dozen yards before toppling over a shadowy shape and plunging headlong to the ground. An unearthly din rose, and he heard many feet thumping the ground around him.

Spider rolled onto his back and brought his knife up in defense—then recognized the sound and smell of sheep. He recognized the foul smell of dung, too, and wiped his face with his sleeve.

"Fuck and bugger!" He tried to regain his feet as the animals stampeded away from him and the Widow Coffin continued yelling behind him. He slipped twice getting up, and by the time he finally arose he was convinced an armed party must surely be ready to clamp manacles onto his wrists.

There was no one around aside from the terrified widow, but her shrieking would not go unnoticed forever.

Spider picked up his hat and looked about for someplace to flee. He noted the lights of the town to the north and west. Pursuers, if they heard the clamor, would come from that direction. Spider turned toward the widow. "I did not kill him!" Then he trotted toward the town, watching for sheep this time, and shouted again. "I did not kill him!"

Once he thought himself beyond the widow's sight, Spider turned north, toward the bay. With any luck—he laughed bitterly at the thought that luck would have anything to do with the likes of him—the Widow Coffin would tell anyone who answered her call that he had run to town. If he could elude pursuit for a while, he might just think his way out of this mess.

What a goddamned mess it is.

Spider reached the water's edge, out of breath. He tried to think. Had he left tracks in Nantucket's soft soil? Probably. He could only hope sheep would obliterate those before they were found.

He plunked his butt down on the thin strip of wet sand and stared out across the dark water. He could hear the bell of a vessel out there somewhere in the fog, probably a fishing boat at anchor. He wished he was on a ship, far away, with his mates by his side and weapons in his hands. You could see an enemy across the waves. You could count on your crewmates to fight for their lives, and yours.

"Hob. Odin," he muttered. "Jesus."

He spat violently, and reached for his pipe before remembering he'd traded his tobacco for the liquor that muddled his thoughts now. "Goddamned fool," he whispered to himself.

Spider listened for the barks of hounds and shouts of armed pursuers, but heard no such thing. He stood up, brushed sand from his breeches, and strolled eastward. He felt just a tad safer with the water to his left, and focused his attention to his right, where men may very well be searching for him this instant. As he walked, he tried to sort out the information they might have.

A dead man at the widow's doorstep, possibly bludgeoned with a sack of coins, judging by the pieces of eight scattered about.

A man assaulted on the south shore, knee shattered by a short seaman wielding an oar. A man who'd grown angry upon hearing how Emma Rush had turned whore. A man who'd gone off to hunt down Jeremy Stoneham.

A cooper, who would tell of a drunk man flashing a knife and demanding to know the whereabouts of Jeremy Stoneham, and whom he'd told to look at the Widow Coffin's house.

The same Jeremy Stoneham who had leaked his life away at the woman's doorstep.

Spider rubbed his hands up and down on his face and fought off tears. It would get worse as word spread. There were not many colonists on the island, but there were enough to hunt him down. If they enlisted the Wampanoags, and there was no reason they wouldn't, it would probably be easy to find him.

Spider halted and weighed his options. He could stow away aboard a ship. Swim, climb an anchor chain, steal aboard, head below. It did not matter where the ship was bound. All he needed to do was stay out of sight for a few days, until the ship was out to sea. He'd likely be caught, eventually, because the need for food and water would force him to forage about, but no captain was likely to turn about just to take him back to Nantucket. Captains had schedules to keep, and money to make.

There was always the chance, too, that they would not connect him with Jeremy Stoneham's death. He would have time while hiding to concoct a story, something credible. They might clap him in irons, but he'd escaped such situations before.

He glanced back toward the west. He could do all that. It would be easy.

Then he turned east and started walking, away from any ship that might carry him to freedom.

This island was home to Emma Rush and Little Johnny. They might come back here one day, and, by thunder, he did not want them to hear how he had clubbed a man to death in a fit of drunken anger.

He stopped, doubled over, and actually laughed. "Of all your crimes, Spider John," he said, "the one you don't want them to hang on you is the one you didn't do!"

He dropped to his knees, and prayed. Once the tears stopped, he rose again and started walking.

He saw a light ahead, and heard a familiar sound.

Someone was sawing wood.

23

Spider peered around a corner and watched a reed-thin man expertly saw a plank. A stack of wood by his side indicated he'd been at it a while, as did the sweat soaking his shirt. He worked by lantern light in a wide barn. Whaleboats were stacked on racks beyond him, sporting fresh paint that Spider could smell even from a distance, and a dozen new oars leaned against a wall to one side.

Spider was still trying to decide whether to announce his presence when the man stopped sawing and turned. His hand reached toward a jug on the ground behind him, but he froze when he saw Spider. The man looked as though he had seen the angel of death.

"My lord," Spider said. "What happened to you?"

The man, who seemed to be younger than Spider, stared at him from eyes surrounded in black bruises. His jaw was crooked, or swollen, or both. His lower lip was cut in three places. Spider had seen plenty of injuries in his day, and reckoned these had been inflicted a few days ago.

The man forgot his jug and stood. He reached behind him, without taking his eyes off Spider, and found a mallet. "Got beat," he said. "Not gettin' beat again. You just go away. I don't lose the fight when I can see the bastard coming."

Spider lifted both hands into the air and stepped forward, slowly. "I don't mean to fight you," he said. "Got no reason. I know wounds. I might be able to help a bit."

"I never seen you before."

"No," Spider said. "I'm a visitor to the island, ran into some trouble. Looks to me that you ran into some trouble, too."

"That happens, sometimes."

"Who beat you?"

"No," the man said, but he lowered his mallet. "I don't want to talk about it. That won't do no good. I'll be fine. What happened to you?"

"Aye, then," Spider replied. "Well, I won't pry if you won't. May I come in? I'm a carpenter, willing to work."

The tall man waved him in. He pointed to the jug. "Whisky?"

Spider almost said yes, then thought better of it. "No, but thanks. If you've some tobacco to share, though, I'd be grateful."

The man turned, walked to a pouch hanging from a nail in the wall, and tossed the pouch to Spider. "Help yourself."

Still wary, Spider thought. *Not willing to come close. I don't blame him.*

Spider nodded and began stuffing his pipe. "Why do you work so late?"

"Lady needs a sheep pen, and her man's away at sea," he said. "Extra work for me, extra money."

"Plenty of ladies on this island with men at sea," Spider mused. "Extra work is good." Then he went to the lantern and brought the pipe to life. Part of the stem had broken off somewhere along the way, but he had enough left. He inhaled deeply, counted to ten, tilted his head, and then blew out a heavy stream of smoke. "Thank you, friend. I can't tell you how much I needed that."

The man picked up his jug. "Probably not as much as I need this." He popped out the cork and took a big swig. Spider smelled the aroma, and regretted turning down a drink. But he needed a clear head, and he could hear Odin in his imagination, berating him for drinking too hard.

"I'm John," Spider said.

"I'm Isaac," the other man answered. "You look a bit beat up. Mud all over. Been in a fight?"

"With some sheep," Spider said, popping his pipe back into his mouth. "I lost."

Isaac laughed. "Yeah, I smell that. They are everywhere."

"Aye. You weren't beat by animals, though."

"No." Isaac did not elaborate.

"Well," Spider said, "let me fix up some planks to help you."

"You hiding from someone?"

Spider blinked. "No."

Isaac pointed to a saw on the wall. "You can use that one. It's not as good as this one I'm using, but it's good."

Spider nodded.

Isaac took up his saw. "I asked if you were hiding from someone, because you keep glancing toward the door."

"Oh," Spider answered. "No, not hiding."

Isaac set up a couple of sawhorses for Spider. "You can use one of my planks to measure."

Spider hung his hat on a nail and got to work, and after a few minutes of effort he could feel the last of his drunkenness fade away. He was sleepy, but determined to keep up with Isaac. It felt good to have something to do, something he was good at. His problems still crowded his mind, but he felt more able to think now. The sound of the saw, the scent of freshly cut wood, the sweat of labor, all helped to settle him down, at least to the extent possible.

"You know your work," Isaac said as he noted Spider's growing stack.

"Thanks. So do you."

Spider noticed then that Isaac had picked up the pace. Not to be outdone, Spider did likewise. Both men shot glances back and forth, and worked up a good sweat as the friendly competition continued.

Once they both stopped to catch their breath—a decision reached mutually, and silently, and agreed to with nods—Isaac pointed at all the lumber.

"Might have saved me a whole day, mister. Thanks."

"You are welcome."

"Listen," Isaac said, turning toward him. "I . . . I appreciate you working and not asking a bunch of stuff." He pointed to his face.

Spider nodded. "Your business. But if I can help, I will."

"Who are you hiding from?"

Spider looked at Isaac a long time. Neither man blinked.

"You will hear it soon enough," Spider said. "They'll be looking for me. A man got killed today, and they'll say I did it. I did not do it."

Isaac gulped. "Well," he said. "That's worse than what they accuse me of."

"What do they accuse you of?"

Isaac thought about that. "I don't want to say it."

"Aye, then," Spider said. "Your business. I am getting sleepy, Isaac. Can I sleep here?"

"Sure, I guess," the man answered. "I work mostly by myself. Nobody's likely to bother you."

"I reckon you might be wrong about that," Spider said, ducking behind a stack of wood. "Someone's coming."

Moments later, he heard a voice from the doorway. "Isaac, you seen anyone about?"

"Short man," another voice added. "Missing a finger on his left hand. Wears a bad-worn hat, floppy brim."

Shit. That hat's hanging from a goddamned nail, in plain sight.

"Hello, Joseph, Ben. No," Isaac said. "Seen no one. Been working."

"The man we are looking for killed Stoneham," one of the interrogators said.

Isaac spat. "Jeremy Stoneham?"

"Yes, Jeremy Stoneham."

"Good," Isaac said. "Somebody needed to kill him, if you ask me."

"We don't care what you think of the man," came the answer. "But I guess Stoneham was not the kind of fellow you like, was he?"

The other man laughed. "No. You like them more dainty, don't you, Isaac?"

"Get off my property," Isaac said.

"Now you don't push us. Looks like someone already beat you up and down, you don't need us doing it, too. You just keep an eye out for this killer, and you come to town and tell us if you see him or hear of him. Zachariah's house, that's where we are organizing this manhunt. Do you understand?"

"Yes," Isaac said.

"Just look for him," the other voice said. "You like looking at men, right?"

No one spoke. Spider could not see them, but he could feel the tension, and he imagined Isaac's grip tightening on the mallet's handle. Spider took a knife from his belt. If it came to a fight, Isaac would not be alone.

It did not come to a fight. Spider eventually heard laughter fading into the distance.

"They are gone," Isaac said.

Spider climbed out of his hiding place.

Isaac would not look at him. "You can leave now, if you want."

"You could have turned me over to those men," Spider said. "You did not. Why?"

Isaac stared at the sawdust that littered the floor. "When I saw you, you looked haunted," he said. "You looked like someone who had troubles way past mine, like pain just was eatin' you. But when you saw me," he gulped, "well, you worried about me."

"You've been beaten bad," Spider said.

"You heard what they said about me." The man still would not look up.

"I do not care about any of that," Spider said. He'd heard similar accusations at sea. "I don't understand it, I'll tell you, but I reckon I don't need to. Is that why somebody beat you?"

Isaac looked up.

"Yes."

Spider nodded. "Well, if they don't catch me and hang me for a killing I didn't do, maybe I can help you teach some fellows to leave you alone."

Spider reached out his hand. Isaac strode forward and took it.

"I think we have a deal," he said.

24

Spider had napped only a few hours, tucked into a heavy wool blanket in a far corner of the barn. He awoke when Isaac returned.

"Have you decided what you will do?" Isaac carried a kettle of tea in one hand, and two mugs in the other. Spider inhaled the aroma and winked. "You make it strong. That's good."

Isaac approached, allowing more morning light to seep into the barn from the door. Spider sat up and took a mug, and pondered Isaac's question as the man poured steaming fluid. He had told Isaac some, but not all, of his story after the interrogators had left.

"I have a plan, of sorts, mostly reckoned out. I need to go into the town and figure out who killed Jeremy Stoneham. If I can reckon who really did it, then I can leave Nantucket with a clear name. As clear as it can get, alas."

He would never be able to erase the stain of piracy from his soul, he knew, but he had committed those crimes out of necessity, not choice. He'd been coerced into the pirate life at a young age because the wild men who had attacked *Lily* needed a carpenter to repair their battle-worn ships. If Spider had not possessed skill with wood and tools, they'd have consigned him to the deep with the other victims. After agreeing to their terms, he had quickly learned that every man on a pirate ship is expected to participate in the crimes. "I will not worry about having coconspirators and accomplices by my side," Bent Thomas had told him. "But I will not have witnesses, with no blood on their hands, looking down on me and telling the judge what an evil son of a whore I am while playing all innocent. No. You shall fight, damn your eyes, and you shall steal and you shall kill. Or you shall die, right now."

Spider, to his shame, had chosen to live.

He had rehearsed his explanation to Em in his mind a million times, of course. He'd had no choice. Joining the pirates and doing the bloody work was the only path that would lead him back to her, and to their son. He did not think, however, that he could so easily explain the murder of Jeremy Stoneham, a sneak attack from behind. He winced at the very thought of Little Johnny hearing that account. No.

He would just have to find the true murderer.

Isaac filled his own mug. "That is foolish, going to town. Everyone on the damned island will be looking for you. No one liked Stoneham, but no one likes murder."

"Last night, it sounded like you did not like Stoneham." Spider had almost mentioned that the night before, but weariness had overtaken both of them by the time they'd stopped their work. Spider did not think Isaac was the killer, though. For one thing, the man had been hard at work when Spider found him. For another, neither of his earlobes had been ripped open by the snatched earring Spider had tucked into his tobacco pouch. And though he clearly had been in a fight, it had taken place before last night.

"He was a drunk, and a bad one." Isaac shrugged. "I'm a drunk, too, sometimes, but I don't hit women nor anyone else. I just get drunk."

Spider considered that. "I've a good thirst, now and again. One reason I'm hiding here, I suppose. I made some fool choices, and liquor helped me make them. Did Stoneham ever beat you?"

"He tried to, twice. Too drunk, both times."

"Did you know a woman named Emma Rush? She hung with Stoneham, I hear." Spider steeled himself for Isaac's answer.

"I know who she is, but I never talked to her nor had any relations with her," the man replied, seeming to choose his words carefully.

"Many men did know her, though," Spider said, quietly. "That is what I hear."

"Well, yes, a few," Isaac said, sitting down in a patch of sunlight. "Her husband got lost at sea, or something, and her father did not stand by her. A preacher, he is."

"I know him," Spider muttered.

"Well. Stern fellow. So, she sold herself. Pretty. She survived that way. Her father did not like that."

Spider swallowed hard. "I reckon not. She took up with Stoneham."

"Yes. He treated her bad." Isaac winced. "Not long after they started up, I remember seeing her with bruises on her face. Not as bad as these," he pointed to his own swollen jaw and eyes. "But bad enough. I think Stoneham got tired of other men touching her, maybe. Or maybe it was about money."

"And that is why she left? Because he beat her?"

Isaac nodded. "Probably. Good enough reason."

"And she took her boy with her."

"I believe so."

Spider drank his tea. *Sorry I was away, my love.*

Once the hot liquid was gone, Spider resumed his questions. "Did anyone else have a jealous nature, regarding Emma? Anyone who might have been mad enough to kill him for what he done?" *Anyone besides myself, that is.*

"Well, there was some knockin' heads and cursing, to be sure," Isaac said. "Some gents kept coming around, and Jeremy did not like that. And some did not like Stoneham anyway. He didn't pay debts, he cheated at dice and cards. So there was fightin' and such with him all the time."

Spider pondered this. He wished Hob was at hand, to ask fool questions. The young man often rushed to wild conclusions, but his guesswork sometimes aimed Spider in the right direction. Here, he was rudderless.

"Emma left about a year ago?"

"I think so," Isaac said, nodding.

"If someone killed Stoneham over Emma, it's an odd thing to wait so long to club him over the head."

Isaac considered that and scratched his beard. "Probably. There's lots of other reasons to kill Stoneham, though. He was generally a rough and brutal man. Stole from people, they say, started lots of fights. Hell, I do not know why anyone cares that he got killed."

"Well," Spider said. "A man is supposed to be able to go about his days without getting killed, I reckon. Most folks don't like it when such things happen. It ain't like pirate life, where a bleeding skull is just a thing that happens to someone now and then."

"Pirate life?" Isaac's eyebrow lifted.

"Well," Spider said, "that's what I imagine pirates to be like, fighting and killing and such." He wondered if he sounded convincing. Isaac did not look convinced, nor did he look concerned.

"I have to go fetch a wagon and haul these planks," he said. "John, you can come with me if you dare, but you might best just hide here. I should not go into town, if I were you. I should not."

"I may be safer than you think," Spider said. "By and by, if anyone should catch me hiding here, you must pretend you did not know. Or you can say I forced you to hide me, held a knife to your throat or something of that nature. I don't want you to take on a burden for my sake."

"I don't think it right to abandon people," Isaac said.

"Do it just the same."

Isaac did not commit. "I can go to Zachariah's later, see what people are saying, maybe ask some questions for you. It'll be safer than you going."

"No," Spider said. "Thanks for that, but no. It's my worries, so it'll be my risks. And you have a fence to build."

"You'll be captured, and hauled over to Massachusetts to be hung."

"I have some thoughts on how I might prevent that," Spider said. "Might I use your tools, and some of that scrap lumber?"

25

*H*e was rather pleased.

Everyone was looking for a short man with long brown hair and beard, a wide-brimmed relic of a hat and a missing finger on his left hand. The man hobbling along the waterfront now had short hair and a somewhat shorter braided beard, and was at least a foot taller than the man they sought.

Even the finger had been replaced, or seemingly so. He'd attached a small stick to his hand with cloth and string, then bandaged the hand up tightly. It would take a close look to determine that his small finger came from a pine.

He'd wrapped his head, too, adding some red paint on the forehead to simulate blood. For a while, he'd covered his left eye, but then decided it was better to be able to see properly. He did not have Odin's long experience of getting along with just a single eye, nor was his friend here to teach him.

Spider was most proud of the stilts, though. Short pieces of lumber, strapped to his feet, with blocks shaped to represent his feet stuffed into his tall boots. Splints flanked his lower legs, further supported by tightly bound cloth. A long coat and breeches borrowed from Isaac completed the disguise. He missed his hat, which he'd hidden along with his own coat in a barrel of nails at Isaac's barn. The hunters the night before had specifically mentioned that, so he dared not wear it.

He had tried walking on the goddamned things, but that had

proven impossible. So he'd fashioned himself a pair of pine crutches as well, and now looked every inch the wounded sailor, hobbling slowly along.

He'd wasted a good bit of the morning practicing his gait, and he'd found it necessary to halt now and then to ease the pain in his legs. Isaac had a wagon and had offered to give him a ride, but Spider had declined so the man could go do the work he'd been hired to do. *Stupid of me*, Spider thought, wishing he could reach down to rub his cramped calves.

The walk to town had been an adventure in itself, with the crutches frequently burying themselves in the sandy soil and him fighting the temptation to wander past the Widow Coffin's place to look for clues. He figured there were people already doing that, and decided there was no need to put his disguise to such a stern test.

Spider worked his way slowly along the waterfront, after finding no crowd at Zachariah's. That old man, Isaac had explained, had retired from the sea and now ran a tavern, of sorts, from his home. He had whisky, rum, and beer brought over from Falmouth or Boston, and sold it to all comers. Spider had found the place empty, however, except for Zachariah himself, snoozing in a rocking chair before a tidy fire, jug on his lap. Spider had nudged him awake.

The old man had opened beady black eyes surrounded by gray beard and gigantic eyebrows. "Did they find the killer?"

"I have no idea," Spider had said. "I am new here. Someone got killed?"

That had elicited a lengthy tale, in which someone had bashed the skull of Jeremy Stoneham, probably to get at the Widow Coffin.

"Handsome woman, she is," the old man had said, laughing. "Plenty of men probably thinking of visiting her. That's my guess. Others have a different idea, though."

"Oh?"

"Aye. Fellow got beaten out by the whale watch, said some man came looking for Emma Rush and beat him when he found out she was a whore. Stoneham was her man, for a while."

Spider swallowed hard. "You don't believe that tale, though?"

"Hell, could be. That widow, though, she's a fine-looking woman and she's lonely. I've thought of heading out there to see her, hee hee. I'd not be surprised if someone just wanted Stoneham out of the way."

The old man lifted his jug. "Don't want nobody killing me, though, just to get at her. No. Hee hee. What the hell happened to you?"

"Shark," Spider said. His lower legs felt like a fucking shark was still gnawing him.

"Thought maybe you'd been up to see the widow, too, hee hee."

The old man's leer reminded Spider instantly of Odin, so Spider had left rather quickly. He wished he'd tried harder to get the one-eyed son of a bitch and Hob to accompany him. He knew he'd likely be in a better spot now if they had come along.

He explored the docks and wharves, listening for any talk of the incident at the Widow Coffin's home. Someone who wanted to flee the island after committing a murder almost certainly would come here. He scanned the bay for ships that seemed ready to depart, and wondered if Stoneham's killer was hiding on one of them. Of course, the murderer could have boarded a ship that had already embarked. That, Spider reckoned, would be just his luck.

Two ships were taking on cargo, a bark and a schooner. Each seemed Boston-built to his trained carpenter's eye, and neither had seen a lot of years on the ocean. *Maybe I should get on one of them and leave*, he thought.

"You seek passage, do you?" That came from a young man, pulling a cart with two hogsheads. Spider detected a whisky aroma, the angel's share seeping through the barrels. He very much wanted a drink.

"Passage? No," he said.

"Not work, then? You seem to have had it rough enough already." The young man, dark-haired and smiling broadly, pointed at Spider's crutches.

"Shark," Spider said. "No, I am not looking for work, either. Just dreaming, I guess. Are you crew on one of those?"

"*Tyrone*," he said, pointing at the bark. "Bound for England. Never been there."

"Keep a weather eye for pirates," Spider said.

"Aye. And sharks." The man resumed pulling his cart toward the waiting tender.

Spider followed, his crutches drumming on the wood. "I hear there is a manhunt."

"Aye," the young man said. "Or so I hear. It was a lot of talk last night, and I helped search about. Did not find anyone, though."

"Who got killed?"

"A drunk, named Stoneham. Over a woman, they say."

"Aye," Spider said. "Keep an eye out for them, too. Along with pirates. And sharks."

"Aye," the young man said. "Pirates, women, and sharks. I'll beware. I am Jacob."

"I am Ezra," Spider said, borrowing a name from a friend he'd lost long ago.

"Well met, Ezra. I have to load this and then go fetch two more, and I'll need to be quick about it." He glanced at Spider's crutches.

"Go, lad, go. Thanks for talking with me."

Spider saw another fellow nearby, lighting a pipe from a flaming brand, and started a similar conversation while taking the opportunity to light his own pipe, full of tobacco provided by Isaac.

"Aye, I know Stoneham," the bald man said. He was Welsh, judging by his accent. "Or knew him, suppose I ought to say. Right bastard."

"Who do you think killed him?"

"Hell, heh, well, that is a fine question, my friend. Fine question. He cheated at cards, fucked men's wives, blasphemed every day and night, spat on the natives, and heaven alone knows what he did to the goddamned sheep, heh."

The man waved his brand to extinguish it and tossed it into the water. "I believe there to be at least a dozen men on Nantucket who wouldn't mind spilling Stoneham's blood, so this tale of a stranger come to town to kill him does not sit well with me, no sir. It sounds very contrived, very convenient."

"Do you have a favorite suspect among that dozen?"

"Heh, no, sir." He puffed on his pipe. "If I knew who killed him, I'd toss in a day's wages to give him a reward, and I believe there to be a crowd who would help me raise a prize, I truly do. But . . ." He glanced about, as though watching for eavesdroppers.

"Well?"

"Well," the man said, "it just seems to me convenient, like I said, that this Dawes is one of the men who tells this story about a mysterious stranger, and he's one of the men who don't like Jeremy Stoneham. Or didn't like him, I should say."

"Oh?"

"Dawes and Stoneham, well, Stoneham rented a room from Dawes, right, so those two was in each other's way a lot, even though Dawes don't much like him. Didn't, I should say."

"Well," Spider mused, "it is not Dawes alone who tells the story of the strange short man with a missing finger—handsome devil, I hear, and certainly a bold clever fellow. I hear a man got beaten, down by the watch posts."

"Name of Wood, aye," the man replied. "A drinker. Probably misses more whales than he sees, with his head always tilted back for the jug. I would not put much store in what he tells anyone."

"Is he alive?"

"Oh, yes. He may not walk again, not unless he does a turn like you and gets him some crutches. But he'll live. He's the one started the talk about a stranger looking for Stoneham, you know. Says that is who attacked him."

Spider nodded. "But you don't believe him?"

"I am just saying there are at least a dozen men right here on Nantucket that would like to see Jeremy Stoneham dead. We don't need to have strangers come about to kill our right bastards, no sir. Someone here done it, I'll wager."

Spider thanked the man for the spark, drew deeply on his pipe, and blew a stream of smoke into the air. He exhaled with force, the way he always did to prevent the fumes from gathering beneath the brim of his hat—then realized he was not wearing the hat. No hat, no Hob, no Odin. No Em. No Little Johnny.

No chance of finding the killer and clearing my name.

He turned south, then caught a motion out of the corner of his eye. Someone was running toward him, from an alley between a fish stall and a warehouse.

Fuck.

Spider hobbled onward, no longer so proud of his disguise. There was no way he could move at speed on the stilts, and no way he could doff them quickly.

He forced himself not to look toward the pursuer. The man, whoever he was, had some distance to cover between the buildings before he could emerge onto the street, and Spider could get out of his sight simply by moving forward. Once he had done that, he looked about for a place to hide. He spotted a wagon headed toward him, loaded with barrels and pulled by a mule. A black man handled the reins.

Spider hobbled as quickly as he could toward the wagon. "Mind if an injured sailor comes aboard?"

The driver smiled and halted the mule. "You don't look like you ought to be walking, sir. Climb up."

"I'll ride in the back, easier for me. Thanks." Spider clambered over the wagon rail, and hoped he did not look too nimble doing so. He deliberately chose the side away from the alley's mouth, and tucked himself out of sight between barrels. He considered it good fortune that the wagon was headed in the opposite direction he himself had been walking when he spotted the man in the alley. The pursuer would exit the alley and look southward, while Spider was heading northward.

"Oh, my goddamned shanks," he muttered, as new pains shot through his legs now that he was no longer walking.

Spider took a quick glance at the alley mouth, but did not see the man emerge. He wished he'd had a chance to spy him. *Did he have a feathered tricorn, and a shiny earring, like the man he'd spotted the other day? Did he have a thick black beard? Did he have a gashed earlobe?*

"How far do you go, sir?"

"Oh, I'll just go where you do," Spider said. "Wanted to see the town, but my legs ache now." *And they probably will ache for however many goddamned days I have left*, he thought. *Jesus*!

"You look like you have had it rough, sir. What happened to you?"

"Shark. And pirates. And a woman."

26

*H*e'd hoped to make it back to Issac's barn by nightfall, but was coming to realize that was impossible. He'd hidden in a fish shack until he'd convinced himself that he was not being pursued, then slowly hobbled back southward along the docks. Once he'd gotten away from town, he'd plopped onto the beach and removed the damned stilts from his screaming legs. He'd suffered sword gashes in his day, and knocks on the skull and hot musket balls lashing his skin. He still winced whenever he recalled the cutlass that had claimed the small finger on his left hand. The shooting, burning, throbbing pain in his legs and feet from those fucking stilts, however, were worse than any of that.

"Good riddance," he said, snarling at the small pile of wood. He tossed the short stilts into the harbor.

Spider rolled up the britches—now too long for him—and picked up the crutches. He would carry them back to Isaac, so as not to waste good wood.

A gull's call echoed across the water in the lowering light, and the fog was beginning to form. Spider walked, keeping an eye out for the bearded man with the earring and for birds and wishing there were more trees on this island he could use for cover. Then he stopped. He could hear Odin in his mind: "The trees are where the fucking birds are, you lobcock!"

The memory of the man in the tricorn got him to thinking. *Had the sack of silver been intended for Spider's skull, and not Stoneham's? Had someone followed him there, intending to kill him, and simply missed in the fog and confusion?*

He could not dismiss that idea, though he thought it unlikely. The man in the pasture might have been looking for anything, a wayward sheep, for instance. Spider had no real reason to suppose he'd been the man's prey, and no one seemed to care enough about Stoneham to protect him. Maybe someone had sought to avenge Wood, though.

Spider looked at the clouds rolling across the darkening sky and moved on, sending new throbs of pain up his legs with each step. That's when he heard a voice.

He halted, and crouched.

"This way." It was a man's voice. A whisper, so it had to be close. It came from somewhere behind him.

Spider glanced over his shoulder. He saw two shapes in the distance, and possibly another beyond, illuminated by a lantern one of them carried.

Fuck and bugger.

He considered his options. He could creep into the water, and simply hide, watch, and listen. He might freeze, but that was better than being shot or stabbed or dragged to the gallows. They might not spot him in the dark, and he might learn something that way. It would be risky, though, and he had no weapons save for his knife if they caught him.

He could try to swim to safety, but his aching legs scoffed at that idea, and he'd have to lose the heavy coat and his boots.

Spider decided. He took a deep breath, rose, and ran in a low crouch, choking down the screams his agonized legs demanded. He ran away from the approaching party and toward Isaac's barn. It was a risk, but he deemed it his best chance. If the shadowy figures behind him were seeking the killer of Jeremy Stoneham, they'd likely move slowly, looking for him. He knew the way, and had traversed this area earlier on his way to town, so he felt he could move faster.

Unless his pained legs failed him.

Or unless they spotted him, and gave chase.

Then they would catch him. And they would hang him.

27

"I am followed," Spider said, out of breath. "And I can scarce walk. Jesus!"

He fell to the floor and grabbed his calves as Isaac ran to close the doors.

"How far behind?"

"I have no idea," Spider said, wincing. "I did not look back. I have not heard them for some time, though. I might have left them behind."

Spider crawled toward the hiding place he'd used before. "I don't know if they'll come here," he said. "I heard them behind me and I just ran. I am sorry."

"Are you certain they seek you?" Isaac picked up a mallet.

"I am not sure of anything," Spider muttered, then ducked out of sight. "Don't fight them. If they come here. Trick them, if you can. Tell them a tale. But don't get yourself hurt. My legs are dead. I can't fight with you."

He heard Isaac remove something from a wall. "Here," he said, reaching over the crates Spider hid behind. It was a hand axe.

"Thanks," Spider said.

Isaac went toward the lantern, and turned down the light. Then he went back to his sawhorses, and Spider heard the scrape of an adze across wood. Spider caught the scent of maple, and figured Isaac was fashioning oars.

Isaac paused. "I heard something," he said softly. Then he went back to work, humming a quiet tune.

Spider's grip tightened on the axe hilt. He'd used an axe many times, of course, but not as a weapon. It would be fine at close quarters, but he doubted he could throw it with any real accuracy. He knew he could throw a knife, though. He'd practiced that skill for years, and won a lot of bets. Even with this knife being fairly new to him, he felt confident. The range would be close, and he was sober now. So he tore away the fake finger, then freed his knife and wielded it in his right hand. He took up the axe in his left.

He heard movement in the brush outside. Isaac ran to a shuttered window and peeked out. "I hear them, but I don't see them," he said.

So, Spider thought, *that means no lantern or candle. They are sneaking, then, for there isn't enough moonlight to depend upon, and they walk through fog.*

Sweat threatened his grasp on his weapons, so he took a second to wipe his hands on his britches.

He heard Isaac spit. "I've had enough," the man whispered. "Don't know if they come to hang you or beat me, but I've had enough. One of them is right outside the door."

Spider said nothing, but prepared himself to spring into action. He gnashed his teeth to prevent a scream as lightning pain shot through his right leg.

"Come on in," Isaac said, loudly. "I know you are out there."

"Aye," came the answer.

Spider heard the barn door open.

"Who are you?" It was Isaac, and Spider could hear the tension in the man's voice.

"Drop the adze, sir. I mean no harm. I am looking for a friend."

Spider rose. "Hob!"

Then he fell down again, dropping his weapons and grabbing his leg. "Fuck and bugger, damnation and . . . fuck! Goddamn it, boy, cut my fucking legs right off!"

28

"Spotting you was simple," Hob said, unable to keep from grinning. "Good disguise, Spider John, very damned clever, indeed, but it did not fool me."

They all sat around Isaac's table—their host, Spider, Hob, Odin, and Ruth in a man's garb—drinking rye whisky from wooden cups. A good fire blazed, and a kettle of boiling clams and onions filled the humble room with a savory aroma. Isaac had fetched the jug while Spider introduced his friends. The shipmates spent most of this time staring at Spider and looking concerned. Their eyes asked unspoken questions.

"How did you spy me out, boy?" Spider massaged his calf.

Hob inhaled sharply. "Well, you were taller, different coat, shorter hair, less beard, but you still smoked a pipe and I've seen you blow smoke hundreds of times, Spider. You always tilt your head back just so"—Hob demonstrated, forcing a whoosh of air out the left side of his mouth—"and you pop the thing in and out of your mouth in a peculiar way, too."

"I do?"

"Aye," Odin said. "You always cross your mouth. If it's in your right hand, you poke it into the left side of your mouth." Odin snatched Spider's pipe and demonstrated. "And if it's your left hand, you pop it in the other side. You do it all backwards when you take it out. Right hand if the pipe is to your left, other hand the other way."

He illustrated by removing the pipe, planting it in his own mouth and then returning it to Spider. The carpenter glared at the hideous old man and snapped the end off the pipe stem before returning it to his mouth—quite pointedly using his right hand and inserting the pipe into the right side of his jaw. "I think you tell tales."

"I've seen it a hundred times, or a thousand," Hob said. "Knew it was you as soon as I spied you, even with all the crutches and all."

"Well," Spider said. "It is nice to know you pay attention to something. And you even knew Isaac was holding an adze! I would not have bet money on that!"

Hob winced. "I am not such a horrible carpenter as you think, Spider."

"Nor as good as you'd be if you paid more attention."

"I pay attention," Hob growled. "I saw you, didn't I? And I knew you could not have run far, nor fast, not on whatever you'd built to make yourself taller. So I figured you'd hopped in that wagon. Nowhere else you could have gone, aye? So I watched where it went, got these two and followed. Found your stilts, we did, floating in the harbor. And we . . ."

Spider stared at him.

"We what?"

"Followed your footprints," Ruth said. "You were walking and running on sand part of the way, Spider."

Spider shrugged, and removed his pipe from his mouth. "Footprints. I should have reckoned on that. And here is my pipe in my goddamned left hand, though it was on the right side of my mouth. I'll be damned."

They toasted that remark, and Isaac filled their cups again.

Spider beamed. "I am damned glad you are here. All of you. But why did you come? And how?"

Odin scratched at the scars that covered his face where he'd lost his right eye long ago. In the flickers of light from the hearth, he looked like a warlock. "We got back to *Minuet*, and that German bastard was gone."

"Seitz?"

"Aye."

Ruth drained her cup and placed it on the table with a thump. "He was in a bit of a fit after you three went ashore. Heard him rattling around in the galley, throwing things, cursing a lot. I think it was cursing, anyway."

"Anything a German says sounds like cursing," Odin muttered.

"Well," Ruth continued, "he was mad. And he certainly paid a great deal of attention to you three when you rowed away from the ship."

"She told us when we got back," Hob added, "and I went looking for him, thought I'd do some spying. But he wasn't in the galley. We searched the ship and he wasn't aboard. Found his clothes piled on the floor, though, and his boots."

"Is that so?" Spider scratched his head. "I'll be damned."

"Thought maybe he was looking for that map," Odin said, "and took a little swim to come chase us. We didn't want him slicing into your neck or anything, so we came ashore, too."

Spider looked at Ruth. "And you came with them."

She glanced down at her empty cup. "Didn't want him slicing into your neck or anything," she said.

"We grabbed some things—couldn't get guns, though, I tried—and we stole a boat. Quite a little adventure, that. They tried to stop us and we had no guns, so we had to fend them off with belaying pins."

"Did you not have a grappling hook hidden somewhere?"

Hob shrugged. "This time, no. We made a good job of it, though. Hated to steal a jolly boat from Cap'n Bellows, but we had no choice."

"I reckon he will not write a nice letter to the Admiralty on your behalf, after all, but I am certain you were quite the swashbuckler," Spider said.

"Oh, he will not commend me to His Majesty's service, he won't. He'll thrash me if he ever sees me again, or he shall try, I should say. But it is no matter. I don't want to be in the Royal Navy."

"Hob was quite valiant, Spider, and they'd all seen what he'd done to those bastards who tried to take the ship," Ruth said. "Not a one of them tried to rush him. They were completely unmanned, the whole lot of them."

Hob glanced at Ruth. "She changed clothes while we rowed ashore."

"We were in a haste, were we not? And surely you did not expect me to change my garb there in front of all the brave fellows who were afraid of you and your damned belaying pin."

"Pins. I had one on each hand."

"Forgive me, I forgot. Pins, then. And I probably should have changed clothes in front of the entire crew, because it would have been less dangerous. You nearly steered us into a seal, Hob, because you weren't paying attention to your duty."

"Fucking big seal," Odin said. "Would feed us for a month."

"Too big to ram the jolly boat into," Ruth said, "It was ridiculous, you trying to row the boat and see my body at the same time, Hob. Surely, you've seen a woman before."

Hob nodded. "And I hope to see many more. But they all don't look like you."

"Belay that," Spider said, smacking Hob on the head. "Ruth is pretty, certain, but she is too smart for you. So is the fucking seal. I am glad you all came, because I think you smoked it out. I do believe Seitz did swim ashore."

"Aye?" That was Hob. "You've seen him, then?"

"Aye. I saw a man, dark beard, and it seemed he was following in my wake, and now I know why. Seitz! The man I saw wore a blue coat and a blue hat, which I never saw him wear aboard *Minuet* but I reckon he stole after he stripped naked to swim ashore. Damn, that must have been cold."

The others shrugged.

They drank in silence for a while, and then Hob finally asked the question. "Was your woman not here, Spider?"

Another awkward silence followed that.

"No," Spider said. He looked Hob in the eyes. "It seems I was not worth awaiting."

Ruth glanced down at the table.

Spider continued. "They tell me she took up with a fellow named Stoneham. Then left Nantucket with another man, name of Westcott, maybe for England, maybe for the Main, with my boy in tow." He tried to keep the bitterness out of his voice, but failed.

"I heard that name when we were looking for you," Odin said. "Stoneham. I heard he got killed."

"Aye," Spider said. "Someone crushed his skull with a sack of Spanish silver."

"I heard it was a not very tall sailor, missing a finger," Hob said.

They all looked at him. Finally, Ruth asked. "Did you kill him?"

"I think I was about to kill him," Spider said quietly. "I know I was going to ask him some questions, where my Em was, what did he do to her, all that. After that, I don't know. Maybe I would have killed him, but someone beat me to it. Maybe not, though. Maybe they meant to kill him, but maybe they meant to kill me. I was thinking it was him they wanted to kill, Stoneham, but if Seitz came ashore, then, well, maybe he tried to kill me and just hit Stoneham instead."

He told them then of his misadventures—the dreadful discussion with Em's father, the unfortunate drunken encounter with the man he'd beaten on the beach, and his manhunt for Jeremy Stoneham. He left out the part about Em selling her body.

"It's a bad way," he said. "Everyone on the island probably thinks I followed Stoneham to the widow's house and clubbed him with a sack of coin. I'll hang for it, and I didn't even get the pleasure of killing the son of a bitch."

"What shall we do, then? Find a ship, and go off treasure hunting?" Hob tapped his boot.

"I want to find out who killed Stoneham, so Em and my son know it wasn't me, if they come back here, or if word reaches them."

"We'll help you," Ruth said.

"I'm for leaving," Odin said. "Whole island smells like sheep."

"I'll not hold you all here," Spider said. "You might get caught up in all this and hang with me."

Odin, Hob, and Ruth all exchanged glances.

"Last time we left you alone," Hob said, "you got all drunk, beat a man with an oar, chased down another man and got blamed for killing him, then nearly broke your own damned legs strolling about on goddamned sticks. You don't want that happening again, do you?"

29

Spider had limped off a couple of dozen yards to piss. Once he'd finished, Ruth came up behind him, humming softly. That, Spider surmised, she did to let him know it was her and not some bounty hunter from the town, come to find Jeremy Stoneham's killer.

She came up beside him, holding a smoldering pipe. "Do not blame Em overmuch, Spider."

He spat. "I'm trying. You were right. She changed. She . . . she sold herself, Ruth. To get by. She sold herself."

"People sometimes are left with hard choices," she said. "You know that to be true, for certain."

Ruth drew some smoke, the light from the pipe bowl glowing on her face, then handed the pipe to Spider. "You've told me the story, how you became a pirate. Bent Thomas and his lads gave you no choice, right? They needed someone to keep their goddamned ships afloat and you just happened to have the skills. So they let you live, on condition you served them. And you chose to accept."

Spider nodded, and blew out a cloud. He handed the pipe back.

"Aye," he said. "I chose to accept. It was really the only bloody thing to do, unless I wanted to die."

"There were other conditions, too."

"Aye," he said, remembering. "They made it clear, when we robbed and killed, I was to get bloody hands, too. There wasn't no holding myself above them, no. We were all in the bloody business together, and anyone who was not willing to shed blood, well, he'd have his own blood shed."

"And you did what you needed to do."

"Aye."

Ruth let him think about that for several heartbeats before continuing. "And how, then, do you reckon Em's choice was any different?" Ruth clamped the pipe between her teeth and stared at him intently.

"She . . ." Spider stammered. "She sold herself."

"Aye."

"To men."

"Aye."

Spider stared at her. "What are you saying?"

Ruth removed the pipe and poked the stem toward him. "Well, she didn't have no flintlock nor sword, did she? No bloody ship to go about the high seas robbing people, like you. No mates fighting by her side. She needed to survive. She had a babe in arms, and a husband off to sea and no idea whether he'd ever come back. What did you think she would do?"

"Not whoring," Spider said.

"My, my. Well. She was going to find a man, Spider, or a bunch of them, wasn't she, one way or another." Ruth handed him the pipe and sighed. "You'd told me her pa was a right bastard when she got pregnant."

"I never called him that."

"No, but that's what you described. I didn't think your Em would want to live under his roof, even if he never said a word of rebuke to her. I've had some experience with a father who loathed me, you see. I felt his disapproval all the time, whether he spoke it or not. I could not wait to escape his gaze."

Spider looked at her. "Why did he disapprove?"

"That is my business." Her tone left no doubt that he'd better not press her further.

"Aye, then," he answered. Ruth was always careful about discussing her past, in the manner of most pirates.

"So," Ruth said. "Think of your own life, Spider John, and the things you've done, out of necessity, while you ponder hers, and consider this. You hope that she will just forgive your bloody deeds, aye? Well, can you not do the same for her? If you can forgive her, as you are hoping she'll forgive you one day, well, then, maybe, you can still have the future you want. Maybe. You will just have to work a little harder for it."

"I reckon . . ."

"It is worth working for, is it not?" She smiled, and Spider surprised himself by laughing.

"Right fucking mess I've made of it all, haven't I?"

"Aye," she said. "A right fucking mess indeed. We all make those."

Ruth snatched the pipe from his mouth, a bit roughly, he thought, and headed back to the house.

30

"It's a council of war, then," Hob said, lifting his cup. "Hip, hip!"

"It is not a fun lark, you whelp," Spider said. "We're in deep waters."

"Full of sharks," Odin added. "And a storm brewing. And ol' Blackbeard's ghost swimming up to snatch us below. Ha!"

Isaac, cutting a loaf of bread into chunks they could eat with their clam soup, looked confused.

"Odin is saying things are really bad," Ruth explained.

"Oh," Isaac said. "No ghosts, then?"

"No." Ruth dipped hot brown bread into her bowl. "Thank you. This will ward off the chill."

Spider clapped his hands together. "Very well, then, let us consider our position. The man who beat my wife got killed right in front of me, everyone thinks I did it because I wandered around beating folk and saying I wanted to kill him, and there is a German sea cook who thinks we have a bloody treasure map and he would like to get his grimy fingers on that map, and probably on all our throats. Did I forget a single fucking thing?"

"You forgot to mention Blackbeard's ghost."

"Quiet, Hob." Spider took a bite of soup. "This is good."

"Thank you," Isaac said. "Sorry the bowls are not so full. Wasn't expecting a crowd."

"Oh," Spider said. "Aye. Sorry. We've crowded your home like a forecastle, we have. Maybe our first thing to do is to find someplace else to hide out. Not to take advantage of your kindness."

"No," Isaac said, quietly. "You can stay. You and your friends seem good people, even with all the talk of ghosts and pirating and, um, murder. I don't mind company."

Spider nodded. "Thank you. We'll see if we can lay in some supplies to help. We got paid."

"You got paid," Odin growled. "The rest of us jumped ship to keep Seitz from killing you."

"This is true," Hob added.

"I have some money, but not much," Ruth said. "You are welcome to it, Isaac."

"Where did you get money?"

"That is my business, Spider John."

"Paying will be nice, thanks," Isaac said. "Thanks."

Spider looked at the man, who was staring at the floor. "Isaac?"

The man looked up. "I grew up in Boston," he said, quietly. "And, well, I . . ."

Ruth touched his arm. "You don't need to explain anything. You are our host. We owe you. You do not owe us."

Isaac moved her hand away, gently. "I want to tell you. Some of it. I had to leave Boston. Too many fights. Came here a couple of years ago, to find quiet in a place where no one knows me. But there's a lot of ships come and go, and they bring wood and pots and pans and, and rumors. People talk."

Spider nodded.

"So," Isaac said. "You all don't ask a lot of fool questions or pry, and you made this place I built feel like a home, so you can stay as long as you need to stay."

"We appreciate not having to explain a lot of things, too," Spider said. "Although that ugly bastard"—he pointed at Odin—"will tell you all of his gruesome crimes if you let him."

"Ha!"

Laughter and small talk followed, and tension melted.

"Aye, then," Spider continued. "So what should we do about all these problems following us around? Seitz probably jumped the ship because the three of us left it," he said, pointing at himself, Hob, and Odin. "Don't know if he saw you lads returning to *Minuet*, or if he saw you returning ashore here, or, hell, who knows what he knows. But he thinks we have that damned map . . ."

"Which we do," Hob said, earning himself a smack on the arm from Odin.

"People with treasure maps don't go around talking about it all the time," the old man grumbled. "Suppose Isaac here put something in our booze or our soup to put us to sleep—or worse—so he could take the fucking map?"

"I would not do that," Isaac said. "Really."

"He's Spider's friend," Hob said, defensively. "Did you even listen to all things he just bloody said, about home and all?"

"Friends? They just bloody well met!" Odin roared.

"Odin."

"What, Spider John?"

"Isaac isn't going to kill us for the map," Spider answered. "Aye, and I will tell you what else I think, if any of us live through this mess and go fetch the fucking gold, Isaac is owed a share for helping us out. Isaac, don't you mind Odin. His mind wanders and he says fool things, hell, he's probably threatened to stab me a hundred times, but he always proves true when we need him to."

"All a damned act, I say," Hob said, quietly. "Keeps everyone off their guard, he does, wondering what he'll say or do next."

"Ha!"

"Is that true, Odin?" Spider winked. "Do you just play daft? Tell us your real name, and where you are really from."

"No," he said. "I tell what I wish, and no more."

"Ireland," Ruth said. "It's in his voice."

"Except when he sounds Scottish," Spider said.

"I thought you said you grew up in London," Hob said, looking at Odin.

"Told me Plymouth," Spider added. "And then Cornwall. And then the Isle of Man."

"I'm a bloody Frenchman, I am! Ha!"

"That's likely as true as any of the rest of it." Spider rubbed his face.

Ruth smiled. "And I think our friend Isaac has earned a bit of treasure, should you find any. What do you say, Hob?"

"I'll come back and pay handsomely for my lodgings, aye!"

"Well," Odin growled, "I don't know why we've all decided to start fucking trusting people, but I won't kill Isaac if he don't try to kill me."

Isaac smiled, and his bruised eyes widened. "I'll open another jug!"

Spider sighed heavily. "Is the nonsense settled, then? Can we talk about Seitz now? Seems we ought to go find him, and . . . well . . . find some way to keep him from killing us for the map."

"I know a way," Hob said, drawing a finger across his throat.

"Aye." Spider glanced around and was glad to see Isaac rummaging about in a pantry, apparently unaware of Hob's murderous gesture. Spider whispered. "Let us avoid that, if we can. We're honest men now, aye?"

Isaac returned with a large corked jug. "Rum," he said. "I like whisky, but someone gave me this. I built a barn, and this is what I got." He wiped the dusty bottle with a cloth. "I hope you all like rum."

He placed it on the table. Spider's hands reached the handle first, barely beating Hob and Odin.

"I thought you decided to drink less," Odin said.

"I did drink less. Then I drank too much. Now I'm going to drink more. Seems heaven shits on me the same way, no matter how much I drink." Spider pulled the cork and started to lift the jug to his lip, but Ruth's hand on his arm halted him.

"He's bringing cups," she said.

Isaac returned with a tray of cups and a small chunk of cheese.

Once they'd all had a round, and Spider had refilled his cup, the plotting resumed.

"If we just go poking around, we'd better spot Seitz first," Spider said. "He knows all of our faces, and he might think any one of us has the map."

"You should not go looking for anyone, Spider," Ruth admonished. "Everyone in Nantucket is looking for you."

"Maybe," he said. "At least they were, but maybe they aren't anymore. Nobody liked Stoneham. He was a right bastard. Ask Isaac."

"Bastard," their host whispered. "Absolutely. A bastard."

"It seemed to me the search was short. People were talking about it when I was hobbling about on those goddamned crutches, but they were going about their business, too, and seemed to think the manhunt was all done with. They probably think I stowed away in a ship and got away."

"But," Hob said, "you beat up that fellow, Wood, and he's going to remember your face, shorter hair and beard won't help that. And Em's father, and that cooper, and probably the widow . . ."

"Aye," Spider growled. "I'm fucking famous."

"Your disguise was good," the lad said.

"And my legs still feel like rats are gnawing at them."

"Saw them off, make yourself some genuine wooden legs. You've made plenty of them for other people. Remember Half-Jim? Ha!" Odin filled his cup.

Taking up his pipe and tobacco pouch, Spider walked to the hearth. "I'm not sure I want to try that disguise trick again. Maybe we can prowl at night." He reached into his pouch, and found the bloody earring he'd ripped from the attacker. He held it up, and turned.

"Have any of you seen Seitz wearing this?"

None of them had.

Hob rushed forth. "Can I see?"

Spider handed the jewelry to him and looked at the image etched onto it. "Is this Satan?"

"Looks like him," Spider said, taking the disc back.

"Does that mean anything?"

"I don't reckon," Spider said. "But it might. The fellow who killed Stoneham, and clubbed me, was wearing this, and now he's wearing a bloody red gash, or maybe he's bandaged it. So, if we find Seitz and his ear is ripped, we'll know he was trying to kill me, and got Stoneham by accident."

"And if the killer was not Seitz?" That was Ruth.

"Then, most likely someone had it in for Stoneham, and I got in the way. I mean, Em's father tried to kill me, but he can barely see and he's not going about the island at night. And that fellow Wood, he might want to kill me because I broke his leg, but . . . well, I broke his leg. He didn't cross the island to track me down and kill me. No, this is about Stoneham. Probably. Unless it was Seitz."

"Well, what we need to do, then," Hob said, "is search the town for Seitz, or someone else with a torn ear, without Seitz seeing us, or without anyone seeing you."

"Aye," Spider said. "Bloody simple, aye?"

"Ha!"

Ruth shook her head. "It sounds impossible."

"I could ask around," Isaac said. "No one is looking for me."

"No, no," Spider said, quickly. "Me and my friends here, we're used to fighting. You're a brave fellow, no doubt—I've seen you grab a tool for a weapon, ready to stand up to fight—but you live on this island and don't need to be risking your own neck just to keep mine out of a noose. Hell, you're risking enough already just having us here. Remember, if things go bad, we forced you to help us."

"You put your liquor at risk, for certain, ha!" Odin reached for the jug again.

"Save me a dram, you smelly scraped-up old fuck," Spider said. He returned the earring to his pouch, then stuffed tobacco into his pipe. Soon, he was puffing away.

"A good pipe always settles my mind," he said. "And I can prove that. By thunder, I have a plan."

31

"The more I think on it," Spider said, "the killer had to be looking to murder me. Hob, move your goddamned foot or I'll slice it off and stow it up your ass."

"Sorry, Spider."

"Hush, fools." Ruth opened a flap in the canvas and peeked back at them. "We are almost to town."

Spider, Hob, and Odin were hiding in the back of Isaac's wagon, newly covered with fresh canvas stretched across a wooden frame built by Spider, with help from Hob. They'd sent Isaac with a good portion of Spider's pay to a sailmaker, and Odin had done a masterful job of cutting the purchased cloth and stitching it just so. Experts all, they'd made short work of it, and found themselves rolling into town before noon.

"Simple work," Odin had said. "Hell, I usually do this kind of job on a rolling deck or way up in the trees. I've even done it with four-pound balls flying past my goddamned head. Ha!"

Now, they hid beneath the sailcloth, peering through small gaps made for just that purpose. They'd elected to have Ruth guide the mule. "You look the most changed, now that you are wearing britches and a shirt," Spider had explained. "Seitz saw you wearing a dress aboard *Minuet*. If you could grow a beard it would be better, but just keep your face behind the brim of your hat, and if you can, try to look less pretty."

"She can't do that," Hob had said. "Pretty or not, though, it is far better to have her hold the reins than Odin. Last time we let him do it,

163

we cracked the wagon against a stone pillar and almost got shot! And there were fucking bombs!"

"That was all your fault, you little skirt-chaser. Ha!"

"Quiet, I said. The cover will keep him from seeing you back there, but it won't keep him from hearing all your babble."

Spider peeked out a slit to port, while Hob used a peephole to starboard. Odin watched to their rear, and Ruth was keeping an eye out from the driver's bench. Spider continued with a whisper. "So we'll be silent as ghosts now, and watch out for Seitz."

"Why are you so sure it was you that was supposed to get killed? You said nobody liked Stoneham."

"Aye, Hob." Spider used his fingers to part the canvas a bit more. "But he's lived on this island a long while, right? So why would someone wait to kill him now? Just when I happened to be there? No, it's the timing, you see. Any enemy of his might know he'd be at the Widow Coffin's, true, but it just seems a bad bet that someone looking to kill Stoneham would show up right there, right then, right when I was waiting around to . . ."

"Kill Stoneham," Odin growled quietly.

"I don't know I would have killed him," Spider answered. *And I don't know that I wouldn't have.* "And it don't matter much now, I reckon."

"It matters if they catch you," Hob reminded him.

Under his breath, Spider muttered. "Does it?"

Em was gone. Johnny was gone, too. And even if he cleared his name of this deed, there were hundreds of others that had left his hands dripping red. Even if he found her, she might not be able to look him in the eye.

People change, Ruth had said. *Maybe I've changed too much for Em.*

"Anyway," he continued, just loudly enough for Hob and Odin to hear him, "we know there was someone come ashore looking for me, right? Or looking for us. He must have thought we three were off to follow that bloody map to the treasure. We don't know for certain anyone was set to kill Stoneham, but we know we've got someone prowling after us, so let's just reckon on that."

"That all seems right," Hob said.

"Aye, it's the safest bet. Seitz came ashore, poked around, and I foolishly left an easy trail Odin could follow with his one eye tied behind his back. He followed that trail to the Widow Coffin's door, and struck when I came out of hiding."

"Not a good idea to whack you with a sack of coins, was it? We could use that fucking money. Ha! Why didn't you scoop it up? Are there any whores in Nantucket?"

Spider was about to answer Odin with his fist, but Hob grabbed his arm. Odin peered outward, seemingly unaware of Spider's anger.

"Just look for Seitz." Spider turned back to his peephole.

"What will we do if we see him?"

"I don't know, Hob."

"That's a nice simple plan. Ha!"

Ruth guided the wagon along the waterfront. Hob's view included the bay, where only one ship stood at anchor but several fishing boats were tied up at the docks. "There's a schooner working into the harbor," the young man announced. "Flying the king's colors."

"Good," Spider said, spying the storehouses and the shops that sold firkins, candles, wool, fish, tobacco, lye soap, clothing, tools, and more. "If Seitz thinks we are seeking a ship, he'll keep an eye on her. I'll bet he's here."

"I'll keep an eye on her, too," Hob said. "She's sweetly made. If we save your arse before she puts to sea, I might just go treasure hunting on her!"

The wagon rocked, hitting a rut. Spider bit his lip. He stared at the baskets of tobacco hanging on a nearby porch, and briefly considered a mad dash to increase his supply. He'd used up a great deal of Isaac's, and he could smell the aroma from the shop.

Ruth tapped on the frame, three times in rapid succession, a prearranged signal that meant she'd spotted Seitz. Spider waited a few seconds for the second signal. It came. Two sharp raps.

"He's on your side," Spider whispered, moving over to join Hob. He found the second slit, a feature added to his plan at Ruth's suggestion. "If you've only got the one spyhole on each side, you'll end up fighting over it," she'd said. "You don't want to wreck the entire goddamned plan because you idiots fought over a spyhole, do you?"

"There he is, ahead," Spider confirmed. "Strolling pretty, calm as can be. Black beard. Big shoulders. No tricorn, though."

"Looks like he's got an earring, though."

"Aye, Hob. Just one of them, I see."

The wagon stopped, and Ruth lifted a flap in the cloth and peered at them. "What is our plan?"

"I wish we had got guns," Hob said.

"That would be a bit loud, don't you think?" Spider watched Seitz pace to and fro. "And we can't beat a confession out of him if he's dead. There is a toolbox. Isaac's a good carpenter. Something in there will serve, no doubt."

He did not peek at the tools, though. He gazed across the water, squinting a bit at the hundreds of bright sun reflections and trying not to think of the damned gulls skimming across the surface. "Seitz is watching that schooner, for certain, and looking about for us."

Ruth blew a stray strand of hair away from her eyes. "What shall we do?"

Spider watched. "He goes a dozen steps toward us, a dozen away, then repeats," he said. "He seems nervous. I think he's afraid of us seeing him, or him not seeing us, or maybe us already being gone, or maybe all of that."

"Well," Ruth said, "thank you. How does any of that help? What the bloody hell do we do?"

"Run alongside him, as he's walking away. Nice and slow."

Ruth scoffed. "You don't think he'll notice that?"

"We could just be heading toward a dock. Business as usual. And all the folk who are about here have work to do. They'll not pay us attention, if we be quick and quiet."

Spider took his knife from his belt, and started cutting a long vertical slit in the cloth cover. "Hob, grab a mallet. Odin, you and I shall land this fish once Hob clubs him. If we do it nice and fast, well, maybe no one will see us."

"What if they do?"

"Well," Spider said, "then we'll just run for our goddamned lives like we always do and hope they don't catch us. Are you ready, gents?"

Next, Spider sliced a horizontal cut across the vertical one. He held the new corners together in his hand lest they flap in the breeze and expose them to sight, and he grinned as he did so. They'd have a good ready opening when the time came.

"What if I kill him?" Hob examined the wooden mallet.

"Then he can't kill us," Spider answered. "That would be fine, to be sure, in some ways, but not so good regarding our plan, aye? We need him to talk. Probably. Just don't hit him too hard. Just knock him out."

Hob fought not to laugh. "I've only ever learned how to kill a man, Spider, not to give him a nap. How hard is too hard?"

"If he dies, it was too hard."

"Jesus, help me," Ruth muttered, disappearing behind the flap. The wagon started forward again. "Shall I stop behind him?"

"No," Spider said. "Roll up slow, and as close beside him as you can. Don't let him see your face."

The wagon bucked a bit. Spider watched Seitz. Ruth was timing her approach quite nicely. Seitz, facing away from them, was watching the schooner intently.

"One," Spider said.

Seitz was nearing his twelfth step. If he held to his pattern, he would turn any second.

"Two."

Seitz halted, and began to turn.

"Three!"

Hob reached out through the opening Spider had created and clubbed Seitz so hard Spider expected a splash of blood. Spider leaned out, his left hand clutching the wagon's new frame, his right grabbing Seitz by the upper left arm and yanking him toward the wagon, fiercely.

Hob rolled backward, to get out of the way. Odin mirrored Spider's maneuver, then the two men hauled their prey into the wagon. Seitz landed hard on his back, and Hob poised over him, ready to clobber him again if he moved. Spider grabbed the canvas corners and clutched them together, shielding them from view again. Odin cackled.

Spider glanced at Seitz. "I think you hit him hard enough, boy."

"I'm not a boy, Spider."

"I know. We got him, Ruth!"

"Aye." She cracked the reins and the wagon's speed increased.

Spider listened, thankful that he heard no shouts. If anyone had noticed their sneak attack, they weren't raising an alarm.

"Well, I do not believe the gods let us get away with that one," Odin said.

"Nor do I. Hold your canvas here, Odin," Spider said. "I want to get a closer look at this sea cook."

"Aye."

Spider surrendered his grip on the sailcloth and let Odin take over the job of keeping the canvas opening closed. Then he scooted over to Seitz and bent over him.

"Well, fuck and bugger."

Spider was examining Seitz's ears. Both lobes were intact, and the small silver hoop in the left ear was no match for the trinket Spider had grabbed from the killer.

"I didn't rip an earring from this bastard's ear."

32

*H*ob shrugged. "So he wasn't after you?"

Spider slapped Hob's forehead. "Of course he was after me, you dolt. He wants the map, doesn't he? Never paid us any bloody attention before that little skirmish when Gray and his boys tried to take *Minuet*, then can't stand to see us go after. Swam to shore, didn't he?"

Hob nodded. "Aye."

"But he didn't kill Stoneham. I yanked a bauble out of the killer's ear, and it had to have made a big gash. Blooded my hand doing it, anyway. And this here man," he pointed at Seitz, "his ears are clean. No gash. And the ring he's wearing is just a hoop, like mine, not the mate to the devil's head I snatched."

Spider and Hob sat back.

"So, what do we do?" Odin pointed at the toolbox. "Toss me that line."

Spider gave the old man a small coil of thin rope. "I don't know, Odin. Let me think on it."

Odin took his knife and poked a small hole in the corner of each flap, then used the line to improvise a stitch. An expert topmast man, he finished it quickly, and there was no longer any danger of a breeze revealing the opening they'd cut in the canvas. "So, what do we do?"

"I said let me reckon on it, for Christ's sake."

"The Lord don't smile on pirates, does he? Ha?"

"Former pirates," Hob said.

"Former pirates clubbin' people and carryin' around a bloody treasure map," Odin said. "I don't sail with Blackbeard no more, lads, but this is not very bloody different from that."

"Fuck!" Spider punched an upright on the frame he'd added to Isaac's wagon. The wood cracked, and Spider wondered for a moment if his hand had, too. "Fuck!"

"Spider," Hob whispered.

"I need to find the killer," the carpenter answered quietly, nursing his right hand. It was swelling already, but as he massaged it with his left hand he felt no broken bones. It hurt like hell, but it would heal. "Until I find out who killed Stoneham, I can't wander about Nantucket asking after Em. And that's the question that really matters, Hob. I don't give a damn who killed Stoneham. I really don't. But I need to know where she's gone. I need to know about this Westcott she supposedly left with. I was told some thought him a pirate. I need to find her."

"Aye," Hob replied. "I understand." He reached into the unconscious man's coat pocket. "Well, this is going to prove handy."

He lifted a flintlock pistol, short-barreled and missing a chunk of wood from the butt, but probably functional. "Bet he's got some balls and powder."

Hob jumped like a frog over the man, twisting in the air and landing in a crouch. Spider imagined trying to do such a thing himself on his sore legs and winced.

After poking around for a couple of seconds, Hob pulled a small wooden cylinder out of the cook's other coat pocket. He waved it around like it was a medal given him by a king. "Indeed." He pulled the lid from one end and peeked into the cylinder. "Lead."

He flipped the container and pulled the lid from the other end. "Powder. Need wadding." He fiddled with the gun for a moment, then aimed it into the air and pulled the trigger. He grinned at the solid snap. "It's not easy to hold, with half the butt gone, but it'll fire true enough if I stick it against a man's head, it will."

"Well, do not put it against his head," Spider said, pointing at

Seitz. "At least you didn't kill him with the mallet, Hob. There is some good in that." Spider got onto his knees, lighting a fire in the pain still burning in his feet and shins, and peeked out to talk to Ruth. "Take us back to Isaac's. We'll sort it all out there."

"Already on the way, cap'n." She winked at him. "No one is pursuing us. I can't believe we pulled that off!"

"Hell," Spider said. "That was the easy part."

33

Seitz had thrown up twice as they'd bound him, although he had not yet wakened.

"You hit him hard," Odin said. "And now this place smells. I don't know what this son of a bitch ate but it smells like seal shit. If we find out this bastard ain't the one who tried to kill Spider, hell, maybe hit him again, and harder. What's he worth? Why keep him around?"

"I told you twice now," Hob said, shaking his head. "Spider wants to ask him questions."

"Ha!"

Isaac poured a bucket of water on the mess, then started sweeping it all toward the door.

Odin crossed the barn, and sat on a sawhorse.

Spider knelt by Seitz, staring at the man and muttering the whole time. "Wake up, you bloody bastard. Wake up, I say."

He used his left hand to slap Seitz, as his right still felt full of broken glass and was wrapped in wet cloth. His knife lay among the sawdust on the floor, at the ready should he need it. "Wake up."

"Pardon me," Ruth said, pushing her way past Hob. She carried a large jug. "I'll wake him. Isaac, you might want to go to the house. You are not really a party to all this."

"No," their host said. "I'll stay. I want to know what happens. Besides, I think the magistrates would call this abetting, me giving you shelter and lending you a wagon. If you all hang, I likely will, too."

"No," Spider said. "Remember, we forced you to help us. Put a knife or a gun to your head, or both, and made you help us. I do not want you to get hurt by any of this, Isaac."

"Aye," he said.

"We shall keep you from harm if we can, then. Very well." Ruth stepped forward and poured water onto Seitz's face.

Seitz shrugged, spat, muttered, tried to sit up. "*Scheisse*! *Hör auf damit*! *Hölle*!" His words were somewhat muffled by the heavy beard and mustache plastered across his mouth by the water.

"I could have just pissed on him. Ha!"

"Where are you going, Odin?"

The old man looked dumbfounded. "I'm going to piss, Hob."

"Oh."

Odin stepped outside.

The water streaming from Seitz's head carried just a tinge of darkness from blood. Hob really had whacked the man. Seitz struggled, realized he was bound, and cursed again. Then he heaved.

"Careful." Hob dropped low and rolled the man away from Spider. Seitz gushed vomit again.

"We'll need more water." Isaac rushed out, holding a hand over his own mouth.

"*Scheisse*! *Scheisse*!" Seitz coughed between the words, and gasped for air. Hob rolled the man onto his back, then stood up.

"*Gott verdamme dich*!"

"Silence!" Spider picked up his knife and waggled it in front of the man's eye. "I'm in a foul mood, and I've got questions, and I might leave your nose where it is or I might cut it right off. I might go on carving, goddamn it, until you answer me right or until you run out of things for me to slice."

"Jesus, Spider."

He ignored Ruth's whispered comment. "Who else is with you, Seitz, and where are they?"

Seitz coughed. "John Coombs. Hob." Then he noticed Ruth. "*Scheisse*!"

Spider loomed over him. "Talk!"

"I do not know what mean you," the cook answered. "What mean you?"

"You did not attack me by yourself," Spider growled.

"*Scheisse!*"

"You were not alone," Spider repeated. "I know that, because you don't have a bloody rip in your ear." He brandished the knife again. "Not yet, you don't."

Spider reached for his tobacco pouch, and tried not to cry out as lightning pain cursed through his injured fingers. He tossed the pouch to Hob. "Show him."

Hob opened the pouch and found the earring. He held it up, making sure to turn it so Seitz could see the devil head stamped upon it. "Did your friend lose this?"

"What mean you?" Seitz looked at the earring, then Spider's knife. "Not mine! Not mine!"

"I yanked it off your man's ear when you tried to kill me," Spider said. "I'm certain you must have noticed his bleeding lobe."

"What mean you? No!"

"Where is your friend?"

"No friend! I heard, they all look for you, John. Little man, missing finger. You kill a man, and want to blame me!"

Spider raised the knife and brought it down hard. It punched into the floor within an inch of Seitz's left ear. The German cook closed his eyes and began to cry. "*Bitte nicht! Ermordet mich nicht!*"

"Where is your friend?" Spider roared it that time.

"No friend! Please! No friend!"

An awful tang filled the air, cutting through the stench of vomit.

"Jesus," Spider said, "Did he piss in his britches?"

"No," Hob said. "Odin came back. He's standing right behind you."

"Jesus," Spider muttered.

"Ha!"

Spider stood up with a groan. He wondered how long his legs would hurt. "Let us confer, gentlemen, and lady. A council of war, as Hob would say."

They walked to the rear of the barn. Isaac walked in, and Spider asked him to stand watch over Seitz.

"Well," Spider whispered. "Do we believe him?"

"There wasn't no one with him when we kidnapped him," Hob said. "And we didn't see him signal anyone."

"Aye."

"And he didn't show no reaction to this." Hob held up the earring.

"Aye."

"He doesn't seem the courageous sort of fellow, does he?"

Spider inhaled sharply, then sighed. "No, he does not."

Odin grinned. "What do we do with him?"

"I do not have a notion at all," Spider said. "Fuck and bugger."

He walked back to Seitz. "Why did you abandon *Minuet*?"

Seitz shook his head. "Understand no."

Spider kicked him in the ribs. "Yes, you bloody well do understand."

The captive cried out, then growled. "Very well. Very well. It's the map!"

Spider and his friends exchanged glances. "You were in on the mutiny with Gray and Simon and the others."

"No! No! No!"

"Don't lie to me. I have a knife, Hob has your gun."

"No! I am not with them, those bastards! I do not want map! I heard them, on the ship, they talk about map, tell stories. I do not want map, not on my soul! I did not come to take map! I came to warn you!"

They all looked around, confused. Spider was the one to ask. "Warn us about what?"

"You do not want map! Trust me, aye? Do not go to that island! Do not, if you value your souls, do not go to that island!"

"Oh, hell," Spider said. "Why should we not? Whose map is it?"

"Red Edgar," Seitz answered. "Red Edgar Moore!"

"I ain't heard of him," Hob said. Spider and Ruth shook their heads.

"Red Edgar? He's dead," Odin said. "Ship went down, he went

with it. French frigate caught up to him, off Bermuda, some dozen years back. Shot his ship full of holes, shot him full of holes while he swam around in water red with blood. Then a shark swallowed him whole."

They stared at him.

"Blackbeard told me himself," Odin said.

"Aye!" Seitz was smiling. "Aye! Red Edgar, he is dead. That map is where he buried his takings, a great deal of gold, they say. But . . ."

Spider waved the knife. "But what?"

"They say he went to that island, on the map, and went ashore with ten men. They bury three chests, full of Spanish gold, pieces of eight, French jewels, Moroccan silver, rubies and opals. And then they drink. They drink hard. And they drink poison."

Hob gasped.

Spider twirled his knife. "Poison, you say."

"Aye! Red Edgar, he kill them all with poison! Drink, he says! Drink! But he give them poison, some foul potion he got from Greece, they say! Some sorcerer's brew! He give them that, so they don't come back some day and steal the treasure!"

Everyone exchanged glances, and Spider shivered.

"Then, Red Edgar, he bury them all, right there with the chests, and death like that means . . ."

"What does it mean?"

Seitz's eyes widened, the whites bright among the dark mess of his hair and beard. "*Geister!*"

"I don't speak bloody goddamned German, you piss-licking bastard!"

"Ghosts, John! Ten ghosts!"

34

"Cow-slaver!" Spider jumped, landing hard on his feet and then screaming in pain. "Ow! Jesus! Fuck my feet, bloody hell!"

Hob tried to steady him, but to no avail. The others scurried away from Spider and the knife he flashed wildly about as he writhed in pain. Then he fell on his ass.

"Ghosts!" Hob spun about slowly. "Jesus! Ghosts!"

"I do not believe in ghosts," Ruth said. "I do not. I do not." Her eyes said otherwise.

"I believe in ghosts," Odin said. "Hell. I've seen them. Blackbeard fucked a ghost, too."

Spider John didn't believe in ghosts, or so he told himself. He could recall a few times in his life when that belief was shaken. This, however, was not one of those times.

Spider sat up and glared at Seitz. "Goddamned blather and drivel! Fucking cow-slaver, I say!"

Seitz shook his head. "*Nein*! *Nein*, John!"

"I've heard that tale a dozen times, you goddamned bubbly-jock, and a different pirate buried the poor bastards every fucking time! Odin's told me Blackbeard done six men that way, and then it was a dozen! It is just a tale. You lie, Seitz!"

"*Nein*!"

Spider stood up. "Oh, my feet. Friends, this man did not come here to warn us of anything. He's trying to save his ass. He didn't even bother to get all my food in my fucking bowl at grub time, but now he leaps off of a good ship and risks his life in the cold, cold sea to swim here and warn us about bloody ghosts? It's cow-slaver, I say, slobbery dripping wet smelly cow spit!"

Seitz shook his head.

Spider pointed the knife at him. "You came for the map, you tried to kill me for it, and you have someone else helping you."

Seitz's face changed. "All my friends dead, or soon will be, because of you," he said. "You and your crew. All I have left is that map."

Hob spat at the man. "Your friends tried to take the damned ship." The young man's eyes narrowed. "They are mutineers."

Seitz coughed. "I told them, not take the ship! I had no part of that! I say to them, we will find ship in Boston, we will find crew! I know people there, we can find ship! That was the plan, I swear it to you."

"What changed?" Spider thought he knew the answer, but he wanted to hear Seitz say it.

"That man, he heard us talk."

"Calvin Garrick."

Seitz nodded. "Aye, Garrick. He heard us, we think. We were talking in galley, and saw Garrick near door. He left, but we thought maybe he heard us talk about map."

"So you killed him."

"They did, not me!"

Spider shook his head. "Not so easy to clean your hands of the blood, Seitz. Did you know they were going to kill him?"

"I tell them not to, it was too dangerous. I thought they listened to me, but no. They were scared he would tell others and they would take the map from us. So they killed him."

Hob spoke up. "And they decided to take the bloody ship just in case anyone else knew about the map. They did not want to risk waiting."

"Aye," Spider said. "Bloody stupid, that was. Did they think no one would stand up to defend the ship, or try to take their precious map after they showed themselves to be criminals?"

Seitz tried to grin. "I tell them exactly that, I did. But they would not wait. No. They would not wait. I did not want to mutiny, or murder, but I was the one who told them of the map to start all this so I am due! They never would have had it if not for me, and neither would you. I say it is mine, and I have no blood on my hands. I want my map!"

"Maybe we shove it up your ass and sink you," Spider said.

Hob shook his head. "No. I want the map, remember?" He looked at Seitz. "How did you get the map, without blood on your hands?"

"Loose talk in a Plymouth tavern," Seitz answered. "Some men, they drunk, they talk of map, they dream big. I hear it, I tell Gray, we stole the map."

"And now Calvin Garrick is dead, one of your friends is dead, and the others will hang," Spider muttered. "For mere gold."

Spider hobbled away to the back of the barn. None of this had anything to do with anything he cared about. He wanted a pipe, and a clue to Stoneham's killer, and a clear path to Em. *But I've got a god-damned German thief tied up and nothing to do with him! What the bloody hell do I do?*

35

"**W**hat do we do, Spider?"

"I don't know, Hob."

They all were whispering in the back of the barn. Seitz remained on the floor, tightly bound in rope and knots probably no one among them but Odin knew how to untie. It was evening, and Isaac was in the house fetching bread, cheese, and beer.

Ruth untied her ponytail and shook out her dark hair. She looked back at Seitz. "I believe him, about not having a friend with a bloody ear, anyway. I am not so certain he was not the planner of the murder and the mutiny."

"Aye," Spider said. "Odds are poor that he has none of Garrick's blood on his hands, but odds are just as poor he just happened to have an accomplice right here on Nantucket, right when he might need one to help kill me and steal his map back."

Isaac came back with a platter. "There is not much."

"We can pay our way, help buy food tomorrow," Spider said. "I have some pay left." He took a small piece of warm brown bread and popped it into his mouth.

Isaac passed the platter around. "If that guy over there didn't try to kill you, who else would?"

"Em's pa?" That suggestion came from Hob.

Spider considered that. "Em's pa already tried to kill me once, but I don't see him planning a murder. He was caught unaware, I surprised him, he was in a rage, he grabbed a gun. I can say certain, though, he's been praying on it ever since. It's his way, and the Lord ain't telling Ephraim Pierce to kill me." *The Lord's probably assuring him that I'll spend eternity in hell,* Spider thought. *That will be good enough for Ephraim Pierce.*

"It could not have been him, anyway. I just don't see him wandering around Nantucket at night. He can't hardly see and his leg's bad. The killer got away from me fast. Besides,"—Spider tapped his tobacco pouch, where he'd replaced the bauble—"Ephraim Pierce don't wear gold on his ears."

Hob shrugged. "Then I guess it was someone trying to kill that fellow Stoneham, after all."

"Most likely," Spider said. "I need a pipe. I'll be back."

He hobbled to the house on his pained legs, then went to a small desk where he'd seen Isaac stash some tobacco. He moved a quill and a jar of ink aside and found the leaf in a cubby. By the time he'd filled his pipe from Isaac's supply and gotten it lit, he had the glimmer of an idea. He returned to the woodshed, a tobacco cloud wafting around his head.

"Well, mates, what we need to do is ask around in town about who might have wanted Stoneham dead," he said. "That ought to be simpler now, aye? They might be looking for me, but the only one looking for you three is trussed up over there. Hob, you and Ruth and Odin can go into town, ask some questions, see what you find out. And then, if we find the guilty party, I can go after Em and you can go after your treasure."

Hob rubbed his hands together. "I will not let you down, Spider."

"I know. Isaac, I can't go into the town because they have a noose waiting for me, so I'll have to stay here with you and stand guard over Seitz. I'm thinking I'll need your gun, Hob."

"Really?"

Spider grinned. "I know you like having one, but Nantucket ain't Port Royal. If you aren't wanted for a killing, hell, the worst thing likely to happen to you is some sheep shit on your boots. But I'll have to guard him, and I think we've upset him something terrible."

They all looked at Seitz, who was straining at his bonds and muttering in terse German phrases.

Hob shook his head. "What's he saying?"

"Whoever knows what a German is saying? Ha!"

Spider stared at him. "What is it you got against Germans, Odin?"

"Same thing I got against everyone else. Why don't we just sink the son of a whore in the bay?"

"Because we're not pirates anymore. Remember, you lobcock? We're honest now."

Odin's lone eye widened. "Since I met you, Spider John, we've done very little except for getting shot at and stabbed at and shooting and stabbing back. And hiding. We've done a lot of that. Seems to me we're still pirates, and it's going to seem that way to the law, too, if we ever run afoul of the bastards."

Spider blew out a puff of smoke, and grimaced as Hob grinned. The young man had caught Spider doing that familiar maneuver with his pipe again. "Well, Odin, we're not going to murder Seitz."

"Then what?"

"I have a plan to deal with him," Spider said. "I think you lot will fucking hate it, though. Get him some water, and let him have a bit of food."

36

*T*he next morning, Spider was alone with Seitz. Hob, Odin, and Ruth had gone off to town, with a mission to buy food and see what they could learn about the manhunt for Jeremy Stoneham's killer. "And keep ears out for any word about Emma, or a ship called *Margaret*, or a sailor named Samuel Westcott," Spider had told them. "The ship disembarked a year or so gone."

Isaac was away as well, taking a wagonload of lumber so he could continue work on the sheep pen he was being paid to build.

"So," Spider said to his bound prisoner. "It is just you, and me, and this pistol. We are going to talk, maybe make a little deal. If you are wise, and quiet, this will turn out very well for you and me and all the rest of our merry band. If you make a lot of noise, or cause me any sort of consternation, I'll certainly shoot you in the head. Do you comprehend me?"

"*Ich muss pissen.*" Seitz sounded tense.

"I don't understand your language."

"I must piss! Goddamn you! I hurt, and I must piss! Can't you free me?"

Spider lowered his gaze to the floor. "Aye, that's a problem. Odin bound you up, and mad as he is, he's a very bloody devil with a knot. I don't know I could untie his knot with two hands, and right now I just have the one." He held up his right hand, still swollen and red from cracking the frame on Isaac's wagon.

"Well, tell Odin free me, damn it!"

"He's away," Spider said. "You'll just have to wait. Or soak yourself."

Spider was glad to have something to do. His mind was with his shipmates, wishing he was with them so he could look things over and ask questions. He tried to console himself, remembering that Hob was sometimes sharp as a nail and had done an excellent job of piercing Spider's disguise. Ruth was sharp, too, and would do her best to keep them all out of trouble.

Still, he wanted to be there with them.

"John! I must piss!" The man was almost rolling on the floor.

"Well, then listen to me and we might make an arrangement."

Seitz stopped fighting against his ropes and stared at him. "Well?"

"You found the map, and think you are owed a share."

"It is mine!"

"You don't have it, do you?"

"*Nein*! You have it!"

"You think we do."

Seitz spat. "I know! I know!"

Spider paced, slowly. His legs and feet still hurt, but the pain was greatly subdued. He could deal with it now. "Aye, we have the map."

"It's mine!"

"We have other things you need," Spider said, stopping and looking squarely into Seitz's eyes.

Seitz seemed surprised. "What do you have?"

"We have a fine carpenter, me; a fair navigator, Hob; and a sailing master, Odin." He started pacing again. "You might recollect your partners are on their way to the gallows, well, except Woodley. You are on your own."

Seitz moaned.

"I have friends, though, as you have seen. All of us can fight. You've seen Hob in action, aboard *Minuet*. Odin is fearless, and he's seen a lot of guns and swords pointed at him in his long, long life. The gents that pointed them are all dead. Ruth knows knives and cutlasses and guns as well. You might find sailors in Boston, if luck be with you, but can you find men who've been on the account? Who've spilled blood, and won't cower when blades are drawn?"

Seitz looked confused.

"Suppose someone gets in your way, or someone else has a map and comes looking, or knows where the island is and decides to just keep digging until they found the gold. You'll need a crew with backbone, Seitz. That'll be us, and some other mates we can find."

Seitz pondered that.

"We have another thing you'll need."

"What's that?"

"We have a ship."

This was a bloody lie, but Seitz's eyes opened wide.

"A ship?"

"Aye. Isaac's brother has a schooner, sweet little thing called *Ezra*. He's got a few hands, too, gents we can rely upon. We'll all be in it together, and we can set sail as soon as Mordecai, that's the brother, gets in from Boston. Any day now."

Seitz started rolling again. "I must piss!"

"Think on it. We'll let you join us," Spider said, ignoring the man's discomfort. "It would be fair, I reckon. You found the map, after all, and we're reasonable . . ."

"Reasonable? You attack me and wrap me up, I can't move, I need to piss!"

Spider nodded. "We're reasonable. We didn't kill you when we had the chance, did we? You could be wrapped up and sunk already, aye? Are you drowning, man? Are you shot?" He waved the gun. "Think on it, aye? If we wanted to kill you, nothing at all is stopping us."

Seitz stopped struggling. "How can I trust you?"

"I just explained all that," Spider said calmly. "We are true to our mates. We signed up on *Minuet*, so it was our duty to defend her, and we did. If we sign up with you, we'll be true to you as well."

"I'll be in command?"

Spider laughed. "No. I'll be cap'n."

"It's my map."

"And it's my plan, my crew and my ship," Spider answered. He waved the flintlock. "And it's my gun."

"It's my gun."

"It was."

Seitz nodded. "We have a deal. Now let me piss."

"I still can't untie you," Spider said. "And my mates will need to vote. They might not want you with us. You'll have to wait until they come back. I will do my best to persuade them, though."

"*Verdammt noch mal!*"

"Not so loud, mate."

37

"**W**e have news," Ruth said, strolling into the barn with Hob and Odin in her wake. Odin carried a leather sack that looked heavy.

Hob pointed at her. "You should have seen her, Spider John. Men will tell this woman anything."

"Well," she said, dancing a slow twirl. "I will not deny it."

"Spider once told her our entire damned plan, and he'd just met her," Odin said, grinning. "Do you recall, Spider?"

"We need not discuss it," Spider growled. "But I do know a little about her talents."

"Do you?" She winked at him, then turned toward Seitz. "Is he crying?"

"He needs to piss awful bad, and he's too proud to just soak his britches." Spider handed the pistol to Hob. "Seitz is with us, lads, if you'll have him. I think it fair, as he has a stake in the map. If he'd never brought it aboard *Minuet*, well, we'd not have it now, I reckon. And we do not wish to kill him, do we? No. But he'll join us, he will, for an equal share. We parlayed on that, did we not, Seitz?"

"Aye."

"We can write articles on it, if Ruth does not mind."

"I can write," she said.

"So let us vote on it, then, as we did when we were on the account. I propose a fair and equal share for our man here, uh . . . I do not know your first name."

"Artur."

"... our man Artur Seitz here, I propose he join our company for a fair and equal share, so long as he take upon him a fair and equal risk. If you be in favor, tell it now."

Everyone lifted a hand and a cheer, except Odin.

"Not sure I ought to take less so he can have any," the old man growled. "Why should I? Why should any of us?"

Spider paced, and nodded. "I see this, Odin. You make a fair point. But consider, there is strength in numbers. You have fought, you know that. And Seitz here, well, we have to do something with him. If we don't take him with us, what do we do? Murder him?"

"*Nein! Nein!*"

"Well." Odin paced, too. "Don't want to murder him. Killing a man who has a gun or a knife is right by me, but not . . . No. You are right, a murder, well that would be wrong."

Odin trying to sound reasonable sounded rather unconvincing, Spider thought.

Then the old man snapped his fingers. "Could I duel him?"

Spider gave Odin a dagger glance. "Odin . . ."

"That would be fair, aye? Ha!"

"Hardly," Spider answered him. He noticed Hob suppressing a laugh.

"Aye." Odin stopped walking and raised his hand. "Another man for our crew is fine, I suppose, if he doesn't shirk."

Spider looked at Seitz. "Will you shirk?"

"*Nein!*"

"Will you take the same risks we all take?"

"Aye! Aye!"

Spider nodded. "Ruth, when time allows write our articles and we'll all sign them, or mark them if that be the best we can do. Odin, loose your knots and then you and Hob take him out and let him empty his pipe. Away from the house, if you please. Let him walk, let him work his joints, but keep him under guard."

"*Scheisse!* I thought we all were mates now!"

Spider shook his head. "Once we sign articles and we're away at sea, where you can't try to steal a map and run off from us"—*or run to town and tell them where I am, he thought*—"then you can go about free. Until then, you are under guard."

"My plan is better," Odin muttered. He placed the sack he'd been carrying on the floor.

Seitz looked doubtful. "What is his plan?"

"You will not like Odin's plan."

"Ha!" The old man grinned.

Spider leaned close to Seitz, and whispered. "This is for your own safety. Trust me. All will be well. Just don't give him any trouble. You need a chance to prove yourself, aye?"

Seitz looked dubious.

Odin approached the prisoner. The gray hair framing his hideously scarred face made him look like a witch, and for a moment Spider thought Seitz's bladder might empty in his britches after all.

Moments later, though, Seitz was walking stiffly outside, under the watchful eyes of his guard. He muttered in German, drawing a laugh from Ruth. "That poor bastard. Your plan is reckless, I dare say."

Spider sat on a stack of wood. "Maybe. I don't have a better one, though, that don't mean killing him. I don't want to do that. Do you?"

"No."

"What did you find out in town?"

She started with the items she knew Spider cared most about. "This Captain Westcott, not many believe him to be a pirate. A decent fellow, the sailors say. Aimed *Margaret* at England about this time last year and has not been back. He was last seen headed east, maybe two days sail from here."

"That could have been a ruse," Spider said. "Head toward England, let a few westbound ships see you doing that, and then turn south for Tortuga or some other goddamned place. Emma?"

"She went with him, and your son. Everyone agrees. Folk seem to think it was good for her, Spider."

"Good for her?"

She nodded, slowly.

"Well." He thought on that for a while. *Maybe she's better off with him. Maybe Johnny is, too. But then again, Roger Dawes thought West-cott was a pirate.*

"Did you learn anything else?"

"Besides learning Odin scares people and they won't talk to him? And Hob has no skill at cards whatsoever?" She sat beside him. "We learned that no one truly felt friendly toward your Stoneham. He spread his seed around, shall we say, with little concern as to whether a woman had a husband or not. If her man wasn't about, Stoneham swooped in."

Spider started to reply, but stopped himself. He merely seethed, instead.

Ruth continued. "Gambled a lot, too, and they say he often stole from one pocket to fill someone else's. Hob played piquet with several men, and every one of them claimed Stoneham owed them money."

"Hob played piquet?"

"Very badly, too, but do not fret, Spider. He played with my money, not yours. I had some hidden away."

"Have you any knives or guns hidden away as well, Ruth?"

"I might." She smiled. Once, just after they'd met, she'd nearly seduced Spider and then surprised him with a dirk. Rather than dwell on that now, though, she continued her tale. "We were at the home of a man named Zachariah. Whisky was flowing. Hob stole a flask for you, I am happy to tell you, it's in his coat pocket. Hob played cards, Odin sat in a far, dark corner—not really far enough or dark enough for that face, I fear—and he watched for reactions while I sat and talked and flashed my eyes and played the coquette and made sure cups were filled often. I was a curious girl, and an outrageous flirt, and they wanted to impress me."

Spider shook his head. "I remember when you played me like a fiddle. What did the poor helpless souls tell you?"

"Well, Spider John, everyone is quite convinced you killed Jeremy Stoneham. They also are quite convinced you left Nantucket aboard a brig that sailed the next morning, and when we had the chance later, your friends and I did all we could to spread that bit of news around."

"Good," he said.

"I don't know if people really believe that, though," she answered. "I rather believe that is merely an excuse, to be honest. No one wants to keep searching for a stranger who killed a man no one liked anyway. They're happier getting back to their work and cards and liquor."

"Good," he replied.

"I dare say you might even be able to go into town with a bit of a disguise, one that won't break your fucking legs."

Spider nodded. "Maybe."

"Clever, that was, no doubt, but . . ."

"Foolish, that was," he said. "So, there is no other suspect? For Stoneham's murder?"

"Well, that fellow Wood, the whale watcher you attacked, told his tale to anyone who would listen, and so did the cooper, Dawes."

"Dawes, aye. Stoneham rented a room from him. He said he wasn't a friend to Stoneham, but he seems to have put up with him, at least, and wished him Christian charity, as I recall."

"They certainly were not friends," Ruth said. "He used to have nothing to do with Stoneham at all, until a few months ago. That's when Stoneham started renting from him."

"That is interesting."

Hob and Odin came back with their charge, who was walking much more easily now. The redness in his face was gone.

"I hope you feel better, Seitz."

"I hope you die and go to hell for making me wait so long," Seitz said.

"Well, I reckon I cannot blame you for that. Toss me that flask, Hob."

"Aye." It was a small pewter flask, stamped with a whale. Spider caught it deftly with his left hand, and was glad he remembered not to try with his injured right hand.

"Should I bind him again, Spider?"

"No, Odin. Not yet. Let him move about. Just keep an eye on him. And Hob, you know what to do if he gives us any trouble."

Hob brandished the pistol. "Aye, Spider."

"I'll not give you trouble. Can I have food, and beer?"

"Aye," Spider said. "Lads, feed our friend." He opened the flask and sniffed the contents. Rum, and not watered down. "Thank you, Hob."

"Don't drink it all at once."

Spider took a sip and handed the flask to Ruth. "Maybe you should carry this."

"Fine," she said.

Odin walked to the large sack he'd brought in. "Some of this I bought, and some of it I stole," he said. He sat down and started rummaging through it. "Bread, with no maggots! I hardly remember bread without maggots. We have cheese, got some fish chunks wrapped in cheesecloth here, some beef—no, I ate that—and a couple of jugs of beer. Not a goddamned maggot in any of it. Ha! I have some black walnuts, too, from the mainland! I have not eaten one of these beauties in years. Still tucked into their cases, so we'll have to let those dry a good long time before we break them. Hell of a mess if we don't. And we'll need that mallet. Hob can crack them, like he did that German bastard's head. Ha!"

"Odin," Spider said, "you were not this excited in Port Royal that night you could afford two whores."

"I have not had black walnuts in years, I said." He tore out a hunk of bread and tossed it to Seitz. "I'll give you a bit of cheese, too. Should we really waste beer on him? And I am not giving him any of my goddamned walnuts."

"We're building trust," Spider said, with a wink aimed at Seitz.

"Aye." Odin pulled a jug from the sack. "I still won't give him a fucking walnut."

Spider turned his attention back to Ruth. "You say Dawes only recently took up with Stoneham?"

"That's what the fellows said. Dawes is a bit of a snob, they say, and would not have anything to do with Stoneham. Called him a whore-monger, and an apostate."

"Apostate?"

"Aye."

"Dawes spoke of Stoneham in somewhat decent terms when I asked about him. Spoke of the Christian thing to do and all that. But if he thought Stoneham an apostate, well . . ."

"It seems they grew closer of late. Maybe Stoneham got religion?"

"Maybe. Did any of the gentlemen you flirted with say anything of that sort, that Stoneham had changed his ways?"

"No. If anything he's been worse lately. Drinking more, that sort of thing."

Spider considered that. "So then, if Stoneham didn't change his evil ways, why did Dawes start treating him kindly?"

"Maybe Dawes is a decent fellow."

"Maybe. I don't know a lot of decent fellows." He nodded toward Odin and grinned. "But now I am wondering something."

Ruth waited for Spider to explain, then grew exasperated when he scratched his beard and stared at the ceiling instead. "Well?"

"Roger Dawes knew I meant Jeremy Stoneham harm . . . but he didn't try very hard to stop me going over there to the Widow Coffin's house, now did he? His plea to me was half-hearted at best, now that I think on it."

"Oh," Ruth said. "I see. Well, could he have stopped you? I've seen you fight."

"I was stunk drunk, Ruth, and he'd never seen me fight anyone. Had a knife, but . . . well. Seems odd he did not even try."

"I see."

"Aye. And I hid in that burnt barn a good long while. If Dawes is such a good Christian man, why didn't he alert anyone right away? He did not have to try to stop me himself. He could have roused a whole goddamned army against me. There was plenty of time to gather help, to stop me from doing anything rash. But no one came. So, why would he wait and then tell his story?"

"So you think . . ."

"I think we need to take a closer look at Roger Dawes."

38

"**D**amn it, woman, be careful with that blade! Do you mean to flay me?"

Ruth smiled. "Well, Spider, I have never used a knife to cut a man's beard. His neck? Yes. I've done that. But never a beard. If you stop squirming, you'll be safer."

She was using a small piece of wood as a cutting board, in her left hand so she'd have something to cut against without pulling on the hair, and slicing through Spider's dripping wet beard with the sharpest knife Isaac owned, honed once again by Spider. The aim was to repair the clumsy job Spider had done previously to alter his appearance, but it wasn't going well and Spider and Ruth both cursed.

"I've never really done this," she said. "Don't move."

"I shaved with a real razor, once," Spider said. "Stolen. Hardly ever seen one before. Soap and a sharp blade, got all the way down to the skin. I remember that, I do. Glorious, that's the word the angels would say about it. Glorious."

"And where is that razor now?" She shook her head.

"Some bastard stole it."

Ruth continued working as Odin came forward. "Tied Seitz by the ankles and arms," he said, using the pistol to point back toward the prisoner. "He does not like me very much. He thinks he's a full member of our little crew now, and ought to be treated as fair as Hob or me."

"He won't like you if you shoot him," Spider growled. "Be careful with that damned thing."

Spider called across to Seitz, who sat on the floor against the wall. "I told you before. Once we are at sea, where you can't knock anyone on the head and take the damned map, we'll let you wander free. But until we reach that happy point, we are going to bolster our newfound friendship with some stout rope and a pistol. It helps build trust."

Ruth slapped him gently on the head. "I said hold still."

Another ten minutes of work and Ruth was finished. "Well," she said. "It is atrocious. I really thought I could make things more even. At least it is short."

"Maybe it will look better when it dries," Hob suggested.

"No." Ruth collected her water bowl, cloth, knife and cutting board and turned to go. "No. You are just going to have to steal a real razor, I say, before I can make you look decent. Scrape all this off and start a whole new beard."

"I finished your new crutches," Hob said.

"Good," Spider said. "If we need to leave the wagon, those will be handy."

"I made a good job of it, too," the young man said. "You will be pleased."

Spider laughed. "So making me a disguise is more fun than sawing deck planks, it seems."

Hob blinked. "Aye."

Spider ran a cloth across his damp hair and beard. It all certainly felt much shorter.

Ruth returned. "I asked again, and Isaac insists he does not need the wagon. He's got it hitched up. Are we ready?"

"Aye," Spider said. "Seitz, Odin is going to stay with you. He won't kill you if you behave."

"This is not fair," the prisoner said. "We made pact, you and I, John! Oaths to each other."

"Aye," Spider said. "And we are going to make sure you keep yours. Odin, watch him close, and don't . . ."

"I know," Odin answered, tapping the leather pouch on his belt. "You don't have to tell me things three times, Spider."

Spider thought about answering, and decided against doing so. *I am trusting you, old man.* "Aye. Ruth, Hob, we're off to the cooperage."

"Hey, Odin, this will keep you company," Hob said, tossing a flask to the one-eyed pirate. "Good whisky, I say. Grabbed it in town for Spider, but it's yours, since you have to stay here with the cook. It'll make a boring duty less boring, I dare say."

Odin caught it deftly. "Obliged, Hob, my boy!"

"I'm not a boy."

"You sure as hell are a boy. Old as I am, you're all boys to me, except for that one." He pointed at Ruth. "Ain't no disguising that. Ha!"

Ruth actually blushed. "Odin, please. Behave."

"I will not," he said. "I have sailed with Blackbeard, killed more men than I can remember, and there is no use trying to make amends, because the Lord won't be fooled. I'll do as I please."

She glared at him, but couldn't quite hide a smile. "You are a salty son of a bitch."

"Aye," he said, proudly. "Every goddamned inch of me."

Spider took Ruth by the elbow and dragged her toward the wagon, before Odin could elaborate on what he meant by "every goddamned inch."

"He's deranged," Ruth said, climbing up onto the driver's bench.

"Oh, certainly," Spider said, "but he is on our side." He climbed into the back of the wagon, where Hob awaited him. "Let's be on our way, Miss Copper."

Once they were beyond sight of Isaac's barn, Ruth halted the mule.

Spider, in the back of the wagon, looked at his young friend, "Go, Hob. You know your duty."

"I'd rather stay with you, Spider. This Dawes may be dangerous, if he's a killer like you think."

"I'm dangerous, too," Spider answered.

Hob spat. "And you are crippled."

"I am not lame, boy. My legs hurt, my feet hurt, but I've suffered worse. And Ruth is dangerous, too, so I won't be fighting alone, if it comes to that. We will be fine. Now go."

"Aye." Hob jumped out of the wagon. "But you've got to be careful."

"We will. Go."

Spider got out, too, and clambered up beside Ruth.

She shook her head. "This plan of yours sounds complicated, my friend. I have doubts."

"Aye, but if you think it's complicated now, just wait until musket balls start flying and the law shows up. That will be complicated, for certain."

Her eyebrows arched. "Is that going to happen?"

"Well, it ain't in my plan," he said. "But that's the kind of thing that generally happens, aye."

"Jesus," she said. "This life."

"Aye," he said. "This is why I am trying so hard to find a better one."

39

"So, then, I don't think I have all this reasoned out," Ruth said, urging the mule to pick up the pace. "Tell me again why you think this Dawes killed Stoneham."

Damn it, woman, Spider thought. *Let me think.*

He knew why she was pestering him. He could feel the tension inside him growing as they approached the town. While he'd been puzzling things out—what to do with Seitz, how to approach Dawes, how he might prove the cooper was the killer—he'd been too busy to dwell on thoughts of Em, out there somewhere in the world with his son. But now, riding alongside Ruth with a plan laid and nothing more to do at the moment, his mind was far off. *Was she at sea, or in England, with this Westcott, living a happy life at last? Or was she on the Spanish Main, dressing like a man the way Ruth does and fighting like a man, too? Was Little Johnny by her side, learning to swing a cutlass and jam a flintlock right into his victim's chest before squeezing the trigger?*

It was all too much. And Ruth, bless her, had noticed his state of mind, despite his efforts at humorous quips and playing the captain, calmly pacing the quarterdeck. She was trying to bring his thoughts back to their present problems. It seemed to Spider as though she could open up his mind and peer inside, and that both annoyed and worried him.

It also shook him a bit to realize how real Ruth was, sitting here beside him where a hint of perfume seemed so at odds with the man's britches and shirt she wore, while Em seemed almost like a ghost, more dream than real. In his mind, he could easily see the beginnings of a smile on Ruth's face, or hear her voice, anytime he wanted to do so. He did not even know how Em wore her hair now, or if she still knew how to laugh, or if time and cares had started to show on her face.

All these thoughts made him want a damned drink. But he didn't have a drink, so he decided to let Ruth distract him. It never hurt to turn a puzzle over in his mind a few times, anyway.

"Well," he said, "here's the first fact. You tell me that Dawes could not stand the man, Stoneham, until a few months ago. Then, there's a change, and he's suddenly willing to rent the man a room."

"Aye."

"That is an odd thing, it is," Spider said. "It's not like selling him a barrel or a firkin, where Stoneham would just pay him and go away. Dawes rented the man a room. That implies sort of an ongoing relationship, does it not? He'd have to be around the man, and often, probably."

"Aye," Ruth said. "A landlord is likely to see renters frequently."

"Aye," Spider said. "If I looked down on a man, considered him beneath me, you know, I don't think I'd let him rent one of my rooms. No. From what you tell me, Dawes thought Stoneham to be rubbish. Aye?"

"Aye," she said.

"Very well," Spider said. "So that's one thing to ponder. Here's another. Dawes knew I might strangle or stab Stoneham, but as near as we can tell, he took no precautions to stop me doing that, right? Did nothing at all that might have kept me from killing the man. As far as we know, he kept quiet about me until Stoneham was dead."

"Aye." There was just the hint of a smile on her face, and Spider realized she was gloating a bit. He'd been wallowing, and now he wasn't. Ruth had sought to distract him from despair, and it had bloody well worked. *One little victory for you, woman.*

He tried to hide his irritation.

"Well," he continued, "he spoke of Christian charity, wanting to help poor Stoneham see better days again and all that rot, but he did not stop me, a man who—as far as Dawes could tell—wanted to gut the fucking son of a bitch Stoneham like a goddamned tuna."

"Which, I might remind you, Spider, is exactly what you wanted to do."

"Goddamn it, woman, it don't matter what I thought, does it, if I did not actually kill the son of a bitch?" He wasn't so sure the Lord would look upon it that way, of course, but that was what he kept telling himself.

"That, I think, is more of a question for the Lord than for me," she said, again echoing his own thoughts. Then she turned her pretty face and looked right into his eyes. "As for me, I want you to know that I am on your side, John Rush, whatever the Lord may say, or the devil, or anyone else."

He tried to answer that, then gulped, then turned away from her gaze. "Glad of that, I am. Well, my point is this. Dawes could have done the Christian thing and gone about telling folks hey, there's a man out there, heading to the Widow Coffin's house, I think he's going to kill Stoneham. But he didn't do that, did he? No. So, then. Why?"

"Why?"

"Because he wanted Stoneham dead," Spider said. "That's it."

Ruth nodded. "Fine, then. But . . . why would he then go to the trouble of killing the bastard himself? He thought you'd kill him, you said."

"Aye."

"Well?"

"I have been thinking on that, and it's a puzzle, to be sure, but I think I have it. You have to imagine what Dawes saw, when I came looking for Stoneham. I was a mess, Ruth. Drunk, stinking of liquor, covered in wet sand. I was the very devil, I was."

She shook her head. "So?"

"So," Spider answered, "he knew I'd try to kill Stoneham, but . . . he had every reason to believe I'd foul things up. Drunk as I was, maybe he thought Stoneham was too much for me. Hell, maybe he thought I'd pass out before I got a chance to attack."

Ruth thought about that. "So, you think Dawes followed you."

"Aye, intending to do the bloody deed if I failed. He waited, hiding somewhere nearby, and when Stoneham arrived, and I pounced, well, I think I got off course, maybe nervous, I don't know, I was still not quite sober, I admit, and sort of recall veering a bit. I'd wager that Dawes, watching, saw me stumbling about like a mad fool and maybe he decided he had to take a chance and make sure Stoneham died that night. He had to make sure of it."

"But why, Spider? Why did he want to kill him?"

"That's what I want to know, too," Spider said. "But I suspect it has something to do with his change of attitude toward Stoneham. Hates him one day, then he rents him a room and talks charitable about him to me. I walked out of that cooperage thinking Stoneham and Dawes was old mates, but that wasn't the situation, was it? No."

"I see." Ruth nodded.

"I think Stoneham knew something about Dawes, something Dawes didn't want anyone else to know, and that was his lever. He used that against Dawes."

"He extorted him?"

Spider nodded. "Aye, lass. I reckon so. It fits, don't it? Stoneham sounds a right bastard, the very type to extort someone. I'm willing to bet our Mister Dawes has a secret, and that Stoneham smoked it out, and then here I come, a drunk bent on revenge, and whoa! Dawes says to himself, this is my chance! I can kill Stoneham tonight, and let this fucking drunk bastard swing for it."

"Jesus."

"Bloody brilliant, it is," Spider said. "Brilliant. But I was a mess, so he followed me to make sure the job got done. Sort of the way I have to check up on Hob with the tools, and end up putting them aright myself."

Ruth sat in silence for a few minutes before asking, "Well, what could that secret be?"

"I don't know," Spider said. "He was a sailor once, he said, and he talked a bit about pirates, seemed to think Westcott was a pirate. It might be something connected to that, or it might be something else. But we're going to find out."

40

Spider, hiding in the back of the wagon again and using a peephole in the canvas cover, watched Ruth enter the cooperage. The barn-style door was open wide, but the interior of the building was hidden in shadow. Spider could hear the thumps of a hammer inside.

He grumbled once Ruth was out of sight. It had been a good plan to send her in, he had admitted begrudgingly, because Roger Dawes had gotten a good close look at Spider before. A shorter beard and shorter hair and a set of crutches were not likely to fool him. Still, Spider was eager to get this Stoneham murder resolved and then begin his search for Em. It irked him mightily to crouch in hiding while Ruth did all the work. He wondered how Hob and Odin were doing with their tasks, and envied them.

All I am going to accomplish here is to cramp my damned legs again, he thought.

He startled a bit when he saw a man emerge from the cooperage. It was Dawes, walking quickly. Spider widened his spy hole a bit, and cursed. Dawes was wearing his hair down, not tied back as before, hiding his ears. Spider could not make out an earring, nor a bloody ear.

He watched Dawes walk southward, then turn to the west between buildings. He saw no sign of Ruth following him.

Spider crept toward the back of the wagon, aiming to follow Dawes, before the scent of burning tobacco and the sound of footsteps compelled him to halt. Someone was approaching the wagon. He ducked back out of sight.

Then he heard conversation, growing louder. Spider stayed away from the peephole, and remained motionless. His hand went to his knife.

The strangers stopped, right outside the wagon.

Damnation!

The men resumed talking, and the first word he could make out distinctly was "pirates."

His grip tightened on the knife handle, and he had to clamp his jaws shut to avoid screaming in agony. His injured right hand was getting better, but it was not ready to clutch a hilt. He freed the weapon from its sheath with his left hand and tucked the right one against his belly, hoping the contact would remind him to not use it.

He closed his eyes and listened more closely. He discerned two distinct voices, one raspy and one that sounded bored. They were not whispering, he noticed, and so he relaxed a bit. This was not likely an attack.

Still, he heard the words "pirate" and "execution," and his heart began to race a bit. He dared not risk a peek outside, though.

"Aye, it all sounds bloody horrible enough. Our girl went in there, I think," said the bored voice.

"Aye."

Spider held his breath. *Jesus, are they looking for Ruth? Former shipmates, maybe, looking to greet an old friend? Or to avenge some past slight? Or were these men working with Dawes, covering his tracks to see if she followed him?*

Spider shook his head. *No, damn it, these are not Dawes's men.* The cooper had no reason to expect a visit from Ruth, nor any bloody reason to think she was anything more than a pretty girl wanting to buy a keg from him. *Think, Spider John, you fool!*

He opened his eyes. The sun was bright enough to throw shadows against the canvas, and he tightened his grip on his weapon once again. Whoever these bastards were, they had halted beside his peephole. The taller one stood to the left of it, the other to the right. And for whatever reason, they seemed to be waiting for Ruth.

Spider risked a crouch, and ignored the pain in his calves. He could not tell if these men were facing the wagon, or facing the cooperage. They were standing in plain sight, though, not hiding. That might mean they were not, in fact, planning to ambush Ruth. *Or it might mean they were not even a little bit afraid of being seen.*

"Thirty or more, it was, I tell you," the raspy voice said. He was the taller man. "All of them pirates."

"Aye, you said that," the other man answered.

Spider's mind raced. He glanced at a hand axe in the tool chest, then back at the shadows. The aroma from the taller man's pipe told him they were very close to the wagon, and a plan took shape in Spider's mind. With a weapon in each hand, axe and knife, he could aim an overhand axe stroke at the shorter man, swinging right through the canvas, and take him out of the fight at the first sign of trouble. The dirk would pierce the canvas, too. If he pounced quickly enough and with sufficient strength, he could at least even the odds, or perhaps even put them in his favor, in an instant.

Then he looked at his swollen right hand, and his plan sank like a hulled corsair.

So he waited, with a knife in his left hand, and listened to the ghastly talk of pirates.

"Their testimonies were quite moving," the raspy voice said. "All of them imploring God, all of them begging the crowd to not go down that wicked path. I don't think God was listening, though, and I know the crowd wasn't. They just wanted to watch the poor bastards die, that was all they wanted."

"Aye," said the bored voice.

He's describing an execution. Spider prayed silently. He'd seen men hanged, and never wanted to see it again. From his very first crimes under the command of Bent Thomas, the gallows had loomed in Spider's mind. Memories of shipmates stirred.

"This one fellow," the raspy voice continued, "I think he pissed in his britches. But all apologies, he was, and warning people to be righteous and not make his mistakes. He says 'I do stand here a sad spectacle' and 'I pray God it do be a warning unto you.' The crowd just wanted to see him killed but he went on with his begging and pleading. It was shameful. 'Seek the Lord early, while he may be found,' he says. 'Spend not your bloomful years in such things as gratify the sinful flesh. Let God be your monitor, lest the adversary of our souls intercept between God and us.' Quite mournful, it all was. Tears. Shaking. He sounded quite repented, I thought. And then, of course, they killed him anyway."

"Of course."

"Thirty of them that day, at least."

Thirty souls!

Spider gasped. He imagined himself, there among doomed shipmates, making a similar speech and wondering if God or anyone else cared.

Both men outside the wagon moved, and Spider's attention returned to the present.

"Well, as for gratifying the sins of flesh," said the bored voice, suddenly sounding a great deal less bored, "I told you she was in there. Here she comes."

"Hello, beautiful lady," said the taller man.

"Greetings, gentlemen." Spider recognized Ruth's voice. He detected no hint of recognition in it, but there was a definite note of caution.

Not friends, then.

Spider prepared to strike. He could knife one of them quickly, at least, right through the canvas. He could follow that with a stab at the other fellow, but his arm could easily get caught up in the canvas. Still, with one down Ruth would have a fair fight on her hands.

"I do not believe I have ever seen you on Nantucket before," said the shorter man. "I know I'd have recalled that. I am Edmund, and my friend is Henry."

The shadows moved away, toward the front of the wagon. They were going to block her path, Spider reckoned. He moved carefully toward the back of the wagon, took the knife hilt between his teeth and climbed out onto the road as quietly and quickly as his injured hand and sore legs would allow.

"I am Prudence," Ruth lied. "I need to get up to the driver's bench, gentlemen." She sounded friendly. Spider could almost hear the pretty smile.

He still could not determine if this was an ambush by bounty hunters or simply two men taken with a beautiful woman, but he decided it could be trouble either way.

Spider moved, keeping the wagon between himself and the interlopers. He took up the knife, ready to stab. Spider was quite adept at throwing a knife, but he'd never tried that with his left hand, so if it came to a fight the bloody work would have to be done at close quarters.

Spider was quite adept at that, too.

"Maybe we could ride with you," Henry said.

There it is. Trouble.

Spider ducked and peeked beneath the wagon. Neither man had moved aside. Ruth had stopped about ten feet short of them.

"I do not think you'd enjoy that as much as you might suppose," Ruth answered. Spider rose, moved, and peered over the hitch. He could now see Ruth, reaching beneath her left sleeve and scratching her arm. "I have a rather horrible rash. Is there an apothecary nearby?"

"I don't mind a rash," Edmund said.

"Well, then." Ruth's right hand reappeared, bearing a knife. She closed the distance frighteningly fast. In a second, that knife was at Edmund's balls, while her other hand grasped his neck and shoved him against the wagon. The mule brayed, and bucked a little, but did not bolt—still, the moment of confusion kept Spider from stepping onto the hitch and leaping into the fight.

"I have absolutely no time to waste with you," Ruth whispered, pressing the knife further between the man's legs. She looked at the other man. "Or with you. If you'd like your rude friend here to have any luck with the ladies in the future, you'll wander off, far and away. Once I see that you are beyond hope of doing me any harm, I'll free him, pecker and all. If you don't comply, I'm keeping his balls, and I'll get yours, too."

Henry raised his hands and laughed. "You are very pretty, miss, but perhaps not worth so much trouble. I should have guessed it. You dress like a man." He blew her a kiss, then turned to go.

Ruth laughed. "And what do you say, Edmund? Hmmm?"

"Look . . ."

"Want to keep that thing between your legs?"

"Aye."

"Then run like hell's hounds are on your ass the second I release you. Any other action on your part, any words, any hesitation, and I take a trophy. Do you understand? Nod, don't talk."

He must have nodded, Spider decided, because soon his footsteps were drumming on the road. He saw the man dashing off in the direction of his friend. They vanished between a candle shop and a fish stall.

Spider sheathed his knife, climbed up to the bench and reached down to give Ruth a hand up. "Remind me to always treat you with respect," he said.

"Why in all the devil's names are you not hiding in the back as we agreed, John? That was the bloody plan!"

41

The mule ambled up the street, in the direction Dawes had taken. The damned beast apparently had upset bowels, because loud gurgles and a foul stench kept emanating from its ass.

"Jesus, I hate mules," Ruth said.

Spider ignored that. "Why did you not follow Dawes? I tried, before your admirers got in my way." He'd been too eager to hear what she'd learned to do the sensible thing and hide again, as she'd suggested, so he was sitting next to her and keeping his head down.

Her quick response showed she had been anticipating the question, which Spider had held back only long enough to assure he could ask it without sounding angry. "Because," she said, "I thought it would look bloody suspicious if I walked into his workshop and then just turned around and sniffed at his heels."

Spider drew a deep breath. "Aye. I reckon you speak true."

"You need to calm down," she said. "You don't ordinarily fail to think of such things. Usually, it is you telling Hob or Odin to focus on the task at hand, and to pay attention to small details because doing so can keep you alive, and all that. I've heard you say that a thousand times, and your mates rely on you to do most of the thinking."

"Aye," he admitted. "I have too much on my mind."

She nodded. "Yes. You do. That, I'm afraid, cannot be helped."

They rode on in silence for a few moments.

"However," she said, "Despite my failure to follow Dawes, I can happily tell you that this little jaunt was not in vain."

"No?"

"No. There was another fellow working inside, quite handsome, I should say, and I was able to learn a few things from him."

"Handsome?"

She smiled. "Another admirer. Are you jealous?"

"No," he lied.

"Men do notice me, Spider John," she said. "I say that in case you have not noticed that yourself."

He ignored her comment. "What did the poor helpless son of a bitch who could not ignore your charms tell you?"

She looked at him, started to speak, then looked away. "I learned that Roger Dawes, for the last several months, has been sneaking away from work. Often."

"Is that so?"

"Aye. Indeed, Abner . . . that is the name of the poor helpless son of a bitch who could not, well, forget all that, Abner is quite concerned that he and Dawes will not be able to produce all the hogsheads and firkins and such that they need to supply their customers, because Mister Dawes is away so often."

"Well," Spider said. "That is certainly interesting."

"Aye."

"Did Abner have an idea why his employer was not attending to business?"

"Aye. It has to do with a woman."

Spider rubbed his brow. "A woman. Well, those can be inconvenient and troublesome."

"Aye. Men can be quite foolish where women are concerned." She turned to look at him.

"Why is it," he said, "that when you talk about men, I think you are talking about me?"

"I have not the bloodiest goddamned idea," she said, but he noted it took her a full three heartbeats to answer.

"What woman?"

"A woman whose man has gone to sea," she said, "and been away long enough for her to get quite lonely."

"That happens, doesn't it. And there is always some bastard sniffing around to take advantage." He spat, and fell into a brooding silence.

"Jesus," Ruth muttered. "Look, John, I realize that you are quite romantic, and you carry around this idea of faithfulness in your head and came to Nantucket expecting your Em to feel the same way and that she'd . . ."

Ruth stopped talking.

Well, then, Spider thought, *bloody hell.*

"People don't often hold to such notions," she said, finally. "Women get the itch same as you men. This woman, her name is Charity, well, her man went to sea and young Abner thinks she got an itch, and that your Mister Dawes decided to scratch it."

"Well, then, who is this woman?"

"Charity Beall," she said. "Abner says she is quite fetching."

"And Roger Dawes noticed that," Spider said.

"Aye," she answered. "Most men notice such things."

Spider started thinking hard, and wished he had a pipe going. "Suppose Stoneham noticed, too?"

"He was already noticing the Widow Coffin, aye?"

"No," Spider said. "I mean, aye, he was visiting the Widow Coffin. And from what people say, Stoneham might have noticed the Widow Coffin and your Missus Beall and probably chased after both. But what I mean to say is this: Suppose Stoneham noticed that Dawes had taken up with your Missus Beall?"

"So?"

"So," Spider said, "Stoneham finds out Dawes, good Christian man he says he is, is getting his wick wet with this Charity Beall. Maybe Stoneham goes to Dawes and he says, hey, you've got a lovely wife, don't you? Tragedy, wouldn't it be, if she was to find out what you are doing with Missus Beall, don't you think?"

Ruth looked at him. "So, then, Stoneham finds out about Roger Dawes and Charity Beall, and . . . that's the key, to the extortion you suspect."

Spider grinned. "Aye, and suddenly Stoneham is renting a room from a man who would not even look at him before. That's why the relationship changed. Suddenly, Mister Dawes is fine with being around Jeremy Stoneham. Although Dawes might as well have sent Stoneham to the devil, because it seems your friend Abner has it all reckoned out and will tell any pretty face that comes along all about it."

Ruth nodded. "I must admit, this seems to all work out."

"Aye," Spider said. "And then Dawes sees a chance, he does, when I come about all angry and drunk and wanting to kill Stoneham. He, I mean Dawes, follows me, and then he makes sure Stoneham dies, reckoning that I'll swing for it."

Ruth sighed heavily. "That all makes sense, Spider."

"Aye. It does."

"Well, handsome Mister Abner told me where Missus Beall lives, and that is where we are headed now. Perhaps we can catch them at the deed."

Spider did not answer.

Ruth noticed. "What is wrong?"

Spider smacked his lips. "Is that a man with a big black beard and a blue tricorn hat, right up there?"

"Aye," she said.

"I've seen him before."

42

*S*pider muttered to himself.

"What should we do?" Ruth shook her head. "Should we follow Dawes—Abner told me where to find his lover, if the gossip is true and that is where he's gone—or do we follow that man?"

"I don't know," Spider said. "Let me think. But don't pass the fellow by."

Ruth drew upon the reins to slow the mule. "I won't. So, then, is this fellow the one you saw, that you thought might be Seitz? All that beard, and the broad shoulders, he does resemble our German friend."

"Aye," Spider said. "He walks like a sailor, too. Misses the rolling deck beneath his feet." He watched the man tarry for a moment before a shoe shop. "Stop the wagon a moment."

Ruth complied. "Do you know for certain this man was following you?"

"I do not," Spider said. "But he seemed to be following in my wake after my discussion with that Wood fellow."

"Discussion? You beat him with an oar."

"It was a serious discussion," Spider said quietly. "Anyway, I thought this guy might be following me, because of the direction he took. Then you lot showed up and told me Seitz had come ashore and I thought, well, that fellow I saw was Seitz. But he is not Seitz. Now that we get a closer look, I see he is younger."

"And handsomer," Ruth added. "I can go flirt, if you like. Maybe I can find out a name, or something."

"Well, he's walking again." Spider watched the man head southward. "No, do not follow him. I don't really know he was looking for me. He could have been looking for a wayward sheep."

Ruth snapped the reins, and the mule was moving again. "Hide your face. I'm going to pass close by him."

The wagon picked up speed, and Spider saw that the man with the blue tricorn would be forced to rush to cross in front of it, or pause to let it pass by. Spider could see no earring now, nor could he tell if the man had a wounded lobe.

The man with the hat paused, and Ruth guided the wagon past him. "Thank you, sir. Forgive me," she told the man, smiling. "I am in a bit of a hurry."

"It is no problem, miss," the man said. He gazed at her, obviously enthralled, and Spider felt a bit jealous.

Behind them, the man crossed the road. "He's headed southward," Spider said, standing on the bench and looking backward. He ducked. "The fellow just looked back to see where we are going."

"He looked back to see where I am going, Spider."

The carpenter spat. "Aye. He gave you a good look, he did."

"It may serve us well later," she replied, "should we decide we need to know more about him."

"Aye," Spider said, "but to be honest I have no real reason to think he really was following me. It was just a feeling I had, and I was not particularly sober nor thinking right at the time. He goes south now, and he came from the south when I saw him before. So perhaps I am just off course. But . . ."

"But, Spider?"

"He had a bright dangly earring before, and I do not see one now."

"Do you want me to chase him down? He's not following a road, but I think I can get the mule to head that way. And these dirt roads aren't really helpful anyway." Indeed, wagon wheels tended to sink a bit in Nantucket's soil.

"No," Spider said. "That would look a might suspicious, I reckon. Let us stay on the path we're following."

"On to Missus Beall's home, then?"

"Onward."

She flicked the reins and the mule responded. Spider soon lost sight of the seafaring stranger. A few minutes later, Ruth pointed at a small home.

"That place, there, the one with the pretty bench by the road. That is where she lives. And that is where Abner thinks Dawes passes his afternoons."

"Very well," Spider said. "I think we should pass by. I'll drop off, and creep around a bit, and see what I can see."

"He knows your face, Spider. And my crude work on your beard and hair won't change that."

"I know, but . . . I need to do this. Peering from a hiding place while everyone else does all the work is not my way, Ruth."

Ruth sighed heavily. "I'm quite capable, you know."

"I know. So am I." He made certain his good hand could find his knife. He stared at the swollen right hand. "Goddamned useless fingers. Goddamned useless, ought to cut them off and use them for bait."

"It wasn't your fingers that decided to punch a wagon, was it?"

"Quiet, girl. Slow, now. I'm jumping off. Go on a ways, then circle back. If I am not about, go back to Isaac's and I'll find my own way there."

"Bloody stupid man."

"What did you say?"

"Just go."

Spider braced himself for the pain he knew would sear his feet and shins, and landed in a crouch. He rushed as quickly as he could toward the small house, determined to show no sign of the agony because he knew Ruth was watching him. He ignored the bright red door, and instead headed around the corner and toward the back. This was a single-story home, and he reasoned the bedchamber would be at the rear.

Soon he was crouched beneath a bright red shutter, and was absolutely certain he'd found the bedchamber.

"God," he heard a feminine voice mutter. "God."

That was followed by a grunting noise, not unlike the sounds made by a rooting hog.

"God! Ohhh . . ."

Spider closed his eyes, then wondered why an image of Ruth flashed in his mind. *Goddamn it*, he thought.

"Oh, God, Roger . . ."

The following crescendo of cries convinced Spider that no one inside the house was going to notice a bloody thing he might do for the next several seconds, so he made a decision. He rose from his crouch, worked his way around the house to the front door and found it unlocked. He looked behind him, saw no one about who might notice him, then entered.

He stood, frozen, for several seconds, then followed the sounds of swinish snorts and feminine moaning to the bed chamber. He listened, decided things within had reached a natural stopping point, then opened the door.

"Mister Dawes," he said, reaching for his knife. Fire and lightning shot through his swollen knuckles.

"Son of a bitch!" The man rolled off of Charity Beall, and fell on the floor, pulling a quilt with him.

"Goddamn useless chum fingers!" Spider reached with his left hand instead, and brandished the weapon.

The woman gasped, looked up at Spider, then sighed violently. "It is not my husband, Roger!"

"Not . . . wait," Dawes said. "I know you!"

"Aye," Spider said, staring intently at him. The man's hair, wet with the sweat of effort, hid his ears. "We've met. Now show me your goddamned ears!"

Dawes stared back at him. "What?"

"Your ears, man. I need to see them. And I need to see them now. Pull your hair out of the way."

Dawes looked confused. "I don't understand."

Charity Beall reached down from the bed and grabbed the quilt. She covered herself quickly, then closed her eyes. "Christ, forgive me," she muttered. Then she opened her eyes, spilling tears. "Are you a friend of Jack?"

Spider shook his head. "Is Jack your husband?"

She nodded and gulped.

"I do not know him," Spider assured her. "Nor is this . . ."—he waved the knife toward the bed—"any of my business. I came for Dawes, who had better do as I command, or this will be the last time he frolics with you."

Dawes tried to rise from the floor, but halted as Spider squared to fight.

"Stay on the floor, and do not get up. Just brush your hair away from your ears," Spider told Dawes. "And do it now."

Dawes looked at Spider as though the latter was mad. Charity Beall, meanwhile, cried softly.

Roger looked up at her. "Charity?"

Spider snapped at Dawes. "Just show me your goddamned ears!"

Dawes sat up on the floor and lifted his hands to his head. He pulled aside his hair, and stared at Spider. The naked man's eyes followed the point of the dirk as Spider moved it slowly to and fro.

"Turn left, then right."

Dawes complied, revealing one shiny disk hanging from his left ear.

Damn it, Spider thought. *No wounds. He's not the man.*

"Well," Spider said, lowering the knife. "I don't reckon you killed Jeremy Stoneham."

"What? I thought you killed him," Dawes answered.

43

Spider followed Dawes, still nude, out through the front door.

His prisoner complained, but the tip of the knife between his shoulders kept him from trying anything. "What is this?"

"I have questions," Spider answered, "and I'd not fancy asking them in front of your woman back there. She's got enough to cry about for now, I reckon, and she won't like seeing what I do to you if you give me trouble."

"I want my clothes."

"Sorry. I am in haste. I did not consider that."

Spider looked around, and was relieved to see that none of the neighbors were outside at the moment. Ruth had turned the wagon around and was heading back toward them. "We'll climb into the back, you and I. And be swift and quiet about it. Somebody might peep out a window any moment."

Ruth drew the mule to a halt.

"Climb in."

Dawes followed Spider's orders, blubbering under his breath, and crawled toward the back of the wagon, putting as much distance as he could between himself and Spider. Spider climbed in after him. "Onward, Ruth."

The wagon lurched forward. Spider flashed his knife. "If you reach for the tools, or do anything else unwise, you will not live another second. I don't want to kill you, but I know how to do it if I must, and it will be far from the first time. Now, tell me all about your relationship with Jeremy Stoneham, won't you?"

"I hated the bastard!"

"That is what I've heard. But you rented him a room," Spider said calmly. The wagon rattled on, and Spider's gaze moved back and forth between his prisoner's eyes and hands.

"He gave me no choice!" Dawes was crying. "Please, my wife . . ."

"That is your problem, not mine,' Spider said. "If you don't answer my questions, or if you give me even a small portion of trouble, I think I might just dump your naked carcass at her feet. Oh, Missus Dawes, I found your husband, making piggie noises and thrusting himself into a woman named Charity. How do you feel about that, Missus Dawes?"

"Please," Dawes whimpered.

"Don't beg, man," Spider said. "Just answer my questions. You reckoned I was planning to kill Stoneham, aye?"

"Aye," Dawes said. "And you did!"

"I did not," Spider answered. "Someone else did. Was it you?"

"No!"

"Convince me," Spider said coldly, even though he'd already ruled Dawes out as a suspect. *I certainly did not snatch an earring from this man's ear.* But he wanted to hear what the man said. Dawes seemed the type to gush and blab under the threat of sharp steel.

"I . . . I . . . listen to me, please," Dawes said, blubbering through tears. "I hoped you'd kill him . . ."

"Why?" Spider barked it, and poked the knife at the man.

"Christ! Christ! I wanted him dead!"

Dawes shook with sobbing, the tears streaming from his face.

"Don't stop talking now," Spider said.

Dawes groaned, sounding more forlorn than a pirate on the gibbet. "He was going to tell Dolly. About Charity. He . . . he caught us. In my shop."

"You tupped her in your shop?"

"God! Aye! I was weak! Weak! Weak!"

Spider closed his eyes. He could not think highly of Roger Dawes, but neither could he imagine the mewling creature before him actually committing murder, or conspiring with another to do so. This man rolling about and weeping was a coward, through and through.

"Stoneham held that against you, aye? Threatened to tell your wife?"

Dawes nodded, violently.

"Said he'd keep quiet if you gave him a berth? Paid him some money?"

"Yes!"

"And instead of beating him or shooting him, you gave him what he wanted. So," Spider continued, "when I arrived, hell-bent on finding Stoneham . . ."

"Aye!" Dawes shook with sobs. "Aye!"

Spider continued. "You told nobody about me at all, until the man was dead."

"Aye!"

"You hoped I'd kill him, Stoneham. You hoped I'd kill him."

"Aye!" Dawes rolled back and forth on the wagon bed. "Aye! God help me, aye!"

Spider spat out onto the road behind the wagon. "But you did not have the steel in you to follow me, did you? You did not have the balls to make sure I fulfilled your wish."

Dawes just sobbed.

Spider stared at him, thinking. *So, then. If not Dawes, who? Who murdered Jeremy Stoneham and left me to swing for it?*

After a while, Dawes wiped snot from his chin and stared at his captor. "What do you want from me?"

"I want to know who else had reason to kill Jeremy Stoneham. The whole island thinks I did the deed, but I did not. I hear a lot of people hated him. So who? Did you hire someone?"

Dawes gasped. "What?"

"Did you hire someone, to check up on me, make sure I wasn't too drunk to slaughter the man for you?"

Dawes shook his head. "Listen, man. I'm weak enough, aye, to look at another woman and . . . and . . . I'm sinner enough to wish Jeremy Stoneham dead at your hands, or anyone else's, but I could not hire an assassin! You must believe me!"

"You did not hire a sailing man, fellow with a blue hat and a thick beard, to follow me to the Widow Coffin's house?"

Dawes shook his head. "I did not!"

Spider had spent many idle hours at cards or chess, watching for any sign of a bluff. Dawes showed no reaction to the description of the mystery man.

"Do you know the fellow I mean?"

"I do not know the man, I did not kill anyone, I did not hire a killer. Please, I beg of you, believe that."

Spider looked into the man's red, wet eyes. "I believe you, damn it. Ruth!"

"Aye, cap'n?"

"Halt the wagon!"

Seconds later, the wagon rolled to a halt. "Get out," Spider commanded.

"What?"

"Get out!" Spider brandished his knife. "Go!"

Dawes stared at him. "You do not intend to kill me?"

"I will leave that to your wife," Spider said, "unless your cowardly face is still in my sight by the time I've counted to three. One."

"I have no clothes."

"That sounds a great deal bothersome for you, but it is not a thing that concerns me," Spider replied. He pointed the bright knife toward a flock of sheep. "Maybe you can hide among them. Two."

"Don't make me do this, I beg."

Spider sighed. The last thing he needed was another inconvenient hostage. He also thought of Charity Beall and that reminded him too damn much of his own problems. He did not care for Dawes at all, but if the coward was spotted wandering the town without a stitch to cover him, any rumors already in the air would catch fire and Mrs. Beall would be consumed by them, as would Mrs. Dawes.

He looked at Dawes. "We left your clothes on your woman's floor. Let us make a bargain, you and me. We'll take you back to her house, and you can dash inside before anyone sees you. You never tell anyone you saw me, and I never tell Missus Dawes that I caught you diddling another woman."

Dawes nodded.

"We're agreed?" Spider sheathed his knife. "I have not hurt you, and I take a risk letting you go. That should give you reason to trust me, aye?"

Dawes nodded again, but not so enthusiastically this time.

"Ruth, let's take this man back where we found him."

"Aye, cap'n."

Once they'd drawn the wagon as close to Mrs. Beall's door as possible and Dawes had rushed inside, Spider climbed up to the bench.

Ruth started the mule and looked at Spider.

"That was kind, you not making him run about unclothed like that."

"Maybe," Spider replied. "I hope it was not foolish."

"What else could you have done?"

He shook his head. "I've no notion, lass. None at all."

She stayed quiet for a while after that, and Spider sank deep into his own thoughts. Then Ruth spoke hers.

"There are ships, Spider John, right here in the harbor. We could board one, go to Boston, or somewhere else, as soon as we please. There is no need to find Stoneham's killer. No one in Nantucket really seems to care who did it. We could just leave. I can find passage from Boston to Virginia, and you can find passage to anywhere you might wish to go. Or . . ."

"Or?"

"You might go with me to Virginia."

That resulted in a long silence, as Spider resisted the urge to look at her. "No one here really cares about Stoneham," he said at last. "But they all think I did it. What if Em, or my boy, come back here? What tales are they going to be told? A pirate named Spider John came looking for you, Em, and he killed that Stoneham bastard?"

Ruth laughed bitterly. "I suppose she might even find that romantic, in a horrid way. The man did beat her, you said."

"He deserved dying, as far as I care," he said. "But I don't want her to think me a brute. I don't want my boy to think me a killer. Even if I have been one."

He and Ruth had not looked at one another during the entire conversation.

"Well," she said after another silence. "If you ever find her, I hope she sees you for what you are now."

"That's why I have to find Stoneham's killer."

"I know." She spoke very softly, and Spider could barely hear her over the clatter of the mule and wagon. "But . . . why would she ever come back here?"

"Her father is here."

"Her father despises her, from what you've said."

"He hates what happened to her because of me," Spider said. "But she's his daughter. He'll remember he loves her, probably."

"You may speak the truth, there. Perhaps."

They rode the rest of the way to Isaac's place without speaking another word.

44

*W*hen they entered the barn, they found Odin snoring against the wall with a flask tucked under his arm.

Across the room was a pile of ropes that had previously bound Seitz.

Spider walked over and tapped his boot against the old man's knee. Odin blinked. "You are back."

"Aye. What happened here?"

Odin grinned. "Just what you planned. Ha! I drank my booze—it was water, damn it! Whose bloody notion was that?"

"Mine," Ruth said. "I thought it might be best if you were sober for this reckless plan. I thought liquor would be one complication too many."

"And I told her the odds of you following my plan the way I told you were even, at best, whether you were sober or drunk," Spider said. And that was true. He'd known it was a gamble, but he could think of no other way to deal with the German sea cook. He might have left Hob here to watch over Seitz, and thus worried less whether Odin would follow the plan or even remember it, but the younger Hob was much better suited to execute the other portion of the scheme.

Odin resumed telling his tale. "Well, sober I was, and I just sat here drinking my water and pondering the map. I drank some more, pondered some more, drank some more and I started mumbling about treasure and ghosts and all that, ha! Seitz thought I was soaked in liquor, for sure."

"Good," Spider said.

"And then I fell asleep, or so he thought, and he got himself free."

"And he wasn't suspicious when your knot came loose?"

"Ha! It is no easy trick, Spider John, to tie a knot that looks good but ain't good, and comes free easy but not too easy, but I did it. It took him a little while, the fucking lubber! I was stiff from laying there on the floor so long, but he got loose."

Ruth shook her head. "I owe you a bottle of rum, Spider. I did not think that would work."

Odin grumbled. "Give me the bottle," he said. "Spider still owes me one."

Spider shrugged. "I did not think it would work, either, to be honest, but I didn't want to kill him nor tow him along with us. He took the map?"

"Aye," Odin said. "I have to tell you, Ruth, you and Hob made it look pretty good. Almost like the real map. I wonder where it'll take him?"

She laughed. "Nowhere good, I'll wager, but I hope it takes him away from us. We just scrambled the little secret marks from the treasure map, and added a few others in there, too. If that was a code showing latitude and longitude, well, that fake map won't lead him there."

"Good," Spider said. "He's just a cook, so I doubt he can navigate anyway. He might know the code on the map, or he might not. Probably not. Hob found it in a trunk belonging to the mutineers, and they likely didn't let Seitz see it much. I reckon they'd have cheated Seitz out of his share, anyway."

"Probably," Ruth agreed.

"But he's got the map, or, I should say, a map, and he'll be looking for a ship to take him to his treasure. If he shows that drawing to a real sailor, well, the trick might be spotted. So we'll have to keep a weather eye for Seitz. He might come back, right pissed at us and accompanied by armed friends."

"Ha! I'll like that better than hiding out in a damned woodshed or a fucking wagon!" Odin mimicked a cut and thrust. "I could use a good fight."

"I, for one, hope Seitz finds a vessel and sets sail long before anyone realizes the map is a forgery," Ruth said. "Hell, we don't even know that the map Hob is carrying is genuine. It might be a damned fake, too. Pirates and treasure maps and Red Edgar and ghosts, foolish to go off after all that, I say."

"Whether we go or stay," Odin said, "I want a real drink."

They left the barn-turned-woodshed and headed to the mule barn, where Isaac was seeing to the beast. "Did you find the killer, Spider?"

"No, Isaac, we did not."

"Oh." He looked down at the dirt floor.

Spider sighed heavily. "We've been a burden on you too long, I'd say."

"I don't wish to chase you away," the man said. "I truly do not."

"But we are trouble." Spider looked at Odin and Ruth. "We are a Spanish galleon full of trouble, aye? We should go before anything bad befalls here. Maybe you are wise, Ruth. Maybe we ought to leave Nantucket."

She looked at him, but said nothing.

"Where shall we go? Boston's got whores," Odin said. "And it is close, hell, I can sniff the perfume. Ha!"

"We can talk about that when Hob returns," Spider said. "He might have news. Or he might have done no better than me and Ruth. All we found was a couple of fellows talking about a pirate hanging and flirting a bit—Ruth scared them off, Odin, you should have seen that! And we saw the fellow in the blue hat, he gave Ruth a long look, too. And our Mister Dawes, of course. We found him, on top of his extra woman."

"Did you bring her back with you?"

Spider sighed. "No, you old bastard. And we didn't get any closer to finding out who murdered Stoneham."

45

*H*ob, out of breath, dropped his coat on the floor. "That smells good," he said.

"Goat stew," Isaac answered. "Have you been running?"

"Aye, not chased or anything, just wanted to get back and eat."

Isaac handed him a bowl. "Got paid in meat for the fence work. Boiled it all day. Not enough potatoes, really, nor enough goat, to be honest, for all of us to have much of that, but I tossed the rest of Odin's cod and haddock in there, too. I am not one for cooking."

Spider waved his hand. "You could boil a boot, and I could tell you honest, we've eaten worse. Well, Hob?"

"He did just as you thought he would, Spider. Odin did his job, smashing, he was! Then Seitz ran off to town."

"Aye," Spider said. "He did not see you following him?"

Hob grimaced. "Of course he did not spy me, Spider John! I am no fool of a lubber, am I? I've seen action before, I have."

Spider sighed. "Aye, you have. Very well. Where did he go?"

Hob sat, smiling again. "Straight to Zachariah's, he went. Some gents playing cards there, and he talked with them. I stayed outside, listening at the door. I could not hear much, but I peeked in and heard enough. He was asking about a boat, to take him to Boston. This stew is fine, Isaac. Thank you."

Spider nodded once Hob finished devouring his food. "Good, then, no one saw you. Did he find a ship?"

"He says thanks to the gents, and he gets up to leave, so I had to duck away. But I followed him, and he went down to the wharfs and was talking to some fellows there."

"Anyone with a black beard and a blue tricorn?"

"No, Spider. Wasn't Seitz the fellow with the tricorn?"

"Apparently, he was not. Go on with your account."

"Well, I saw no one with a blue tricorn, nor anybody with a rip in his ear, either, and I was looking careful for that. I followed Seitz, and he went up to a boat shed and talked to a man who was painting a hull. I waited for my time, I did, and rolled in behind a barrel, quick as you please! They had no idea I was there, and I heard every word they said."

Hob stood, smiled widely and took a bow. "Our German friend will be sailing in the morning. The fellow with the paint works for a man who hauls wool and such to Boston and comes back with whatever cargo he can arrange. Tomorrow, Seitz goes sailing with the painter's boss."

Isaac returned with a couple of bowls and placed them on the table. Spider pushed one toward Ruth, and Odin grabbed the other. Hob sat down while Isaac fetched more.

"Did Seitz talk about the map?"

"No, Spider. But he talked about having some very lucrative business to do, and the need for a ship, and the painter liked that bit about lucrative business, and soon he was telling Seitz about his boss, called Collins, and the Boston jaunts."

Isaac gave Hob another bowl of stew, then placed one before Spider. It looked thin, and Spider found no hint of spice in the aroma. He took a bland bite. *Maybe we chased Seitz off too soon*, he thought.

"Thank you, Isaac. This tastes fine," he said.

Isaac grinned. "Really?" He walked across the room, came back with a candle, and sat down. In the better light, Spider noted the man's bruised face was starting to heal.

"Aye. It is a good meal. Thank you. So, Hob, you did well."

"Aye," Hob said around a mouthful of goat meat.

Spider sighed. "And let us hope that is the last we see of Seitz."

"I went back to Zachariah's after that," Hob said. "Played some cards. Got the names of a few gents who might get us a ship." He looked up at Spider. "Just so we have one if we should decide to leave Nantucket and go treasure hunting."

"You are for leaving, too?"

Hob shook his head. "No, sir. I will stay with you here as long as it takes us to save your neck. But if you should decide to save your neck by leaving the island, well, I confess I would not try to talk you out of that. And I'd say, well, I'd think it grand if you and the rest of us followed this map I got."

Spider nodded. "I see. Thank you, Hob. That was well said. Odin, what is your thought?"

"Boston first, and some women, and some rum, then a ship for the Spanish Main. This Nantucket is boring, Spider John. I sailed with Blackbeard, by God! I never knew a life beside sailing and pillaging and fighting. Look around this place. Just sheep and lubbers."

"Well, there is no one but lubbers here because so many men are at sea." Spider looked at Ruth. "I reckon you still think leaving is the best course, as well."

"I do," she said. "But I am of Hob's mind on this. I will stay here as long as you need help. I am not going to the Caribbean, though. I am done with that sort of life, I hope. I aim to go to Virginia."

Spider ate his tasteless stew. "I am weary of all this, too. Damned weary," he said. "We could go to Boston, ask after *Margaret*, see if anyone has sighted her. Someone might know her, or her captain, this Samuel Westcott. If we can smoke out where he's sailed, then I can maybe go find my Em and Johnny."

Hob nodded. "Aye. And maybe that course leads us to the Main, after all." He looked hopeful.

"I pray that is not the case," Spider said. "I do not want her or my boy to ever share a deck with pirates. I want us together, that is all, whether it is in England or Boston or anywhere else besides bloody Jamaica or Tortuga or any other godforsaken pirate haunts. I want a home, and a woodshop, some good tools, and a fireplace to keep us all warm. I am done with the seas and roaming."

They all sat quietly, eating their stew.

Hob shoved his empty bowl toward the center of the table. "Well, we'll need passage to Boston as a start. And I can pay for it."

They all looked at him.

Spider sat back and shook his head slowly. "You have money? I can guess how, Hob. We're not pirates now, are we? Not thieves?"

"You don't frown on me so when it's a bottle of whisky or a pouch of tobacco I nab for you, do you?" Hob inhaled deeply. "The man was playing cards, he was drunker than I've ever seen you, Spider, and the damn purse was right there for the taking. Someone was bound to grab it, aye? And we have need, aye? So, I took it. He'd have spent it all on drink, anyway, I wager."

"We could spend it all on drink," Odin said.

Hob reached to his belt and came up with a leather purse. "Another small crime, aye, but another step toward a new life, I dare say. We need the funds, damn it."

He thunked the purse down on the table with force, to emphasize his point. The drawstring was not tight, and two pieces of eight spilled onto the oak. One of them spun on its edge, a dazzling silver dervish in the firelight.

Spider stared at it until it fell flat.

"Sheep and lubbers," he said quietly, "and all of them smarter than I am. Fuck and bugger. Fuck and bugger!"

He looked at his companions, seeing nothing but puzzled faces.

Ruth, sitting next to him, touched his hand. "What is it, Spider?"

"I think I know," he said. "Oh, damn it all. I think I know who the killer is."

"Who?"

Spider stood, not even noticing the pain in his legs now. "I have to go."

Hob and Ruth stood, too, and Odin rose a moment later. "Where," Ruth said, "are you going?"

Spider took his coat from a peg. "I am going to find out if I am right."

"We'll come, too," Hob said.

"No," Spider said. "No. I can sneak about better on my own. I will spy it out, see whether I am right, and then we can make a plan."

"At least take the flintlock," Hob said.

Spider paused, thought hard, and then shook his head. "No. I will not be in need of that."

"Spider," Ruth said, but he was already heading out.

46

Nantucket's thick fog rolled around him, and Spider regretted not grabbing a lantern. Even when he hit higher ground and was able to peer across the lowering mist, the moon hid behind marching clouds.

At least it did not look like rain was on the way.

Spider cursed and grumbled, and tried to decide whether to return to Isaac's for a light or to just stumble forward slowly across the empty landscape. He looked skyward, where the bright moon had been reduced to a mere faint glow behind the clouds. There was open sky to the east, though, and the clouds were sailing along swiftly, like pirate sloops. He decided he could risk the darkness, and pick up speed whenever the moon peeked through. He did not want to delay. He wanted to confront the killer and leave Nantucket as soon as he could.

He looked ahead of him to make sure he wasn't going to wander into a sheep flock or a pile of shit, and kept alert for the bleats of sheep. Then he noticed a shadow ahead of him, surrounded in a fiery glow.

Spider crouched, hoping he had not been seen. He reached for his blade and waited for the man to approach.

The ghostly figure had crouched, too, and Spider suddenly realized he was watching his own silhouette, projected on the fog. Someone was approaching from behind, heavy footsteps drumming on the sandy ground.

Hob, no doubt, bringing me a lantern and ready to beg to come along with me.

"Well," Spider said, rising and turning to face the young man. He saw a lantern raised about a dozen yards away—then something rammed his stomach, hard, like a cannon ball.

He fell backward, instinctively trying to catch himself, and jammed his injured hand into the ground. His wrist bent awkwardly. No cutlass slash, no musket ball had ever hurt like that. The loss of a finger, years before, had not pained him this much. He wondered if his wrist had snapped.

He had no time to check, though. Something heavy had fallen with him, knocking the air from Spider's lungs and trapping him beneath its weight. Spider tried to call out for help, but could not muster the breath. He could not even scream in agony. *This is what drowning feels like*, he imagined.

Blindly, he groped at his attacker. He could not see anything but red, and was not even certain his eyes were open, but he could smell a man's breath in his face, so he reached for that. The one hand he could still use snatched a handful of hair, or beard.

"*Scheisse!*"

Seitz.

"Where is map? Where is map?" The burly cook ignored Spider's grasp on his beard, and hammered at him with his fists. The blows were to his gut, and Spider wondered if he'd ever be able to breathe again. He twisted his adversary's beard and yanked on it for all he was worth, but at the moment, that wasn't much.

"Quiet, you fool," a man whispered. It was not Seitz.

This second man placed a lantern on the ground. Its shutter was adjusted to throw light in Spider's direction, but no other. The man then moved into that light, and became a shadow again. The shadow knelt beside him.

Spider felt the unmistakable jab of a dagger at his right cheek. It was not a blow to kill, or to injure. It was a mere poke, to get his attention.

It did.

Seitz rolled off of Spider and got to his feet. "I want my map!"

"Quiet, Seitz." The blade moved. "My knife is now at your throat," the other man said. "Do you feel it? Just nod. Carefully."

Spider nodded carefully, and tried to focus his eyes. All he saw was darkness, and swirling red. Experience told him that was the shock of pain, and that it would pass—if he lived long enough.

The man next to him moved, and Spider writhed. The bastard knelt on Spider's injured hand and wrist. Spider could not gather enough breath to cry out.

"Seitz," the other man said softly. "Watch the house. Shoot if anyone comes out."

"Aye," Seitz said.

"Now, Spider John," the man moved, removing his weight from Spider's hand. "My new friend here says he has a map, a wonderful map, a map that reveals the location of a great deal of gold and silver. He shows me this map, and then he gasps. It is not his map, he says! The little island is not the same shape, he says."

The man—presumably the Collins mentioned by Hob—pressed the knife flat against Spider's neck.

"The little sigils drawn on the map, he thinks they are not in the right order, he says. So we talk about it, and he says you sons of whores let him run off with a fake map."

Spider blinked. He could just make out the man's silhouette, looming above him. He could definitely feel the knife, though, and could not decide whether the moisture running down his neck was sweat or blood.

"So, if you tricked my new friend with a fake map, this leads me to believe you still have the original map. And this leads me to ask where it is. Do you have it on you? Just nod."

Spider shook his head.

"Does one of your friends have it?"

Spider shook his head again.

"Tell me where it is," the man said softly, "right now." He moved the blade, slowly, and its cold touch settled lower on Spider's throat. One quick gesture would lead to a red gush.

Spider blinked, and writhed, and took a wild, useless swing with his left hand.

The man jumped back and inhaled sharply. "This is foolish," he whispered. "I'll just kill you, and search you."

Spider threw another desperate punch, but hit nothing. The shadowy attacker moved, and Spider thought he could just discern the glint of a knife rising above him.

He steeled himself for the killing stroke. *Better this quick death than the noose I've run from my entire life.*

Next came a thunderclap and rain.

Those weren't storm clouds rolling across the sky.

Then, familiar scents.

I know these smells. Burnt powder and—

The man with the knife fell across Spider's chest. The thunder had come from a flintlock, and the rain was blood.

47

Spider heard a second explosion, and tried to shove the man off of him. That caused more excruciating pain in his right hand, but at least his effort to curse led to a sudden rush of air into his lungs.

Feet drummed on the ground around him, and he heard Seitz swear an oath. Then the man lying across his chest was gone, and Spider rolled away as quickly as he could. He got his knees under him and was just about to rise when Seitz fell, blood between his eyes reflecting the lantern light. It was a horrid sight, the kind Spider had seen all too frequently as a pirate, and the kind he had hoped to never see again.

But at least I can bloody see now.

"Ha!" Odin hovered over Seitz, wielding a hand axe and slicing the air. "That's for all the maggots in my bread, you German son of a bitch!"

Spider saw Hob, as well, holding the other man by his belt and the collar of his coat. Hob dropped the man like a heavy sack, then reached down swiftly to pull something from the man's coat pocket. "On your knees, Collins. And don't reach for your gun. I've got it already."

"Damn you," Collins said.

Spider rose. "Are you lads hurt?"

"Hell, no," Hob said. "Not me."

"No scratches for me," Odin answered. "That German bastard can't shoot at all."

"He won't shoot anyone else," Spider said. "That is for certain." Spider inhaled deeply, and fought the urge to vomit.

Odin spat, looking more like a witch than ever in the uncertain light from lantern and moon that played across his disfigured face. "Hell, I don't think he's dead. Cracked him with the haft, not the blade." He put a boot against the sea cook's shoulder and rolled him onto his back. The man moaned softly, in his native tongue.

"I'll be damned," Spider said, shaking his head. "You didn't kill him?" He looked at the man. Head wounds often looked worse than they were, he knew, so he ignored the amount of blood and peered at the forehead beneath it. He saw swelling, and a nasty scrape, but no deep gash.

Seitz would, indeed, probably live.

Spider looked at Odin. "You didn't try to kill him?"

"You did not wish it, aye? You always go on about how we're honest men now, aye?" Odin shrugged. "So I flipped the axe backward and slugged him instead of slicing him. I am telling you, too, it wasn't natural, Spider John. Felt damned wrong, it did, all that thinking instead of fighting and doing a thing that might let him get back up and kill me."

Welsh, Spider John decided. *In a hot moment, Odin sounds Welsh—not Scottish, not Irish, nor any of the other heritages he's claimed at various times. The old bastard is Welsh.*

"Don't expect me to do such a fool thing next time, Spider John. I don't think I'll do it. A man caught thinking when the blood is flying around him is going to die."

Fuck. That sounded Irish.

"Well, it is likely good you did not kill him this time," Spider said. "Considering one of us is already accused of murder, I dare say it is well you listened to me for once. How about the other gent, is he going to live? This Collins?"

"Collins is going to kill you," Collins answered.

Clouds parted for a moment, and Spider saw Hob place a foot on the man's shoulder. "You won't be doing us any harm today, Mister Collins, not with a ball in your shoulder already and me here with another one to put in you anytime I please." Hob aimed at his prisoner's nose. "You'd best not make yourself too much of a burden for us. We don't wish to kill you, but that does not mean we won't. Do you comprehend?"

The man nodded.

Spider looked around, flexing his wounded hand. It hurt like sharks were chewing on it, but nothing seemed to be broken. "Where is Ruth?"

"Over here," she said. "I was rear guard. Seems it was just these two. I don't see anyone hiding in reserve."

"Well," Spider said, eyeing the scene. "We've made worse messes than this."

"Ruth was watching, saw a flash of a lantern, and we remembered you did not take one," Hob said. "So we thought you'd likely found trouble."

Ruth rushed to his side. "How badly are you hurt, Spider?"

"I'll live. Thank you all for the rescue."

Ruth picked up the lantern and spied the surrounding ground. "I told you that plan with Seitz was a big risk."

"Aye," Spider said. "You did. I hoped he'd just move on, but here he is."

"Ha!" Odin shouldered the axe. "You ate his fucking biscuits, aye? No pity at all if I'd killed him."

"I've noticed something here, Spider," Hob said, pushing his foot harder into the man's shoulder. Collins cried out as Hob stooped over him. "He's got no cut or rip on his ears."

"I didn't think he would," Spider said. "Stop hurting him, Hob. He's loud."

Collins moaned again.

"Quiet," Spider said. "I know it is sort of lonely out here, but we don't want anyone to hear this man." Then, because he realized he'd just given Collins a ray of hope, "We can kill the bastard very quietly with a knife if he hollers again, or if he tries to, and I say do it, if need be."

"Aye," Hob replied.

Spider saw the defeat in the prisoner's eyes and turned away. "Jesus, what a mess."

"The man did try to kill you, Spider," Hob reminded him.

"Aye, damn it, he did, and he would have." He spat, then gazed heavenward. "But, if God will let me, I'm going to be as good a man as I can be, and that means not killing anymore."

"Bloody inconvenient," Odin muttered.

"Say that again?"

"You heard me, Spider. I know we are supposed to be honest men now, and not bloody pirates, but with you wanted for murder, and Hob carrying around Red Edgar's treasure map, and me here with a man's blood dripping on my axe"—he wiped it on his britches—"well, we haven't got very far from the piracy, have we? Hell, what's one more crime?"

Spider glared at his friend. "This is my choice. I am not killing him, and I am not letting anyone else kill him."

Hob moved between Spider and Odin. "Gents, I must ask. If we're not killing them, what are we to do with them?"

"Yet another inconvenient prisoner," Ruth said, trying to lighten the tension.

"Aye, that seems to be our luck lately. Let me think, damn it." Spider paced. This was a difficult problem, and not just for him and his shipmates. These men had come looking for them at Isaac's place, which could pose future dangers for the man who had helped them out if these bastards decided they were in a vengeful mood.

"Well," he said after much thinking, "we can't just threaten these bastards the way we did Isaac and expect them to meekly do our bidding." He let his eyes convey his thought to his friends, and was happy to see comprehension in their faces. "So, we'll just have to put them somewhere they can't give us trouble."

Spider paced some more, then nodded. "Fetch rope, we'll bind them good. I don't care if you bind them so tight it hurts, Odin. They did try to kill me, after all."

"Ha!"

"Gag them, too, so they don't do no shouting, and drag them that way." Spider pointed toward the southeast. "Not much that way but pasture and wigwams, as far as I remember. Just leave them there. We'll be gone by the time anyone finds them."

"Gone?" That was Hob.

"We will," Spider said. "I reckon we'll be on a ship tomorrow come what may."

Odin looked at Spider. "And what will you do while we are doing all this lugging and wrapping and binding and hard work?"

"Well," Spider said, "I'll stand guard for now, while you fetch what you need. Then I am going to go have a talk with Jeremy Stoneham's killer."

"How about we all do that," Hob said. He made it sound like a command. "We've got three flintlocks among us now. There's strength in numbers, aye?"

"No. See to things here. Keep Odin out of trouble. I can handle what comes."

I think.

48

I t was almost dawn by the time Spider was in place. He'd stood guard over Collins and Seitz while the rest of his crew took care of preparations, and it all had taken longer than he'd expected.

Collins, of course, had tried to talk things over, offering to arrange a ship for them all for a share in the treasure. "You'll need a ship, aye? I can do that. And, I know we all had knives at our throats and guns shot and all that, but, well, I can see that isn't your nature and it isn't mine, neither. Seitz, he was the one pushing violence and all that, weren't you, Seitz? I just want to make a deal, aye? I told him that. Didn't I, Seitz? A lucrative enterprise is all I want, and I dare say Red Edgar has enough booty in the ground to make us all barons and lords."

Spider had listened glumly. "So, I could free you, we'd shake hands, and we'd all sail off tomorrow?"

"Aye!"

"You could go arrange a vessel, while we gather our goods. We could meet up in the morning."

"Aye! Aye!"

"No," Spider had said, punctuating it with some spittle that landed near Collins. "I don't have any reason to trust you."

"And I don't trust you!"

"Heh, well. I did play your German friend a trick, didn't I? Nearly got me killed. I'm going to leave you both with the goddamned sheep."

"We'll die before someone finds us!"

"Maybe. Maybe not. Bad things probably happen to people who

go about sticking a knife against a pirate's throat, I reckon. I could kill you both now, I suppose, if you'd rather."

"Don't leave me in the pasture, damn it! I beg you!"

"Listen," Spider had said, almost laughing, "after we leave you, you just chew your way through the gag, aye? It'll take a while. Then try to wiggle under one of them sheep, a big one, a big ram, and latch your teeth on his balls. Clamp on there real tight, you see, because he's going to run like hell and bleat like the devil. But maybe he'll drag you somewhere so people will hear you, and come cut you free."

Collins had started crying at that point.

"Jesus," Spider had relented. "Wampanoags will find you soon enough, or some shepherd. You'll miss a meal or two, probably."

Then, his friends had returned and he'd spent more time convincing them to stay behind and see to the prisoners. "No," he'd told Hob. "If I am wrong, a crowd of former pirates with flintlocks will just cause problems we don't need. And if I am right, well, I don't think it'll come to a fight."

That had been a lie, of course. Spider expected trouble whether he had discerned the truth or not. But he had good reason for doing this alone.

Now Spider waited, on the south side of the island, near a familiar house with a bright red door. He glanced around, saw nothing but sheep and a Wampanoag sitting in a whale seat and watching the ocean, so he took a long piss. He longed for food, and tobacco. The wind carried a scent of burning peat, and he supposed someone near was preparing a breakfast, probably johnnycake, maybe eggs, maybe both. His stomach growled.

The red door opened, and a broad-shouldered man with a thick black beard stepped outside. He was not wearing a blue tricorn, but Spider recognized the sailor's gait.

The man walked a couple dozen yards, yawned, then stopped to relieve himself.

The man had not noticed Spider John.

Willing himself to be calm, Spider crouched and calculated. He did not suppose he could reach the man before he finished emptying his bladder, but he could wait for him to turn and head back to the house. That was likely to be his next move, since he had no hat nor coat against the chill.

No, he's not headed anywhere. He's going back inside.

So Spider decided to wait. Once the man turned, Spider would veer left or right, as needed, and approach swiftly from behind. It would work. He could be on the man in seconds.

Instead, Spider watched the man finish his piss, then turn back to the house. Spider stayed where he was and watched him until he vanished behind the red door.

"Fucking lobcock," Spider muttered, referring to himself. "Get on with it, you coward."

He rose, sighed heavily, and walked up to the door.

Spider stood there, eyes closed, steeling himself, rehearsing the coming encounter in his mind.

Finally, he knocked.

The door opened thirty or forty seconds later, and the cloudy blue eyes of Ephraim Pierce stared at him.

"You."

"Aye."

Fury rose in the older man. "Why do you haunt me, John Rush?"

"I want to clear my name of a man's murder."

"Go ask God's forgiveness," Pierce said. "You will find none here!"

Pierce tried to close the door, but Spider was ready for that. Spider shouldered his way in, careful to keep his right hand out of the way, and nearly knocked his father-in-law over in the process. He was not worried about the old man, though. It was the other man who concerned him.

Enoch. Ephraim's son, Emma's brother.

"Damn you to hell, John Rush!" Ephraim stumbled to the table, regained his balance and looked up at the gun rack.

But Enoch was already there, with the blunderbuss in hand.

Spider had no idea if the weapon was loaded with powder and

shot, so he assumed it was. He launched himself, ramming his shoulder squarely in Enoch's chest before he could bring the big gun to bear. Spider steeled himself for the thunderous explosion, but none came.

Spider's shove sent Enoch back into the wall, hard. Spider moved forward, leaving his foe no room to aim the long weapon. Then Spider brought his left hand up hard under Enoch's chin, driving his head backward. The head hit the wall with a thud, rattling the gun rack.

Spider stepped back, grabbing the gun barrel and kicking Enoch in the balls. Doing so gave him a chance to finally notice that Enoch's left ear sported a vicious red rip, one that was not healing well.

Well, now, Spider thought, *I knew it.*

"Damnation! Damnation!" Ephraim Pierce approached from behind and wrapped an arm around Spider's neck.

Spider reversed the gun and drove it backward as hard as he could, with both hands. That hurt mightily, but there was no way to avoid that. The cry and gush of air behind him told him he'd planted the gun's butt in Ephraim Pierce's belly. Spider shoved the gun backward again and heard Pierce fall to the floor behind him.

"Damnation on you, John Rush!" Pierce yelled it between gasps of pain.

Spider backed away and aimed the gun at Enoch's face. Before either man had recovered from his attack, Spider had them both covered by the blunderbuss.

"We shall have a talk," he said, as calmly as he could, although tears threatened to blind him and the words caught in his throat. "And then we shall see what comes from it. Sit down." He glanced at the table. "Sit down, I say."

49

The Pierces, father and son, sat across from one another at the table. A blue tricorn hat and Ephraim's Bible rested on the table between them.

Spider hovered nearby, the gun trained on Enoch. Spider's injured right hand was on the trigger, and he had serious doubts about being able to squeeze the trigger rapidly if it came to that. But in the heat of the moment, he'd handled the gun in the way that came natural to him, and now he was stuck with it. He made sure the barrel in his left hand and his shoulder took all of the heavy gun's weight, but he knew it was going to hurt like hell if he had to pull the trigger.

He tried to keep the pain from showing on his face. Spider knew he could handle the older man, Ephraim, but Enoch was a big man of Spider's age, and had the kind of muscles hard work creates and he'd gotten to the blunderbuss quicker than a rattler can strike. The man also had a mad look in his eye.

Spider had seen that before. This was not a man to back down.

"Well," Spider said at last, "you tried to kill me."

"You are hellbound! The devil's own!"

"Silence, father!" Enoch's eyes were blue, like his father's, but icy hard instead of cloudy. "Say nothing! This man is a known criminal, a murderer, and there are witnesses who will attest to that."

Spider John glared at him.

"He assaulted you, father," Enoch said. "And he attacked Bill Wood on the beach, and threatened the cooper. The Widow Coffin saw him standing over Jeremy Stoneham's body before it even began to cool. And I've heard more beyond that."

"Have you, now?" Spider sighed heavily. "And what might that be?"

"You were among those hauled away in irons from a pirate vessel the Navy sunk near the Turks, a year gone," Enoch said quietly. "A damned pirate, killer, and thief, fit only for hanging, and that is what will happen to you."

"Did you hear that kind of talk in Tortuga, perhaps? Or Port Royal? Talking with pirates, killers, and thieves? You are no stranger to action, now, are you, Enoch? You know how to fight."

Enoch simply glared at him.

Spider gulped, and tried to steady the gun.

"Do it," Enoch said, with a defiant fire in his eyes. "Take us to the magistrate. Tell him anything you please. And he will see your tale for what it is, a desperate plea from a doomed pirate, trying to hang his crimes on innocent men."

Spider sighed. *No court was going to take a pirate's word for any-thing.*

"I know the truth of it, Enoch. I know you tried to kill me, and the wrong man died in all the fog and confusion."

Ephraim moaned. "Almighty God . . ."

"Silence, father!"

"It was the coins that told me."

Enoch said nothing, so Spider continued.

"Such an odd choice of a weapon, that. A sack full of silver coins. I got hung up on the idea that someone had murdered Stoneham, so I kept looking everywhere else, but I should have focused on those pieces of eight, aye? That was the clue I missed."

Enoch's eyes blazed, and his lips tightened.

Spider recognized Enoch's intensity for what it was. *No stranger to action, indeed.*

"I hoped it had been an impulse," Spider said. "I hoped you'd come home, heard I had been here, and chased me down to curse me, to vent your anger at what had become of Emma's life."

Enoch remained silent.

"I hoped you'd seen me, lost control, and then hit me with the only thing you had at hand. Your pay. Back from the sea, aye? So, I thought, an angry man, sees me, rushes in, sees I've got a knife, grabs something, anything, to fight me and hits me with the purse from his pocket. But that is not how it happened, is it, Enoch? That is not how it happened at all."

"You tell stories, don't you, John? Are you sure you want to tell stories? I've heard stories, too. I've heard tell of how a man named Spider John killed a Royal Navy lieutenant in Port Royal harbor. Missing a finger, they say." Enoch glanced at Spider's wounded hand. "You are missing a finger there, John. Spider John, I ought to say."

"Aye, there are a lot of stories, to be sure." Spider sighed. "And they tell those stories in taverns and on ships where pirates gather. Is that where you learned to fight, Enoch? Are you a pirate?"

"Hell, no."

Spider shook his head. "Doesn't matter, I reckon. Pirate or not, you did not just let rage take over and swing a purse at me, did you? You showed me here, your eyes are showing it now, you know bloodshed. You came looking to kill me, didn't you? You intended murder from the very moment your father told you I'd come back."

He got no answer.

"How many pieces of eight were there, Enoch? Was it thirty?"

Ephraim roared. "You traitorous devil spawn!"

"Father! Be still!" Enoch placed a hand on his father's, and clutched it tightly.

"Traitorous, aye, that is how you see me, isn't it," Spider said. "You think I betrayed your daughter, led her down a path of sin."

"You seduced her," Ephraim hissed.

It was rather the other way around, Spider recalled, *but I am not going to tell her father that.*

"Judas got thirty pieces of silver for betraying the lord, aye?" Spider blinked the sweat from his eyes. "And I betrayed Em, you decided, so

. . . hell. I should have seen it, Ephraim, but I just tossed the notion overboard. You can hardly see, and hardly walk. I knew you wanted to kill me, hell, you tried to kill me with this very gun. But I decided it wasn't you at the Widow Coffin's house that night, because it did not make any sense."

And because I didn't want to believe it.

"But I forgot about you, Enoch. I just didn't think of you, and I should have. You just came back from the sea. When I showed at your father's door the first time, he was expecting you. He said your name before he opened the door. He knew you would be home."

Enoch glared.

"You got to that blunderbuss damned quick, Enoch. You know trouble, and keep a cool head, don't you? I'm lucky you missed me the first chance you had."

Enoch wiped blood from his chin. "You can't go to the law. The court will hang you."

"No," Spider answered. "I surely dare not risk that."

Enoch stared at the gun in Spider's hands. "If you kill us, that will just be two more crimes to mention when they hang you."

"It is a long list," Spider said.

"You deserve damnation, John. Emma sold herself," Enoch growled, "because you never came back."

"I ran into troubles," Spider answered, "and I could not come back. I did what I could do."

He hoped that Enoch did not notice how he put the weight of the gun on his left hand and his shoulder and kept his injured right hand close to the trigger, but not touching it. He hoped the man did not notice how red and swollen Spider's right hand was. "I am here now, though, but only because you missed me, goddamn it."

"Blasphemer!"

"Nothing so blasphemous as murder, I reckon," Spider said. "You failed to kill me at your door. But Enoch came home from the sea, and by thunder, you had another chance. That should have been a joyous occasion. Hell, anytime a sailor comes home alive it's a bloody miracle,

I reckon. But you told him you'd seen me, aye? And so you sent Enoch off to drop me dead."

"Say nothing, father."

Spider aimed the gun at the Bible, briefly, then covered the men again. "I never read that book, but I've heard it read. Judas, and his silver. I should have reckoned that."

"Thirty pieces of silver, a traitor's price!" Ephraim was frothing at the mouth now.

"Silence, father!"

But Ephraim would not be quiet. "Thirty pieces of silver! But we counted out sixty, for you betrayed my girl, and my grandson!"

"Father!"

"That's an odd choice of a weapon," Spider said. "I should have paid more attention to that. Not really the surest way to kill a man."

All pretenses of innocence vanished from Enoch's eyes. "It's heavy enough if a strong man swings it hard enough," Enoch said. "Or as many times as it takes."

Spider nodded. "Oh, I reckon it would work well enough. But a sack of coins isn't what a man planning a murder would choose, is it? I should have seen that right away. It's what you choose if you are sending a message, maybe to God, maybe to the devil, to show why you were killing me. Thirty pieces of eight for Emma, and thirty for Johnny. I should have seen it. Damn me, I should have seen it."

Enoch said nothing.

"Your father probably watched me head south, after he tried to save you the trouble of hunting me down. You followed in my wake, and found Wood. Jesus, I left you a trail, didn't I?"

Enoch shook his head. "I am not admitting anything. But I heard about Bill Wood. You hurt him bad, you did, before you went off and killed Jeremy Stoneham."

"Aye," Spider replied, sighing. "I said I had a long list of crimes."

"All of Nantucket knows you went off on a murderous course," Enoch said. "No one is going to believe anything you say."

"Oh, aye, indeed. And I drank too much, got in a sorry state. But I hear Wood lived, though, so maybe he has learned to not call another man's woman a whore."

"God!" Ephraim Pierce wailed, and tried to rise, but his son stopped him.

"Father! Do not say a word!" Enoch glared at Spider. He looked ready to pounce.

Spider aimed the blunderbuss directly at Enoch's chest. "I would stay in my chair, if I was you. I have seen the kind of hole one of these opens up in a man. Especially at close range. Ugly."

Enoch sat back.

Spider continued his tale. "You talked with Wood, and he told you I'd gone to the cooperage, looking for Stoneham. You followed. I saw you, you know, trailing behind me a ways. I noticed you, but I did not know who you were. I thought you were someone else who might want to kill me."

He noted the confusion in Enoch's eyes. "That's another long list," Spider added.

The three men stared at one another for several heartbeats as Spider felt a deep chill. Whether that came from being out in the open air all night or from the icy expressions father and son aimed at him, he was not certain, but he moved closer to the hearth nonetheless.

"So," he said, "you found Dawes, and talked to him and found out I was off to the Widow Coffin's place to beat Jeremy Stoneham."

"You went there to kill him," Enoch said. "Everyone knows that. No one is going to believe your wild tale."

"Probably not," Spider said. "But the three of us, we know what happened, aye? We know the truth."

He aimed the gun at the Bible again.

"And God knows it, too. He'll judge us all, I reckon. You went to the Widow Coffin's, looking for me. You weren't sure where I was hiding, or if I'd maybe changed my mind, or fallen asleep drunk somewhere, or what. So you waited, and watched, and when you saw me, you struck."

Enoch shook his head. "You are a desperate fool, telling desperate tales. Let us go to the magistrate, and you can tell him this strange story of yours, and we'll see who they hang."

Spider laughed bitterly, "Oh, they'll have plenty of reasons to hang me. No need to invent more."

"They can't hang you fast enough," Enoch said.

"When you pounced in the dark, and you swung your purse of silver, it was all muddled there, wasn't it? You missed your mark. You killed Stoneham, instead. Not much loss, I guess."

Enoch shook his head. "I do not know any of these things you speak of, John. All I know is you came here, my father defended himself, and now here you are again, pointing a gun at us."

"I ripped a bauble from your ear that night, Enoch. Judging by your ear, it must have hurt. I've got the earring with me, if you want it back."

Ephraim Pierce started crying, quietly, without blinking. He was no longer staring at Spider. He was staring at the hearth, watching the fire. "I should have gone to kill you myself. It should have been me."

Enoch pounded the table. "Father!"

"Two children, I have," Ephraim said. "A whore and a murderer. Both consigned to Hell!" He began shaking and sobbing uncontrollably. "Both consigned to Hell! It should be me! It should be me!"

Enoch rose. "Damn you, John. You should never have come back here."

Spider blinked. "Well, that is gospel, I reckon."

Spider turned his back on Enoch, and aimed the weapon at the hearth. He squeezed the trigger, and thunder filled the house. The smell made Spider think of brimstone. *I suppose I'll smell that again, someday. And these men will smell it, too.*

Then he turned back to the men, and pointed at Ephraim. "He needs you, Enoch. See to your father. I am leaving, and I am going to go somewhere and drink too much and think on my sins."

He stepped toward the door. "And you can think on yours."

Spider halted, still not facing Pierce and his son. "I have fretted, thinking Emma, or my boy, might come back to Nantucket one day. I didn't want them to hear about me killing a man. I didn't want my wife to hear that, or my boy to hear that. But . . ."

He almost choked on the words.

"If they do come back here, I reckon there is bitter news for them no matter what."

He walked out, and never looked back to see if Enoch was following and trying to load the blunderbuss.

50

A squall to the east had sent a brief rain sweeping across the island, and Spider was wet by the time he got back to Isaac's house.

"You don't look much better than you did when we met," their host said.

The rest of them looked at Spider expectantly as he went to the hearth and sat on the floor with his back to it to warm and dry his dripping hair.

"We have a ship," Hob said. "*Presto*, she is, bound for Boston. All arranged. We'll have to work. Can't pay passage for all."

Spider nodded, without looking up. "Good."

"Those bastards, we left them knotted together pretty good, and we took their clothes," Odin said. "Bundled them up together, very naked and cozy. Don't know if they will want to talk much when they're found. Ha!"

"Good," Spider said.

"Hmmmf," Odin replied, seemingly annoyed by Spider's lack of enthusiasm.

Ruth pulled a chair from the table and placed it next to Spider. "This will be more comfortable."

"No," he said. "I'm fine."

"You don't look fine."

"I am. Or will be."

They left him be for a while after that, and he ignored the occasional glances they cast his way. It was Odin who finally asked.

"Did you find out who killed that Stoneham son of a bitch, or did you not?"

Spider looked up and drew a deep breath. One day, Em and Johnny might return to Nantucket. Maybe they would hear the tale of how Spider John Rush had come looking for them, and killed the man who had mistreated them. Or, maybe, they would be talking about it some evening, and Em would look into her father's eyes, or her brother's, and see the hurtful truth hiding there, and learn that her father and brother had the hearts of murderers.

But she will not hear the truth from me, nor from anyone else if I can help it.

"No, Odin. I thought I had it reckoned out. I was wrong."

51

They sat in a tavern near Boston. It was far from the bay and its shipyard, far from all the sailors and harbor workers who might have news of *Margaret*, or her captain Samuel Westcott. But they had spent a whole day at the harbor asking questions and learning nothing before Spider had led them here, to a familiar spot, because he had nowhere else to go.

He remembered how much his friend Ezra had liked the chowder here an eternity ago.

He took a bite of chowder. It was not as he remembered, nor was the beer, nor was the whisky he'd swallowed the night before. Nothing felt quite right anymore.

Adrift. That's what I am. Adrift.

A young girl rushed about, lighting candles and lanterns as the sun lowered. She seemed full of joy. Spider wondered what time would do to erase that joy.

"It is good," Ruth said, her nose hovering over the bowl and taking in the aroma. "I see why your friend enjoyed it."

"It had corn in it, the last time we were here," Spider said. "That's what Ezra liked best, the corn. I don't know why this has no corn in it. Bloody chowder."

Ruth sighed, and continued eating.

Hob wiped his mouth on his sleeve. "I want more."

Spider slid his own bowl toward Hob. "You always want more. Have mine."

Spider watched the younger man eat with delight, and wondered if he himself would ever delight in anything again.

Ruth must have read his mood. "Spider, we'll find *Margaret*," she said, gently placing a hand on his. The pain and swelling were subsiding, at last, although he still had trouble when he made a fist or lifted anything. "I don't care where on the wide sea that ship has gone, we shall find it. Ports record the comings and goings, do they not? And you know how sailors are. They remember details of every ship they meet. This is a busy port, and we know she departed from this part of the world, do we not? Someone will come into Boston with letters or gifts from *Margaret*'s crew. All you need do is avoid trouble, ask questions, and the news will come to you, I wager. Then, you can go to her."

Spider looked at her. "I suppose."

"And for now, no one is trying to kill us. Ha!"

"That can change quickly, like the sea," Spider said. "The last time I was in this place, some bastard picked a fight and then me and Ezra were running for our lives." He lifted his cup. "To Ezra Coombs."

They all drank.

"You'll see your boy, Spider," Hob said. "I know it. Hell, he's probably like you, aye? Wondering where you are, piecing things together, reckoning it all out? Maybe he'll find you!"

"Maybe," he answered. "As for you, I reckon you can't wait to go find ghosts and gold." Spider had not meant it to sound like an accusation, but he was fairly certain it had.

"I'll never be much of a carpenter, Spider, though you are a fine teacher. I learned a lot from you, but . . . I don't take any joy in it. And I don't have a wife to stay with. I want to see the world, make something of myself."

Ruth nodded, as though she'd come to some decision. "I believe I'd like more beer. Anyone else? Let's have a show of hands."

All hands went up, including Spider's.

Ruth looked at him. "So, the chowder is no good, but the beer suits you." She got up and headed toward the taverner.

Spider watched her go. "Is she upset with me? I seem to disappoint a lot."

"She's a fine lass, you know," Odin said. "Don't take two eyes to see that. Of course, two eyes don't help much if you don't use them. Ha! And she isn't upset with you, really."

Spider leaned toward Odin. "What are you saying?"

"I say this, Spider John. You've been chasing your woman since I met you, and maybe she's worth it or maybe she's not. But she's gone, with another man, and got her another life. And maybe she's happy with all that . . ."

"And maybe she's not."

"And maybe she don't need a pirate like you . . ."

"I'm not a pirate anymore."

"Maybe she don't need a former pirate coming back into her life."

Spider stared at him. "And maybe she's in trouble."

"Maybe she's not." Odin sipped his beer, then pointed toward Ruth. "But that one, right there, she fancies you just the way you are, blood on your hands and always whining about the right thing to do and poking into other people's business. She likes that about you, God knows why."

"She wants you to be happy, Spider." That was Hob.

"Well," he answered, "then why does she always seem like she wants to slap me?"

"She wants you to be happy with her, Spider." Hob shrugged. "But you want Emma."

Odin smacked the table. "You are a pain, Spider John, a goddamned pain, complicating everything with your plans and your blather about being a goddamned honest man and your wife and your boy and all that, even if they've gone devil knows where and don't bloody care if they ever see you again. None of that bothers her at all, though, because she wants you to have what you want. She just . . ."

Odin shook his head. "She just wishes you wanted her. Hell, Spider, if trouble comes your way give her a gun and a cutlass and she'll fight right there with you. She'll jump between you and a sword, or you and a gun. And you don't even see all that, do you, with your two good eyes. Ha!"

"Now you sound Irish," Spider said. "Where are you really from?"

"I'm from your nightmares, Spider John. Do not ignore what I say and try to talk about other things. She loves you. Damned if I know why."

Spider saw Ruth approaching with a tray. "Hush, you scary old bastard."

She placed the platter on the table. "An ale for each of you, and I paid for just one. I just smiled at the poor fellow and batted my eyes and assured him you were all family and that I am quite unattached. This one is for you, grandfather."

She handed a cup to Odin, who grinned. "I wish I was pretty enough to get by with such trickery."

"You are the most handsome one-eyed man of a hundred or so years I have ever met," she said, as she handed a beer to Hob. "Little brother."

Hob took the cup. "I am not so much younger than you," he said.

"And yet, younger you are, so do not take offense. I shall always think of you as my little brother. Cousin Spider, this is yours."

"Thank you, miss."

"Try sipping it slowly enough to enjoy it this time," she said. "You'll still get drunk."

Once they each had a cup, Spider raised his. "Well, then, if I am not just pouring this goddamned thing down my throat on the way to my next drunk, I reckon we have time for a toast. Drink, crew, to safe travels."

They clanked their cups together and drank.

Spider glanced at Ruth. "Safe travels. Wherever we may be going."

Historical Notes

In Chapter 39, Spider hides in a wagon and overhears a couple of fellows discussing a horrible trial of more than thirty pirates. The men were describing a true event, one that took place in Rhode Island in July of 1723. Cotton Mather, Puritan minister and noted witch hunter, recorded that twenty-six men were executed after being "advised about the affairs of their souls." Part of that advice was to "shew their love to Christ by shewing their concernment for the Salvation of the Souls of their Fellow Sinners" and to be willing to "warn other Sinners to keep clear from those Paths of Destruction, that had brought them so far into Ruine."

Many of the doomed souls wrote their accounts of piratical murders and thievery, while others spoke to the gathered crowd. They told quite mournful tales of how the sins of greed and of the flesh had led them down the path to Hell. I have no idea how many souls were saved by their confessions.

Spider was in Nantucket, not Rhode Island, of course, but that spectacle was the kind of thing people talked about and such tales moved from port to port, so it seemed likely to me Spider might hear an account of it. I am not sure Spider's soul was saved, but I will advise you, Dear Reader, to not go down the pirate path.

Speaking of Nantucket, I found Nathaniel Philbrick's excellent book, *Away Off Shore: Nantucket Island and its People, 1602–1890*, quite interesting and useful as I wrote this novel. He is a fine historian, and I recommend you check out his other works. I greatly enjoyed *In *the Heart of the Sea*, a detailed account of the deadly encounter between a New England whaling vessel and a rather aggressive whale in 1820. That sea struggle famously inspired Herman Melville's *Moby-Dick*, which in turn inspired Philbrick to explain why you should read that classic novel in a book called, helpfully enough, *Why Read Moby-Dick?*

Philbrick is an historian and scholar, but I am a mere storyteller, so if I mucked up anything about Nantucket history in my book the fault is mine, not his.

I found the lyrics for "The Bold Pedlar and Robin Hood," sung by Jeremy Stoneham in Chapter 19 just before his untimely demise, among the traditional English ballads collected by Francis James Child. It also is known as "Gamble Gold," and you can find recordings of it by various performers on YouTube or Spotify, if you are so inclined. Those old songs tell some bold stories.

Afterword

As I was still writing this fourth Spider John adventure in January 2020, the world learned that legendary Rush drummer Neil Peart had died of brain cancer.

Good friends know why I gave my protagonist the last name of Rush, and it seems fitting for me to let the rest of you in on the secret. Unless you've figured it out already, of course. You mystery readers can be a perceptive lot.

Peart, as a drummer and a lyricist, has been an inspiration to me for most of my years. His passing is a reminder that life is brief, but his life reminds us that it can be lived fully. It's worth pondering.

Thank you, Neil.

As long as we are talking about musicians, I named *Minuet*'s fiddler for Sam Bush, a newgrass pioneer whose driving mandolin and fiddle performances made New Grass Revival one of my favorite bands. Bush is one of those musicians who says to hell with genre and plays whatever he damn well likes on his chosen instruments, whether it be traditional bluegrass or the Beatles. It's an attitude I think we would all do well to adopt.

I have more people to thank, of course. My agent, Evan Marshall, and my editor, Dan Mayer, made it possible for me to put these stories where you all could get your hands on them, so I am forever grateful to them for that. Dan's keen insights were particularly helpful this time out, and I feel lucky that he puts up with me.

My friend Tom Williams helps hunt down typos, and suggests

plot twists that I usually disregard, but appreciate nonetheless. If you aspire to writing yourself, Dear Reader, find friends who read widely and care enough about you to tell you that you really sort of messed up rather badly in Chapter 15.

Many book bloggers have taken the time to say kind words about these adventures, too, and that is much appreciated. Book people are the best people.

I also want to thank all of you who have come along for these journeys with Spider John and his growing collection of friends. If you'd like to reach out and talk more about these books, you can find me on Facebook (Steve Goble, Author) or Twitter (Steve Goble Fiction, aka @Steve_Goble). I always enjoy hearing from readers.

Most of all, though, I need to thank my wife, Gere, and our kid, Rowan. They provide the joy and inspiration that fuels any creativity I can muster, and without them, I sure as hell would not be a published author. Say a false word against either of them, by thunder, and you and I will cross blades at dawn.